SEX RITES

SEX RITES

An Erotic Sci-fi Novel

Brandon Fox

Leyland Publications
San Francisco

First edition 2000

Front and back cover design/layout by Stevee Postman.

Library of Congress Cataloging-in-Publication Data

Fox, Brandon.
Sex rites : an erotic sci-fi novel / Brandon Fox.—1st ed.
191 p. 22 cm.
Sequel to: Conjuring the flesh.
ISBN 0-943595-80-0 (pbk. : alk. paper)
I. Title.

PS3556.O8772 S48 2000
813'.54—dc21

00-42838
CIP

Leyland Publications
P.O. Box 410690
San Francisco, CA 94141
Complete illustrated catalogue available for $1 ppd.

1

THANE ANGLED the delicate blossom to catch sunlight streaming through the greenhouse's vast windows. Droplets glistened like rubies on flame-colored petals as he tilted the flower back and forth. "See the gold specks in its throat?" he asked.

Ander leaned forward. Raven hair fell unnoticed in front of his brown eyes as he peered at the star-shaped flower. He examined the plant intently, radiating curiosity. Thane smiled. Though his beloved had turned twenty the past summer, he still possessed a child's fascination with the world.

"I see them," Ander said at last. "Tiny, almost the color of copper."

"Make sure you don't use a blossom if you see green specks on it. Oils made with those are just as slippery, but will make a cock soft for an hour. An unpleasant surprise when you're ready for love."

Ander looked up and grinned. "I'll remember!" His handsome features were alight at learning the secrets of the art.

Thane put the blossom down and picked up a pale yellow orchid. "You already know this one, I think. The Xu Quan flower. Remember how it's used?"

"Um, you dry and powder it. Then mix it with raffia bark and make a tea. If you drink the tea and then make love while burning dreamsmoke leaves, you can make it last longer. A *lot* longer, Sorel says." He smiled seductively. "Would you like to show me, tonight? We could—"

"Ah, boys, there you are!" A thin man with wispy white hair emerged from the foliage behind them. Dirt stained his green velvet robes. Lord Jeffrey Tolmin, the master of the house and Thane's aristocratic patron, bustled toward them. "I found it. My newest specimen, all the way from Peruskia." He held up a glazed clay pot and proudly displayed a fleshy plant covered with long spikes like spears.

"It's good to have you back in the house," Tolmin said as he set the plant on a potting table. "How long has it been since you lived here, Thane? Five years? It's so hard to remember. With you never changing, it seems like yesterday!"

"Eleven years," Thane said softly, all levity vanished. "To me, it seems like forever."

Tolmin looked stricken. "I'm sorry, I didn't mean to raise ghosts. I've just missed you, my boy. But you were nineteen when you left and don't look a day older now. It's uncanny." The elderly aristocrat was right. Thane still appeared a radiant youth of nineteen, tanned and strongly muscled like a farmer, but possessing beguiling silver eyes and the easy grace of a dancer.

"It's the art," Ander said, putting an arm around Thane's waist. "He'll never change, as long as he keeps using magic. And he owes it to you, Lord Tolmin. You taught him botany, and the estate you gave him is perfect for pursuing his studies."

Tolmin waved a hand, clearly distressed by the discomfort he had caused. "Let's forget the past. It holds too much pain. And there's work to do. Your collection, Thane! We have to restock your greenhouse, as soon as it's rebuilt." He picked up a trowel and began loosening soil around the pot's perimeter. "Take a look at these roots. They're remarkable!"

Thane gave him a hand, carefully holding the prickly plant while Lord Tolmin loosened it from the pot and exposed thick roots. *Jeffrey's fortunate*, he thought. *If only I could forget the past as easily as he.*

It had been eleven years since Lucian, his first love, had died in the zamindar's torture chamber. Lucian and Thane had freed Tolmin's daughter, imprisoned on suspicion of treason, but a guard closed the portcullis at the prison gate and trapped Lucian after the others had already passed through. The young lovers had already discovered the rudiments of the art and shared a deep psychic bond. Thane shared Lucian's agony as the torturers tried to learn how the escape had been accomplished. He almost went mad as his lover succumbed to pain and despair.

Out of gratitude for saving his daughter, Lord Tolmin gave Thane a small estate in the country. For eleven years Thane tried to bury his grief by pursuing the mysteries he and Lucian had begun to explore. Intense pleasure could be a gateway to unseen realms, a different reality beyond the perceptions of everyday life. Creating elixirs, potions, balms and oils to enhance sensation and expand awareness was only the first step. The art required finding comrades who shared his passionate nature and honing their lovemaking until pleasure forged a link between minds. Thane's estate became a Lyceum, a secret training ground for mages dedicated to a common cause.

Behind it all, driving him relentlessly, lurked barely contained rage. The zamindar had ravaged Izmir as brutally as his inquisitors had cut and branded Lucian. Thane's quest for vengeance grew into iron determination to overthrow the tyrant. Ander's arrival at the Lyceum during the past winter had soothed his pain but not weakened his resolve.

"Here, look closely," Lord Tolmin said as he brushed dirt from purple nodules near the root tips. "This is most unusual. I've never seen such—"

"Lord Tolmin!" A servant dressed in green hose and a gold shirt rushed through the door connecting the greenhouse with the rambling mansion. "Two boys are out front, demanding entrance. One of them is armed! They claim to know your guests and want to see them immediately."

Thane looked up, his eyebrows arching. "Did you get their names?"

"Erik was one, the one with a bow. The other had some barbaric northern name."

"Skorri?" Thane asked.

The servant nodded. "That's it. So you *do* know them?"

Thane frowned. "Yes. But they shouldn't be here. Especially not by themselves." He turned to Lord Tolmin. "Jeffrey, whatever brought them here must be important. Your new specimen had better wait."

Lord Tolmin sighed. "If you insist." He waved absently to his steward. "Show them in. We'll see them here." The servant bowed and left.

Lord Tolmin's attention returned to his plants, but Thane wasn't listening. Skorri and Erik, new initiates at the Lyceum, were outcasts from a tiny village in Izmir's northern forests. They had only recently turned eighteen and weren't experienced enough to journey to a sophisticated city like Chanture on their own. Their sudden appearance did not bode well. Thane glanced at Ander while Lord Tolmin theorized about the traits of his new specimen. His lover waited silently, too polite to interrupt the elderly botanist, but the tense set of his shoulders showed he shared the mage's unease.

Though the mansion's galleries and greenhouses were extensive, it took only a few minutes for the servant to return. Two wide-eyed youths dressed in soft brown traveling leathers entered the greenhouse behind him. As soon as they saw Thane they ran to his side. The curly-haired blond reached him first.

"Sorel sent us. You have to leave, Thane. There's no time to waste." He grabbed Thane's arm and tugged. "Let's go!"

Thane put a hand on the boy's shoulder and held him still. "Slow down, Skorri. What's the news? Is there a problem at home?"

The other youth moved to Skorri's side. His chestnut hair was cut short like Thane's, and he moved with the eerie quiet of an expert hunter. A quiver of arrows crossed his broad back and his right hand held a yew bow. While Skorri was excited and flustered, Erik was as serious as a hunter facing a deadly beast. "We need privacy," he said. "There's danger." He glanced at the servant who hovered near the greenhouse door.

Lord Tolmin stared at the new visitors with bemusement, but made a dismissive gesture to his steward. The servant left, closing the door behind him.

"You can talk in front of Lord Tolmin," Thane said. "He'll keep our secrets."

Erik bowed toward Lord Tolmin, then turned back to the mage. "As Skorri said, Sorel sent us. You have to flee, Thane. The zamindar is searching for you. His heralds are riding everywhere, offering a reward for your capture. We even saw heralds in Kielce, a few miles north of here. They're moving fast. In one day they'll be in Chanture. In two days everyone in the city will be looking for you."

A grim frown clouded Thane's features. "What happened?" he asked, his throat tight.

"That's what I was trying to tell you," Skorri said. "A cuirassier patrol came to the Lyceum. They'd been searching the whole province. They had orders to arrest any man who looks about twenty and has silver eyes. They searched, and then announced the reward for your capture. Ten thousand drinars. Ten *thousand*! A fortune!"

Thane slumped onto a stool beside the potting table. "Is the Lyceum all right? Did the cuirassiers find anything?"

"We knew they were coming," Erik said. "We were watching the roads into the valley, like you told us to. We had time to hide all implements of the art." His brows pulled down over his deep blue eyes. "But you understand, don't you? You can't go back. You can't stay anywhere in Izmir. Nowhere in the kingdom is safe."

Lord Tolmin pushed his fingers through white hair, oblivious to the dirt. "How can this be, Thane? What does the zamindar know about you?"

"He's seen me. Face to face." Thane's voice was a whisper. "I was his prisoner, Jeffrey. A few weeks ago, in Pella. There was a trap. They . . . I, I'd rather not talk about it." He swallowed hard and looked aside, sweat beading his brow.

Ander moved behind Thane and began to gently massage his shoulders. "It's a long story," he said to Lord Tolmin. "The zamindar's sorcerers had found a way to extend his life by stealing the lives of others. They were almost ready to use it, but Thane stole the crystals they needed to work the magic. They knew he was guilty because he'd been caught by a cantrip and marked by the spell. They put him to torture by the chief imperial wizard."

"But Thane *still* escaped," Skorri said. "Nobody had ever defeated the zamindar's wizards before. The zamindar must have figured out Thane's a mage, and more powerful than his own sorcerers." The blond shrugged. "At least that's what Sorel thinks."

Lord Tolmin looked more confused than ever. "Sorel?"

"One of Thane's initiates," Ander said. "A crafty one."

Thane stood up. "I've got to get back home." Determination settled on his face, a look the others knew well. "We have to rebuild the Lyceum's greenhouse. Grow the plants we need for magic. Only the art is strong enough to defeat the zamindar. We have to stop him *now*. His chief sorcerer had discovered a way to use blood magic to bestow immortality. The zamindar thinks I stole that secret and escaped with it. No wonder he's desperate to find me."

Erik held up a hand, his expression firm. The youth was accustomed to the silence of the hunt and did not speak often. When he did, it was usually important. "Sorel said that's what you'd want to do. He said you'd be a fool to try and wanted me to tell you so. He thinks you should leave Izmir, at least for now."

Anger flashed across Thane's face. Though he had thirty years experience in life, the art had suspended his spirit as well as his body at nineteen. Feelings burned hot. His stalwart body tensed as he glared at the young messenger. "Since when does Sorel decide what I do or when I go?"

Erik didn't flinch. "He doesn't, and he knows it. But he said to tell you to put the cause first. Staying won't help anybody, Thane. You'll be captured and this time you won't escape. Skorri and I brought supplies. We'll go with you, help guard your back."

"*NO!* I can't run and hide!" He was breathing hard.

Ander stepped between the youths. "Sorel and Nicolai can watch over the Lyceum until it's safe for you to return. Trust them. Sorel is usually right. Things will calm down soon enough. Please, jirí. I'll be at your side whatever you choose. But fighting is foolish if we can't win."

Ander's concern cut through the tumult in Thane's mind. *Jirí. Beloved. He shouldn't need to remind me.* His shoulders slumped and he nodded wearily. "I'm sorry. I should know by now to listen to my friends." He stood and clasped Ander briefly on the shoulder, then turned back to Erik.

"Did Sorel suggest where I should go?"

Erik looked relieved. "East. He said you've been wanting to journey there anyway, to search for the origins of Leif's stories. He thinks a trip to the east won't be wasted."

"Ah." A half-smile brightened Thane's features. "Sorel's clever, as always. He knows how to tempt me."

Leif, Ander's boyhood friend and a recent initiate to Thane's band of mages, had a grandmother from the distant east. Her tales of lost secrets, mysteries of flesh and spirit, had piqued Thane's interest. They hinted that the art, or something like it, might have flourished in another time and place.

Lord Tolmin wiped dirty hands on his robes, then reached into a pocket and withdrew a small leather sack. "Take this, use it to book passage on a ship. It's the only way out of Chanture that you won't be seen." He handed the sack to Thane.

The soft chink of gold was unmistakable. "Jeffrey, I can't. You've given me so much already."

The old man waved a hand. "You're wise to take your friend's counsel. Don't let the damned zamindar catch you. I couldn't bear it."

Thane hesitated a moment, then embraced his old friend. "Perhaps I'll find some new specimens for you," he said.

Tolmin patted his back gently, then pushed him away. "Don't worry about me," he said. His eyes were sad. "You're like a son to me, Thane. Take care. That's all I want."

"We should get ready," Ander said. "There's not much time if we're to leave Chanture on tonight's tide." Long shadows already filled the greenhouse, making it look like deep jungle.

Thane sighed and released his kindly mentor. Plans for rebuilding the Lyceum's greenhouse and defeating the zamindar hovered around him like shattered dreams. But his gaze came to rest on Ander and the tightness in his chest eased. He would be a fugitive, but would not be alone.

Chanture never slept. Narrow streets and canals wove a tangled web around stately mansions and elegant entertainment districts, turning the teeming city into a maze. Though it was early spring and still brisk, doors were open to entice travelers with fine food and exotic entertainment. Erik and Skorri gawked at the marvels as they hurried past, while Thane wore a hooded cloak and kept his eyes downcast. He didn't want any of the revelers to remember seeing a gray-eyed youth when word of the zamindar's reward reached Chanture.

They soon found their way to the warehouse district near the docks. Darkness brought a measure of relief. Thane threw back his hood and looked around. They all wore their traveling leathers and carried saddlebags over their shoulders. Erik had kept his bow in hand and Ander carried his guitar in its leather case. He had made his living as a musician in a brothel before finding his way to the Lyceum and was justly admired for his skill. His musical ability, even more than his beauty, was what had drawn him close to Thane.

Turning a corner, they found themselves in a narrow avenue lined with stone warehouses. Smells of fish and tar hung heavy in the air. They were halfway down the street when a shadow near the next intersection divided into half a dozen figures. Thane saw a glint of moonlight on metal.

He raised a hand to halt his companions. "Nightblades. Too many of them, and we can't fight weighted down like this. Back." They moved away, returning the way they had come, not turning their backs. The nightblades kept pace.

Thane heard the scrape of boots on cobblestones behind them. He spun around. Three more men had appeared at the opposite end of the street. He cursed softly and let the saddlebag he was carrying slip off his shoulder. His companions did the same, preparing to fight.

"There's too many," Erik said softly. "The longer we wait, the worse our odds. Get ready to run." He plucked an arrow from his quiver and raised his bow, pulling the drawstring to his ear and letting fly in a single smooth movement. A man screamed in the larger group of nightblades and curses split the air. Erik turned while notching another arrow and took aim on the other group. The arrow's whisper was followed by more curses. The nightblades dissolved back into the shadows.

"Back the way we came," Thane said. They grabbed their baggage and ran until emerging into a wider street where richly dressed residents still strolled. Thane slowed and pulled up the hood on his cape. "We probably haven't lost them," he said, breathing hard from the sprint. "They'll want revenge. Look out for an ambush. But don't attract attention."

"Can we still get to the docks?" Ander asked.

"It'll take longer, but I know another way. Keep close. And stay away from shadows."

Thane led the way, relying on his memory of the city's labyrinthine streets. They detoured through an entertainment district where brothels competed with inns and taverns. Nobody challenged them, but furtive figures kept pace. Soon they turned downhill again. The slap of water on stone got louder and they emerged quayside. A line of ships bobbed gently on inky water, lamps hanging from booms swaying overhead like drunken moons.

"Which one?" Ander asked.

Thane studied the line of ships. Most were merchantmen, ranging from sleek galiots to four-masted carracks. He started walking down the quay and examining each vessel closely. The others followed, keeping wary watch on the side streets. Finally Thane stopped beside a three-masted vessel with a carved dragon on its prow. The fierce beast was painted red and gold, with black eyes that bulged from its long head.

"This one," Thane said. "It's the only one built in the eastern style. And it's big enough to take on passengers." He put down his luggage and cupped his hands around his mouth. "Is anyone aboard?" he called. "We seek passage. Hello, is anyone on watch?"

Soon a man appeared on the foredeck and ambled over to the taffrail. The tilt of his eyes confirmed Thane's guess about the ship's origins. He peered at them, then spat into the water.

"Go away. Have full crew." He turned and started walking back toward the helm.

"Wait, come back," Thane called. "Let me talk to your captain. We can pay."

The man paused, then turned. "We go tomorrow, home to Xi'an. How much?" The interest in his voice belied his nonchalant pose.

Ander grinned. "We're making progress," he whispered to Thane. He dug a silver coin out of a pocket and tossed it to the man aboard ship, who caught it deftly. "There's more where that came from," he said. "If your captain gives us passage, I'll double it."

After holding the coin up to light and confirming its authenticity, the sailor gave Ander a small salute, then turned and jogged into a companionway.

"He'd better not take long," Skorri said. He pointed to an alley on the far side of a warehouse. "Somebody's over there. I heard him."

"Probably a damned nightblade," Erik said, scowling. "Waiting for his friends. There's no cover here. We're done for if they bring bows."

Thane's stomach knotted, but he stood fast. "A little longer. None of the streets would be much better. Be ready to jump into the river if you have to."

A minute passed, then two. Thane began to fear the sailor had failed, that they had run out of time. Then the companionway door swung open and a tough looking woman in silk robes stepped onto the deck. Two sailors followed her.

While female captains were rare in Izmir, the eastern kingdoms had no such prejudices. The woman walked to the taffrail and looked at them curiously. Her rich robes, decorated with intricate needlepoint, spoke of nobility. The design featured an embroidered dragon that matched the ship's figurehead.

"Thank you for coming," Thane said. "Can you grant us passage? We can pay."

The woman laughed. "My man was right. You *are* the most comely boys ever to turn up on the wharf. But that's not enough to earn you passage." Though she bore the almond eyes and sleek black hair of the east, her strong voice had only a slight accent.

Thane blushed but didn't look away. He pulled a small leather bag from a cloak pocket and poured gold coins into his palm. "Here, see for yourself. We're honest merchants."

The woman snorted. "I can guess what you've been selling. Keep your money, boy. I was curious to see if you were as fair as my man claimed, that's all. But I've carried westerners before and it's more trouble than it's worth. You don't understand our ways. I don't need your fare that badly." She turned to leave.

"Wait!" Thane shouted. The captain ignored him.

Ander suddenly pulled his guitar from its case and sat cross-legged on the quay. He started playing with fierce concentration, a dissonant melody that made no sense to Thane's ears. It sounded devilishly difficult.

The captain was halfway to the companionway, but she stopped and cocked her head to listen. After a few moments she returned to the taffrail. She looked astonished.

"Keep playing," Thane whispered. "Whatever you're doing is working." Ander didn't seem to hear him. A true musician, who felt music to the depths of his heart, he was oblivious to distractions. His fingers flew over the fingerboard as the music whirled and danced. The captain watched him intently. Several sailors appeared at the taffrail and seemed equally awed.

The piece raced to a fiery conclusion. Ander took a deep breath, then rose gracefully and gave the captain a bow. "A small gift," he said when he lifted his gaze. "We understand some of your ways and would like to learn more. That's why we're traveling east."

The captain tapped her fingers on the taffrail, regarding them with a serious expression. At last she gave a single nod. "I judged too quickly. Those with great beauty are often shallow, but it's a mistake to judge by appearances. Would you be willing to play for me during the journey?"

"I would be honored," Ander said as he bowed again.

The captain returned the bow, then gestured to her sailors. They extended a gangplank from the foredeck to the wharf.

Thane sent his friends aboard while keeping a wary eye on the alley where trouble lurked. Figures moved in the shadows as he boarded with the last of their panniers. He took a last look at Chanture as the gangplank was withdrawn. *Will I ever see it again? Or Lord Tolmin?* There was no way to know. He sighed, then followed the others below deck.

2

"HAVE SOMETHING to eat, Ander." Captain Jiang swept her hand over the low table. Blue porcelain dishes filled with aromatic delicacies cluttered its lacquered surface. "I've been a poor host. I've been enjoying myself too much."

Ander laid his guitar aside. He was grateful for the respite, but careful not to show it. They had been at the captain's table for an hour and he'd barely touched the food. "It was my pleasure, captain. An appreciative audience is a musician's greatest joy."

Captain Jiang handed him a goblet of wine. "Fate smiles on the Anshan tonight. I had thought our return to Xi'an would be dreary. But now, I shall relish it."

Ander ducked his head in an abbreviated bow and accepted the goblet. He wanted to eat, not get drawn into conversation. After a sip of tart wine he put down the goblet and started collecting samples of the exotic foods in a small bowl. Captain Jiang turned back to Thane and resumed their conversation.

Ander bit into a springroll. Rich flavors of cured cabbage and grilled chicken filled his mouth, spicy but not overwhelming. His eyes widened with pleased surprise and the morsel vanished before he knew it. Next he tried a dumpling containing bits of barbecued pork embedded in sweet dough. Strange, but pleasing. He chewed contentedly and looked around the room.

They dined in the captain's cabin, a small but elegant chamber paneled with dark mahogany and lit with oil lamps. Skorri and Erik sat across the table from Captain Jiang. They leaned against each other, shoulder to shoulder, their eyes barely open. Both had eaten heartily and enjoyed the wine, more than they were accustomed to. And they had ridden hard to reach Chanture ahead of the zamindar's heralds. Fatigue had overcome them and they were nodding off.

Turning back to the feast, Ander sampled the varied fare and sipped his wine while Thane traded information with the captain. She seemed as fascinated by the mage as she had been by Ander's music. It was hardly surprising. Thane's mind was like a beacon, illuminating unusual ideas and obscure facts that few paused to examine. Ander was glad to see the mage warming to the journey. His greatest fear was for Thane's safety, and he wouldn't breathe easy until they had evaded the zamindar's net.

Ander was enjoying noodles spiced with peanuts and sesame seeds when a sailor entered the cabin and signaled to Captain

Jiang. She uncurled from the floor with surprising grace, then bowed to her guests. "You must excuse me. It's time to set sail. Please stay and finish your dinner. We'll talk again later." She bowed again before leaving with the sailor.

"Why don't you two turn in?" Thane said to the sleepy boys. "I'll stay while Ander finishes his dinner." The young lovers got to their feet, blinking sleepily, and left the captain's quarters. Their saddlebags were already stowed in a cabin near the crew's quarters, a small but clean room with two beds.

Thane met Ander's gaze and attempted a smile. He looked exhausted. "Perhaps she's right. Maybe fate does smile today. I wouldn't have thought so a few hours ago."

"Fate helps those who help themselves," Ander replied. "At least that's what Sorel says. Come to think of it, he said you told him that."

Thane leaned over and brushed a stray lock of hair from Ander's eyes. "Don't believe everything Sorel tells you," he said. "Eat, while it's still hot. You earned your dinner tonight."

Ander indulged himself, sampling and tasting, until he was sated. He wiped his fingers on a napkin and finished the last of his wine.

"Ready for bed?" Thane asked. "It's been a long day."

"Let's get some air first. It'll clear my head."

Thane nodded agreeably. They left the warm confines of the captain's cabin and went on deck. Sails billowed overhead, canvas flapping softly in a light wind. Twilight had settled over the river valley like indigo snow. Chanture was already behind them, its intricate stone mansions dwindling in the distance. Gargantuan columns, made of hard rock that had withstood the river for millennia, stood like sentinels along the bank.

Ander stood at the railing and watched the landscape slide past. "I think Captain Jiang likes you," he said as he leaned against Thane. "Did you see her surprise when you asked her about Quangdo legends? She was pleased."

Thane put an arm around Ander's shoulders. "Your music is what *really* impressed her. For good reason."

Ander basked in his lover's praise. Though he'd received many compliments on his playing, he could feel Thane's sincerity through their bond. Forged by the art and reinforced each time they made love, the psychic link conveyed more than his partner's sensations. He could feel Thane's heart, the core of fierce determination and loyalty that defined the mage's spirit.

"We were lucky," he said. "Leif's mother was a singer and taught me the tunes. It made Leif happy to hear me play them, especially after she died."

"You're too modest, jirí," Thane said as he gave his partner a squeeze. "It's your skill that makes the music live. But never mind. I'm glad we're together now. That's all that matters."

The mage's words were vague, but the melancholy tinge through their bond told Ander more than words could ever convey. Visiting Chanture always reminded Thane of Lucian.

They watched dark fields glide silently past, as if they were stationary and the landscape moved. Moonlight painted the rock pillars with silvery light and cast shimmering reflections over the river's surface. The deck rocked gently beneath their feet. Ander leaned against Thane, enjoying the weight of his partner's arm around his shoulders. The close contact turned his mind to the opportunities presented by life aboard ship.

Thane laughed softly, then turned his head and nuzzled Ander's ear. "I can tell what you're thinking," he whispered. "I always know when you're horny. Which is most of the time, it seems."

Ander's embarrassed smile did nothing to deny the claim. "Look who's talking. You seduced me first, remember?" He turned and put a hand on Thane's crotch, cupping the mound of flesh beneath his lover's soft leathers while using his body to conceal the gesture from any crewmen who might be watching. Thane's virile body responded strongly. Ander's grin widened as he felt the youth's cock harden.

"You're as relentless as Skorri," Thane said. "Why I ever thought you were a shy boy, I'll never know."

"I *was* shy." He stepped back and took Thane by the hand, tugging him away from the railing. "But not any more. Now I'm just horny." He pulled his partner toward the ship's bow. "Enough talk. Let's go to our cabin. Want to wager if Erik and Skorri are sleeping?"

Thane laughed and shook his head, following willingly. They entered a narrow companionway in the forecastle. Faint light shone through portholes, barely enough to find the way to their cabin. Ander knocked on the door. "It's us," he said softly. After a short wait a bolt was thrown and the door opened a crack. Erik peeked out, then moved aside to let them enter.

A single oil lamp, suspended from a rafter in the middle of the ceiling, bathed the cabin's pine walls with golden light. Erik and Skorri had obviously not been totally exhausted. The curly-haired blond reclined on one of the beds with his legs spread wide. His long cock stretched across his ridged abdomen in a hard curve, glistening with spit. Erik's erection speared up from his groin with potent vigor. He shut and bolted the door, then slid onto the bed beside Skorri.

Ander's gaze swept the handsome lovers. Though he had bedded them repeatedly since joining Thane's band of mages, he hadn't seen them naked together for over two weeks. They were a stunning pair, Erik's deeply tanned skin and dark blue eyes contrasting with Skorri's golden radiance and lively green eyes.

Erik stroked Skorri's lean torso from nipple to navel, then gave the blond's rigid penis a gentle squeeze. Precum oozed onto Skorri's flat belly. "Want to join us?" Erik asked while using a fingertip to smear precum along the underside of his partner's cock. "There's not much room, but we could manage."

Ander's cock hardened as he watched Skorri squirm. The last time all four of them shared a tumble had been a lusty and strenuous adventure.

Loud pounding on the cabin door made Ander jump. "Come see captain!" a man said loudly. "She's talking with you!"

Thane groaned. "I forgot she wanted to talk some more after we got under way. But when the captain calls, you go." He put a hand on Ander's shoulder. "Do you want to go too? Be forewarned, she'll probably have you making music until midnight."

"Of course," Ander said, forcing a weak grin. "I can always use the practice."

Thane snorted and pushed Ander down onto a bunk. "You'll never be a slyboots, jirí. That wouldn't have fooled me even without our bond. I'll entertain the captain and try to learn more about our destination. You get some rest."

Ander nodded, reclining on the bunk opposite Erik and Skorri. The mage was right. He was far too tired to perform again. "I'll wait for you," he said as he tugged a boot off.

Knocking resumed as Thane doused the lamp. He tousled Ander's hair, then unlatched the door and left with the sailor.

Ander stripped and pulled a blanket up to his waist while Erik and Skorri resumed their lovemaking. He knew they would have welcomed him, but he wanted to wait for Thane's return. He soon fell asleep, accompanied by soft sounds of pleasure.

Morning light cast a beam through the porthole. Ander stretched as he woke, comforted by the familiar feel of Thane's sturdy body at his side. He rubbed his eyes and tried to remember when his lover had returned to the cabin. Nothing. He must have slept soundly.

A few feet away, Skorri slept with an arm flung across Erik's broad chest and his head resting on the hunter's shoulder. Their athletic bodies gleamed with oil left from the night's lovemaking. A faint scent of cloves told Ander the oil contained sensitizing elixirs. One of Thane's great discoveries had been that plant extracts could be used to heighten pleasure. Exceptional skill in the arts of love, coupled with the discipline to forestall release while pleasure spiraled to fantastic extremes, opened a gate to realms beyond normal perception. Infinite mystery and untold power waited in the kei, but reaching the kei was its own reward even without that lure.

Thane woke as Ander stirred. They embraced, then shared a leisurely kiss. Ander marveled anew at his lover's masculine beauty. Lean and powerfully muscled, possessing alluring features but tanned like a field laborer, he was an uncommonly sexy youth. Kissing him never failed to produce an aching erection.

"Morning," Ander murmured. "When did you get back?"

"Well past midnight. Captain Jiang and I got along well. She's inquisitive and well read. I managed to learn as much from her as she learned from me."

"Did she get you out of your clothes?" Ander pressed himself against Thane, enjoying the feel of his cock against the mage's naked torso.

Thane laughed and rolled on top of Ander, holding him down by the shoulders. His phallus throbbed against Ander's flat belly. "If she was interested, she didn't say anything. She knows you're my jirimandari. And she's far too polite to ask for a tumble. Unlike randy beasts like you!"

"Huh! Feels to me like you're ready to fuck something yourself."

Thane lowered his head and kissed Ander again, pressing their bodies together and rubbing cocks, then rolled off. "I'd like nothing better, but we'll have to wait. The captain told me we'll reach Jaffna by mid-morning. We'll be taking on supplies for the trip down the coast. I need to finish eating and get back in our cabin before we get there. Ports are always swarming with the zamindar's spies."

Ander reluctantly got out of bed and started dressing. Erik and Skorri had woken and were rubbing sleep from their eyes. Soon all four joined the crew on deck for porridge and biscuits.

The river had widened to a broad delta and the sun already glowed overhead like a gold dinner plate. The breeze held a hint of the sea. They watched the scenery, marveling at the comfort and ease of traveling by ship. Thane stayed on deck until the port city of Jaffna appeared in the distance. The zamindar's heralds might not have reached so far south yet, but there was no reason to take a chance.

Ander stayed above deck while the mighty river carried the Anshan into port with surprising speed. They moored at a crowded wharf alongside vessels larger than Ander had ever seen. Erik and Skorri were speechless with wonder.

Casks of rice and salted meat were rolled aboard and quickly stowed. Quayage at Jaffna was paid by the hour and Captain Jiang plainly wanted to avoid delay. The loading was almost done when three unfamiliar figures strode up the gangplank and stepped onto the deck.

Ander watched the newcomers warily from his perch near the helm. There were two men and a woman in the group. The woman wore pale blue gowns and shimmery gold veils; she moved with the studied sensuality that to Ander's practiced eye signified a courtesan. One man was a heavily laden porter. It was the second man who gave Ander pause.

The middle-aged man wore black leathers and boots, and the metal skullcap of a priest of Yataghan. He scowled as he surveyed the ship's crew, his eyes squinting and his lips pressed together inside an oval formed by a closely trimmed moustache and beard. When he saw the captain on the upper deck he beckoned imperiously. Ander edged closer, lurking behind the main mast as the captain responded to the summons.

Captain Jiang bowed to the new arrivals, her face impassive. "You must excuse me. We sail shortly and have no time for business in Jaffna. You'll have to—"

"My apologies," the man with the skullcap said. "I'm Varian, sayyid priest in the Order of Yataghan. An urgent matter requires that I travel east."

"I am sorry, but I cannot—"

"The owners of this ship have guaranteed passage to imperial representatives, by long-standing treaty." A snap of his fingers and the porter handed him a leather folio. He withdrew a parchment bearing a wax seal. "My Order has been commissioned by the zamindar himself. As we now represent the zamindar, you must grant passage to me and my dependents." He handed the parchment to the captain, then turned and gestured for his porter to pick up his bundles.

Captain Jiang read the imperial commission, her eyebrows pulled down in a fierce frown. Even from a distance, Ander could see her anger.

Varian turned back to the captain and crossed his arms. "It's all in order, captain. It's not your decision. Now, where will we be quartered?"

Captain Jiang bowed again, stiffly this time. "I'll have the crew prepare a cabin for you in the stern quarter gallery, master Varian. I'm afraid it won't be much—"

"I'll require two cabins," Varian said as he sat on a cask. "I don't want my porter or woman in the way when I don't need them." Captain Jiang looked furious, but said nothing. She nodded and stalked away from the new passengers.

Ander went below deck and knocked on their cabin's door. Thane opened it, looked relieved to see him.

"We're leaving port?"

"Something's happened," Ander said as he shut the door. "A passenger boarded. A priest of Yataghan and his servants. Varian. He told the captain he's on the zamindar's business and forced her to give him passage."

Thane stood motionless. "Did he say what kind of business?"

"No. But he said it was urgent. And from what Erik said, it sounds like you've become the zamindar's obsession. Maybe we should get off the ship while we still can."

Thane scowled and crossed his arms. Ander felt frustration and anger seeping through their bond, but the mage's determination was even stronger. "No. Things will only get worse here. And we don't know if he's heard about me. He could be on other business."

"But what if he *does* know about you? There's no way to prevent him seeing the color of your eyes."

"I'll stay in the cabin until we're sure it's safe. You can tell Captain Jiang I'm sick."

Ander smiled. Thane's stubborn spirit was as unchanging as his virile body. Relenting, he took one of the mage's hands and drew him near. "Maybe it's a good plan," he said. "At least I'll finally have you to myself." He leaned close and kissed Thane's neck.

There was another way Thane hadn't changed: he responded instantly to a lover's touch. He moaned softly and closed his eyes as Ander's lips brushed his skin. Ander felt the strong pulse quicken in his lover's throat as he continued his gentle explorations. He gripped the bottom of Thane's shirt and lifted it off. His partner's muscular torso, tanned from long hours working in the Lyceum's gardens and fields, flexed with sinuous grace as he shimmied out of the garment.

Ander pulled off his own shirt, then wrapped his arms around Thane. Hard flesh, warm and satiny smooth, pressed against his chest. He lowered his hands to Thane's hips and pulled their crotches together.

Someone thumped the cabin door.

Ander sighed and released his partner. "Ships are too crowded, I think." He turned and opened the latch. Skorri waited on the other side.

The young blond grinned as he glanced at Ander's bare chest and the bulge at his crotch. "Should I come back later? You look busy."

Despite the polite offer, the boy's interest was plain. Skorri's sunny charm was matched by insatiable enthusiasm for sex. Ander returned the grin and opened the door to let him in. "Where's Erik?" he asked.

"Did you see that priest who boarded a few minutes ago?"

Ander nodded as he closed and latched the door.

"Erik has a feel for dangerous animals, and he thinks the priest is dangerous. He wanted to watch without being noticed. So I decided to come down here while he does his spying."

Thane put an arm around Skorri's shoulders and pulled him close to make him feel welcome. They were a sexy pair, Skorri with his blond curls and northern features, Thane with short brown hair and the intense masculinity of a young wrestler.

Ander approached Skorri from behind and pressed against him. He cupped a hand over the boy's crotch and felt his cock stiffening beneath soft leather. The shaft, longer than Ander's hand, pulsed as the youth's excitement mounted. The blond moaned and opened his mouth to Thane's inquisitive tongue.

Ander unbuckled Skorri's belt and unfastened his trousers. The garment slid down the boy's slender hips and pooled around his feet. Circling the embracing pair, Ander repeated the service for Thane before removing his own boots and pants.

Ander moved next to Thane and put a hand on his shoulder, squeezing gently.

The mage released Skorri, who smiled blissfully, then turned to Ander. "He's ready for us. See?" He wrapped his fingers around Skorri's upthrust penis and squeezed it lightly. A droplet oozed from the cock's tip and smeared Thane's fingers.

Ander shivered with anticipation as Thane sat on a bed's edge and pulled off his boots. His athletic body beckoned with taut lines and natural animal grace. Though he was Ander's height, his body was more muscular. Broad shoulders tapered to a narrow waist and powerful legs, and his skin was honey brown except for a narrow band where he wore a loincloth while working in the

Lyceum's gardens. Hard muscle shifted beneath smooth skin, etching his chest and abdomen with clean lines; he was lean as a prize racing steed. His thick erection curved up from a thick bush of brown hair to touch his flat belly above the navel.

Skorri pulled off his shirt and boots. The blond was flushed, and a long strand of precum drooled from the tip of his rigid cock. As soon as he was nude he turned and reached for Thane's cock. Ander put his hand beside Skorri's. Their two hands almost covered the shaft from root to glans.

"Let us pleasure *you* for a change," Ander suggested as he cradled his lover's cock. "Erik and Skorri did it for me the last time we shared a tumble. You'll like it."

"We had him panting like a dog on the hottest day of summer," Skorri said, green eyes sparkling.

Thane laughed and touched Ander's cheek. "Show me, jirí. Then next time we'll see if we can make Skorri pant."

Ander blushed at the blond's claim but didn't dispute it. He went to the pile of panniers in the corner and fetched a small clay pot, then put the pot on the floor and removed its lid while Skorri knelt between Thane's legs.

Thane sprawled on the bunk with his arms propped behind his back, powerful shoulders bulging, long legs splayed wide. Skorri pulled the youth's cock upright, making a strand of precum droop between the dusky glans and his torso. The blond waited while Ander knelt on the bunk on Thane's right, then slid his fingers to the base of the mage's cock.

Leaning forward and supporting himself with a hand on each side of Thane's waist, Ander slid his lips over the slippery cockhead. His bond with his lover strengthened with the intimate contact; the sensation of wet warmth engulfed his own aching cock. He tightened his lips around the crown of the glans and tugged, feeling the soft pressure as if lips circled his own penis.

Thane reached between Ander's legs and cupped his balls, kneading them gently. "You feel it too, don't you? I can tell by how hard you are."

Ander focused on the straining penis between his lips. He let a trickle of spit escape, then followed it down the thick shaft until his nose pressed into Thane's balls. Thane moaned softly, deep in his chest. Ander appreciated the sentiment; his own cock throbbed in resonance with his lover's pleasure.

"That's good," Skorri murmured as he released Thane's cock and brushed Ander's cheek with his fingertips. "Squeeze it. Take him all the way."

Ander eagerly followed the advice. Thane's strong body flexed beneath him, muscles standing out in cleanly etched lines. Thane's right arm rested on his back as he started a slow glide back up the shaft.

Thane moaned appreciatively and lifted his hips an inch off the bed, the muscles of his legs bunching. His cock emerged inch by inch, glistening, from Ander's encircling lips.

When his lips reached the cockhead Ander reversed direction. He sucked hungrily, his tongue pressing the cock with wet pressure, euphoric at the sensations flowing from Thane through their bond. The shaft was as smooth and hard as a bully's horn, yet fit his throat comfortably.

Skorri dipped a finger in the clay pot and stirred, coating the finger with a thick layer of clear grease. Mint fragrance filled the air. He placed his fingertip against the rosette of Thane's ass and the mage spread his legs wider. Slowly, Skorri massaged lubricant over the sensitive flesh and probed until the tip of his finger slipped inside the ring of muscle. He eased the finger in deeper, twisting gently to spread lubricant evenly. Finally, timing his movements to coordinate with Ander's leisurely sucking, he slipped his finger all the way into Thane's clenching ass.

Though his heart raced, Ander maintained his rhythmic strokes as the frisky blond's stimulation of Thane's ass echoed in his own body. The young northerner dipped his other hand in the pot of lubricant, then began to stroke his cock while continuing to slide a finger in and out of Thane's tight ass.

Ander basked in the shared feel of lips moving along his penis and a finger massaging the sensitive spot inside his ass. His cock drooled precum as he pleasured Thane's cock with all his skill, using their link to keep the mage within a heartbeat of coming.

Thane began to writhe and moan. Ander shared the tingling sensation sweeping his lover's body. A pleasurable itch tickled his cock, rapidly spreading and swelling beyond the limits flesh could bear. A red nimbus shimmered into existence around Thane. The aura blossomed, engulfing the trio of youths, as shared pleasure soared.

Skorri gasped as his cock spat a geyser of semen. He threw his head back, blond curls glinting in the dim light, while his long cock pulsed. Cum coated his fingers and cock in white gobs.

Though he was panting, Skorri didn't neglect his partners. He released his cock and reached up to squeeze Ander's penis in his slippery palm while continuing to massage Thane's ass with his other hand.

The slick warmth of Skorri's cum on his cockhead hit Ander like lightning. Semen and lubricant bathed his glans with wet heat. Then Skorri's slick fingers wrapped around his straining erection and gave it a slippery stroke. There was no holding back.

Ander's orgasm rocked him as a bolt of pleasure traveled from his cock through the length of his body. He heard Thane gasp, felt the sensation of Thane's ass clamping tight on Skorri's probing finger, and then a blast of musky cum filled his mouth. Thane's seed gushed over his tongue.

Ander sucked deliriously, coating Thane's convulsing penis with a sheen of semen as their orgasms reverberated between linked minds. Sucking Thane's cock was like sucking his own, and Thane's cum could have been his own. Skorri added to the exquisite torment by capturing Ander's ejaculation in his palm and smearing the thick cream against the glans as it continued to spit.

When their ejaculations finally subsided Ander let Thane's penis slip from his mouth. He rolled onto his back, breathing hard, his head resting on Thane's lap. The mage leaned down and kissed him. The red halo that had been created when they touched the kei slowly faded. The exhausted youths fell into a heap on the crowded bunk, their bodies slick with sweat and cum.

The Anshan had reached the sea and was many leagues from Jaffna before Ander's thoughts turned back to the unwelcome passenger, Varian.

3

Captain Jiang greeted Ander graciously when he arrived at her cabin for dinner, guitar in hand. "Where's Thane?" she asked. "I have much to discuss with him."

"He's not feeling well. I think the sea is making him unsteady. Erik and Skorri are keeping him company until he gets better."

Genuine concern showed in the captain's eyes. "Please give him my regrets. It can take time to get accustomed to the waves."

"I will," Ander said. He bowed and entered the ornate cabin. The low table was set, as it had been the night before, with delicate porcelain dishes and wine goblets.

"Please be seated," the captain said. "I invited two other guests tonight, a priest of Yataghan named Varian and his companion. You might have seen him when he boarded."

"Yes," Ander replied as he sat cross-legged on the floor opposite the captain's position at the table. He laid his guitar by his side. "I don't know much about his order, though. We didn't have a Yataghan priest in Pella, where I grew up. He looked . . . severe."

"Severe is a diplomatic way to put it. The Order of Yataghan is brutal. They use torture as a sacrament. They're also shrewd. They've even insinuated themselves with the zamindar." She scowled fiercely.

Ander looked at the captain curiously. "Forgive my boldness, captain, but you don't seem to like him. May I ask why you're taking dinner with him?"

The captain closed the door and turned to Ander. She looked older than she had the night before, and worry wrinkled her brow. "Take care," she said softly. "The man is dangerous, his superiors have great influence. Even mikados Lanzhou, who owns this ship and many others, fears their power. I don't want to antagonize Varian, and neither should you."

Ander dipped his head, then met the captain's gaze. "Thank you for the counsel, Captain Jiang. I'll heed it."

Captain Jiang's expression softened. "I'm glad you're here tonight, Ander. I'd much prefer your music to priestly lectures."

Ander grinned. "Religion is always a good topic to avoid, captain. It's a lesson I learned early. Did Thane tell you I grew up in a house of companionship? When a customer starts talking about religion, companions always change the subject."

"A house of companionship? Did Thane work there too? I imagine he'd be an intriguing companion."

Before Ander could answer someone pounded on the door. The door opened before Captain Jiang reached it and Varian strode into the cabin. He glanced around the paneled chamber with sour disdain before giving the captain a perfunctory nod.

Captain Jiang bowed stiffly. "Welcome, master Varian. I hope your quarters are acceptable."

Varian sat down and reached for a bowl of figs. "Don't worry, captain. It's a trivial matter. I have far greater problems demanding my attention." He poked through the bowl to find the best fig, then popped it into his mouth.

Keeping his eyes downcast, Ander surreptitiously watched the priest eat. The man moved with force and decisiveness. Whatever his faults, lack of confidence wasn't one of his failings. His black leathers and hard features made him look more like a soldier than a priest, and his aggressive manner bolstered the impression.

Captain Jiang sat at the head of the table, maintaining a dignified bearing despite Varian's provocations. She poured wine into a goblet and handed it to the priest. "I had assumed your companion would dine with us," she said. "I hope she's well."

Varian wiped his mouth with the back of his hand before accepting the goblet. "I didn't hire her for conversation," he said. "Whores should stay on their backs with their mouths shut."

Ander tried to conceal his frown. He saw captain Jiang give him a sympathetic glance, and remembered her advice not to antagonize the priest. He picked up a piece of bread covered with flakes of peppery spice and had started to eat it when Varian tossed an almond at him. Startled, he looked up and met the priest's eyes.

"Brown," Varian said. "Too bad."

Captain Jiang froze, incredulous, with the wine flask in one hand and Ander's goblet in the other. "Brown? The boy's name is Ander. I was about to introduce you."

Varian resumed eating, scooping fried rice with his fingers. "Never mind. Just checking something."

A frown pulled at the captain's lips, but she said nothing. She handed Ander his wine before filling her own goblet. "Eat well," she said. "There's food enough for five, but only the three of us. Unfortunate."

"Five?" Varian asked, looking up from the plate he was filling to overflowing with delicacies. "Us, my woman and who else?"

"A friend of Ander's. A remarkable youth named Thane. You'd find him very interesting, I'm sure."

Varian squinted at Ander and grunted. "I doubt it. I've no interest in pretty boys. But tell me, what color are his eyes?"

The captain blinked at the unexpected question, and panic surged through Ander. Though Thane's eyes could appear either gray or blue depending on the light, it was the silvery gray that most people noticed. He picked up his guitar before the captain could answer.

"Blue," Ander said, a little too loudly. "Pale blue, like a northerner. Um, would you like some music, sir? I'd be glad to play while you dine. No trouble at all." He saw Captain Jiang looking at him strangely and realized he was blathering, but didn't know what else to do. A careless word from the captain would be disastrous.

He began to play a difficult jig. It felt awkward, with the others watching him as if he had taken leave of his senses, but he concentrated on music and tried to draw them into the spirited tune. Soon they returned to their meals. Captain Jiang appeared to appreciate his efforts, while the priest seemed oblivious.

Ander's hands ached by the time the others were done eating. Fortunately, Varian didn't look inclined to socialize after dinner. As soon as he finished his wine he stood and gave Captain Jiang a short nod. "You have a good cook, captain. I think I'll take the rest of my meals here." He turned to Ander. "You're not bad. Not equal to our temple musicians, but of course you haven't had their training. Your technique is better than some I've heard."

Surprised, Ander dipped his head in a token bow. He remained silent, not wanting to encourage the priest to linger.

Captain Jiang looked at Ander sternly as soon as Varian had left the cabin. "Do you mind telling me what that was about? I enjoyed your performance, but I don't like mysteries aboard my ship."

Ander's mind raced. While the captain was no friend of the priest, she was in no position to defy him. "Forgive me, lady. Varian made me nervous, that's all. It made me want to do something, keep busy. And making music was the only thing I could think of."

"Why did he make you so nervous?"

"Um . . . you said he uses torture, captain. Thinking about it made me lose my appetite."

The captain didn't look convinced, but she didn't pursue it. "Well, he *should* make you nervous. He has power and he's not afraid to use it. Do you want to finish your dinner now?"

"Perhaps I should take something to Thane," Ander suggested. "He'll be hungry when his stomach settles."

"Spoken like a true jirimandari," the captain said with a smile.

"It would please me if you share the food with Thane. I hope he's well soon. And I thank you for your gift of music."

Ander gathered fruit, bread and grilled meats in a basket the captain provided, then took his leave. Darkness had fallen and the sea was calm. The distant coastline slid past, a rocky landscape lit only by moonlight. They were not far past Jaffna, the kingdom's eastern-most city. The inhospitable lands in this region had always defied conquest, and had been shunned for centuries.

When he reached the forecastle he entered their cabin and gave the basket to Thane. "There's a problem," he said. "The priest knows about the zamindar's search. He's interested in the color of eyes."

Thane scowled. "I've never seen word spread so fast! The zamindar must be truly desperate."

"So what do we do?"

Thane sat on a bunk and rummaged through the basket. He selected a piece of dark bread and bit off a piece, a thoughtful expression on his face as he chewed. Ander's heart went out to him. His lover worked tirelessly, never wavering, but was never rewarded with good fortune. A lesser man would have been crushed by the disappointments but Thane only struggled harder. It was no wonder he inspired such fierce loyalty in his friends. Even without his beauty he would have been a great leader.

Thane finished the bread and met Ander's gaze. "Tell Captain Jiang I've come down with a fever," he said. "Sailors fear sickness. It spreads fast on a ship, and there are usually no healers around. Nobody will ask questions if I stay here in the cabin. They'll be grateful."

"It should work," Ander agreed. "But you'll have a miserable journey."

"Better than if the priest finds me. Last night Captain Jiang told me we should make port in Xi'an in about ten days. I'll manage."

"Where are Erik and Skorri? I didn't see them on deck."

"They decided to learn sailing, as long as they've got the chance." Thane smiled, rueful. "To tell the truth, I encouraged them. They needed something to do."

"Something other than getting in your pants you mean," Ander said, poking Thane in the ribs. "I know what they're like."

Thane laughed and wrapped Ander in a bear hug, tumbling him onto his back. "You should know! They told me some interesting stories about the last time they bedded you. They were impressed."

"I've had good teachers," Ander said. "And I'm ready for another lesson!"

Ander staggered through the door, breathless. Thane looked up from the book he was reading and blinked, bleary eyed. Three days in a dimly lit cabin had left the mage dazed. Ander was afraid to think what ten days of confinement would do.

"Bad news," he said as he dropped onto the bunk beside Thane. "The crew's been talking about you."

Thane put the book down and rubbed his eyes. "They're probably worried I've got something they might catch."

"That's part of what they're talking about. But some of them saw you the first day, and they've been telling the others what you look like. I heard one of them say you have gray eyes."

Thane went white.

"And the priest has been listening," Ander continued. "Everybody tries to avoid him, but he's always prowling around. He's a snoop if ever I've seen one. Even worse than the girls back at Lady Tayanita's House of Companionship."

Thane began to pace, crossing the cabin in two strides. "A snoop, and from what you've told me he's persistent. I wonder if—"

A soft rattle of the door's latch made Thane freeze. It wasn't locked. The door swung open and Varian stepped into the cabin. He grinned triumphantly when he saw Thane's face.

"So it's true! And you're all mine! The zamindar will—"

Ander sprang from the bunk and hit the priest's body with a solid thud. They fell to the floor and grappled for holds. Thane fell to his knees and laced his fingers together, then smashed his joined fists down on the back of Varian's neck. The man grunted and jerked, then fell limp.

Ander squirmed out from beneath the man's heavy body. Thane pulled a blanket off the bunk and ripped a strip from its edge. He tied Varian's hands while Ander looked down the corridor and then shut the door.

"Anybody see us?" Thane asked.

"I don't think so." He knelt at Thane's side. "Why are you tying him? He's seen you and knows who you are. We can't let him live."

"It's not that simple." Thane ripped another strip from the blanket. He fashioned it into a gag and tied it securely, then rocked back on his heels. "He's here with the sanction of the ship's owner. Captain Jiang will have trouble if he dies. She could lose her position, or worse."

"I suppose you're right," Ander said doubtfully. "But what choice do we have?"

"I have an idea. Find the captain, tell her I need to see her right away."

"Here?" Ander asked, shocked. "She'll see what happened!"

"Some people are honorable, others aren't. I think we can trust Captain Jiang. Now go. There's no time to argue. Tell Erik and Skorri to come too."

Events were moving too fast. Trusting in Thane's greater experience, Ander went on deck. Skorri and Erik were helping rig a topsail. They clambered down the rigging when Ander called, looking pleased with their growing skill as sailors.

"Get down to the cabin," Ander said. "Something's happened."

Their smiles vanished. "What?" Skorri asked.

"Thane will tell you." He put a hand on the blond's arm. "Have you seen the captain?"

"A minute ago," Erik answered. "Talking to the helmsman."

"Good. You'd best hurry."

The boys left. Ander turned and walked quickly to the helm. Captain Jiang had finished with her helmsman and was examining the coastline while referring to a parchment map. He approached her and bowed. She rolled the map and gave him a short bow in return.

"Good day, Ander. How do you fare?"

"I'm well, captain. Thank you. But something has happened, and you need to know. Thane asked that you come see him."

Concern filled the captain's face. "Has he taken a turn for the worse?"

"It's . . . more complicated than that," Ander said, feeling awkward. "The problem is more, um, political. That's why he needs to see you."

"Very well. I've been concerned about him anyway. He's been below deck longer than most passengers who get a green stomach on the sea." She tucked the map under her belt and followed Ander to the forecastle.

They arrived at the cabin and were admitted by Thane. Erik and Skorri stood in front of one of the bunks. After the captain entered the cabin they stood aside to reveal Varian, still unconscious. She stiffened and turned to Thane with a glower on her face.

"Are you mad?" Her voice shook with anger.

Thane held the captain's gaze. "Not mad," he said calmly. "Desperate is more like it. I need your counsel."

The captain blinked and her scowl faded. "Explain."

"The priest was searching for someone. He heard a rumor about me and came to investigate. We subdued him, but he's seen me. I'm his quarry."

"You?" She looked incredulous. "What have you done to earn such enemies?"

"I know a secret. Something the zamindar needs. Something he *has* to have."

"What kind of secret?" Her eyes narrowed.

"Secrets of the earth, and of plants." He picked up a thin black case from the other bunk and opened it. Vials of colored liquid, sealed with cork stoppers, filled both sides of the case. He removed a half-empty vial of pale green fluid and held it up. "I gave the priest some of this. He'll sleep for half a day or more."

"You're a poisoner?" She backed away.

"He's a scholar," Ander said. "If he'd poisoned the priest, why would he have asked you to come here?"

"Why *do* you want to see me?" the captain asked.

"The zamindar's an old man," Thane said. "My knowledge could extend his life. And his tyranny. But I'd die before giving it to him."

"I understand," Captain Jiang said softly. "Many fear the zamindar, few love him. Fewer yet dare to oppose him."

"I could have killed the priest," Thane said. "But I didn't. His death aboard the Anshan would bring you grief. But if you let us take a dinghy ashore, you can pretend to find Varian tomorrow. He'll think we stole away in the night and won't blame you. I'll pay you for the dinghy."

"Why are you asking me? Why didn't you just steal a dinghy and leave the priest?"

Thane closed the case of elixirs and gave the captain a respectful bow. "You gave us aid when we needed it, and treated us honorably. Betrayal would be a poor reward." He met the captain's eye and grinned. "And it would be convenient if you were on deck tonight at midnight, speaking to your helmsman, when the time comes for us to leave. It would be best for all if we left without being seen."

Captain Jiang nodded thoughtfully, then returned his grin. "I was right about you. There's more to you than meets the eye. I hope we meet again."

"My thanks, captain. I share the wish."

Water black as ink splashed into the overloaded dinghy as Erik rowed for shore. The Anshan had already vanished in the darkness. Ander shivered. While their escape had gone smoothly, it was plain their problems were far from over.

"Are you sure you know where we are?" he asked Thane.

The mage thumped a saddlebag and nodded. "The map's in here. Captain Jiang made the copy herself. Nobody knows much about these parts, but she says there's a trade route not too far inland. If we find it, then turn east, we'll find a settlement sooner or later."

The answer didn't inspire confidence, but they had no alternative. Soon there was no time to worry. Waves grew in height as they entered the shallows, and boulders loomed around them. They clung to their saddlebags and the sides of the boat while Erik struggled to guide the dinghy through turbulent waters. The shore rushed upon them.

A bone-jarring thud nearly knocked Ander from the boat as a wave pushed them against a rock outcropping. The boat spun and threatened to capsize. Then, with a dropping feeling, the wave brought them down at the mouth of a small cove. Sand and pebbles grated beneath the keel.

"Get to shore!" Thane shouted as water surged between the boat's sprained planks. They grabbed their packs and tumbled out as the boat bobbed drunkenly. The water was waist deep and an undertow tugged strongly at them. Moments later a splintering crash marked the dinghy's end as another wave hurled it against the rocks.

Ander staggered onto the beach, soaked and shaking. The waterlogged pannier had tripled in weight. He dropped it and collapsed on the sand beside his friends, coughing and clutching his guitar case to his chest. Thane put an arm around his shoulders and held him tightly.

"It's all right, Ander. We made it."

Ander coughed again, looking at the steep bluff that surrounded them on three sides and the churning sea in front of them. He leaned against Thane and sighed. "Maybe traveling by horseback isn't so bad after all."

4

LIGHT GLOWED on the horizon, like a gold band on the lip of the sky's indigo dome. Ander thought he could already feel its heat, though he knew it was only his imagination.

"Time to start looking for shade," he said, pointing ahead. "Maybe someplace with no lizards this time?" he added hopefully.

"Lizards are good eating," Erik said as he walked beside Ander. "And about all we're going to find around here when our supplies run out."

Surveying the barren landscape, Ander had to agree. After four days of hiking they were still surrounded by yellow and russet pinnacles, crags that had been carved into fantastic shapes by wind and sand. At least the map Captain Jiang had given them was proving accurate. They'd found the trade route only half a day after fleeing the Anshan. While they hadn't encountered a caravan, and their feet ached from walking with saddlebags over their shoulders, there had been deep wells along the road. Their water flasks had never run dry.

"A little further," Thane said. He was in the lead as usual, always eager to see what lay around every bend in the narrow trail. "There's something ahead, can't you feel it?"

"I hope it's food," Skorri said. "I'm sick of pemmican."

"Maybe it's one of the old cities Captain Jiang told us about," Thane continued. He stopped to let the others catch up. "You know what I mean, don't you? There's something in the air."

"Dust," Skorri announced. "It's definitely dust."

Ander stopped at Thane's side, grateful for the brief respite. "I think I feel it," he said. "Like singing in a strange tongue, far away." He shivered, glancing at the rocks spearing out of the sand. "I thought I was daydreaming. But if you feel it too, there must be something out there."

Thane grabbed his shoulder. "Look!" He pointed at a distant point nearly hidden between two weathered peaks. A golden point shone like a jewel on dawn's pale crescent.

"What is it?" Ander asked. The point grew brighter as he watched.

"I don't know," Thane said. "But we can't stop now. Maybe it's a beacon of some kind." He released Ander and resumed walking east.

The trail rose gently, weaving its way between boulders laced with quartz. The golden point lured them on, though its sparkle faded as the sun rose and light flooded the sky. Soon they climbed a final switchback and arrived at a plateau. Ander's breath caught at the vista that was revealed.

A green oasis lay before them in a shallow valley filled with palms. At its center, next to a walled city, stood a massive four-sided structure with triangular walls that leaned in to meet in a shining peak. It was four times higher than the city walls, at least two hundred feet of polished limestone capped with gold.

"What is it?" Erik asked, his voice hushed.

"It must be a pyramid," Thane said. "Like a ziggurat but with no terraces. I've heard stories of them, but always thought they were only legends."

Ander wiped sweat from his brow. "We'd best go into the city for shelter. We'll roast if we stay out in the sun."

No argument was required. Intoxicating scents of water and lush vegetation beguiled them as they descended from the plateau and entered fields. Farmers dressed in white robes and headscarves were already at work tending their crops. The caravan trail turned to cobbles and then to stone as they approached the city. Towering wooden gates, painted with red and blue interlocking circles, stood open.

Inside the yellow brick walls, the city swirled with the strangest mix of people and animals Ander had ever seen. Men and women with skin ranging from pale white to darkest ebony haggled over figs, rice, leeks and squawking chickens. Skewered chunks of spiced meat sizzled on grills. Fragrant smoke filled the air and made Ander's stomach rumble.

At the edge of the bazaar they found a low table shaded by an awning. A girl tending a grill sold them sausages and flat pieces of freshly baked bread spread with tangy yogurt. Skorri charmed her into telling them about the city, an ancient crossroads called Skarn, as they devoured the meal like wolves.

At Thane's insistence they bought four horses from a trader and replenished their supplies before finding a place to rest; the mage was determined to be prepared as they ventured into the unknown. It was past noon before they found lodging at a quiet inn surrounded by cool gardens. Whitewashed adobe walls a foot thick kept their room cool, and a jasmine scented breeze blew gently through slatted windows. They piled their packs in the corner before stripping and collapsing on canvas mats stuffed with fresh smelling straw. Exhaustion claimed them.

A deep gong, muted with distance, roused Ander from blissful slumber. Outside the western window the sun was a huge orange ball hanging above the palm fronds. Erik and Skorri had woken earlier and were already entangled; Erik was on his back, legs splayed wide, getting fucked with exquisitely slow strokes. Beads of sweat glistened on Skorri's hard body like golden dewdrops.

Thane stretched and opened his eyes, the last to rouse. Ander caressed his lover's athletic torso, then wrapped his fingers around the erection stretching across the mage's flat belly. "You're well rested, I see," Ander said as he pulled the foreskin back from Thane's cockhead. Thane rubbed his eyes and smiled, then rolled on top of Ander and pressed their bodies together.

"Well enough. And you?" He rocked his hips to rub his cock against Ander's stiff penis. "Erik and Skorri have the right idea. Want to fuck?" He grinned eagerly, youthful lust in his eyes.

"You know the answer," Ander replied, giving his partner a sultry gaze. A pleasurable throb shot from his cock and ran the length of his body. As Thane brought their lips together in a kiss the gong sounded again, followed by the sound of drums beating in the distance. Thane's head cocked to the side.

"What is it?" Ander asked.

Thane rolled off Ander and went to the window. Bars of sunlight poured through the slats and painted his body with golden stripes. In a moment Ander joined him. The pyramid's golden cap towered above the city and caught the sun's rays, gleaming like a torch. At first he didn't see what had distracted the mage. Then he felt a trembling vibration deep in his body. The internal vibration grew stronger, resonating with the distant drumming.

"Remember what we felt in the desert?" Thane asked. "We're closer. I don't know what it is, but something's making echoes in the kei."

Ander's stomach clenched. "Sorcerers? Can you tell if there's blood magic in the kei?"

The mage's eyes closed and his breathing slowed. After a few moments he opened his eyes and shook his head. "There's no hint of blood magic. Or the art." Excitement grew in his eyes. "This is something new, at least to us!"

Ander sighed. "I know that look. Love will have to wait."

Thane was already retrieving his dusty brown leathers from the pile in the corner. "We have to explore this. Maybe we'll learn something we can use against the zamindar." He reached over and patted the hard mound of Skorri's rump. "What about you two goats? Want to go with us?"

"Maybe . . . later," Skorri said in a husky voice. He arched his back and slid his oily cock into Erik again, a blissful smile on his face. "We haven't fucked in a real bed for days. It'd be a shame to rush." The ecstatic young hunter grunted in agreement. Precum oozed from his cockhead, slicking the brown skin under his glans, as Skorri's golden pubic hairs tickled his balls.

Thane and Ander dressed and left the inn. Dusk was settling over Skarn and the afternoon heat was already fading. Deciding how to pursue the mystery was not a problem. Pulsing drums echoed from the direction of the pyramid. The air seemed to crackle with energy as they emerged from the city's western gate and entered the forest surrounding the pyramid. A small stream wandered through the palm grove, bordered by a flagstone trail. The insistent drums were louder outside the walls. Ander felt as if his blood surged in time with the complex rhythms.

Forest soon gave way to a clearing. The stream they had been following fell over the lip of a circular depression two hundred feet across and ten feet deep. A complex sandstone mosaic, curved like a shallow bowl, filled the depression. Water flowed around the bowl's circumference and was siphoned off by carved channels that zigzagged down the bowl's sides before disappearing beneath a round stone at the bowl's bottom. Three men in bright red robes, on the far side of the depression, beat with red mallets on drums shaped like huge barrels. The pyramid towered behind the scene like a ramp to the heavens.

Ander barely noticed the exotic setting. Ten men wearing black loincloths, spaced around the shallow bowl's perimeter, were slowly moving through a series of poses. They ranged in age from adolescence to about thirty. All were extremely fit and possessed amazing balance. They twisted and bent, often with an arm or leg extended, pausing to hold positions that looked impossible. Sweat streaked their lean torsos, revealing the strength behind the illusion of dream-like effortlessness.

"Nicolai would be impressed," Ander whispered. "Though it seems more a dance of some kind than acrobatics."

Thane nodded, his expression rapt. "Feel the kei," he replied. "Something is happening."

Even as he spoke, the figures started moving more rapidly. The transition between poses changed from fluid grace to swift precision. The drummers beat a faster rhythm, accented with sudden syncopation.

Ander felt tightness in his chest. It was as if lightning flashed in the clouds, building in power, preparing to hurl bolts to the ground. But the coiled power lay in the kei, not the sky.

As the orange ball of the sun touched the pyramid's golden apex, the true purpose of the ritual was revealed. The men moved from their stations and converged on the center of the depression, avoiding the broad bands of water that zigzagged down the bowl's sides. Soon they stood in a circle thirty feet across. The drumming stopped. The men bowed once, then raised their fists.

Combat exploded with unexpected fury. Punches and kicks were a blur as the men leapt from one dry place to another while trading blows. Ander winced at the sharp impacts, but the combatants absorbed the punishment without pausing. Their endurance was as amazing as their strength.

One by one, a hand or foot would touch water and a fighter would retire to sit near the drums. The sun dropped lower and the pyramid's shadow cut a black wedge into the circle. Ander's heart pounded as the power in the kei coiled tighter and tighter.

Soon there were only two fighters still standing. One was the oldest of the group, tall and sturdily built. He had used brute force to eliminate his opponents, wrestling them into the water while ignoring the punishing blows that pummeled him.

The other was about Ander's age, a broad-shouldered youth whose whippy body glistened with sweat. He was blinding quick, and had endured by avoiding blows and unbalancing others at the exact moment their weight shifted from one foot to another. His opponents seemed to defy the earth's grip as their redirected momentum sent them sailing through the air.

They circled each other warily. The older man waited patiently for the youth to get within reach. Both were well muscled, but there must have been thirty pounds difference in their weight. It would be a one-sided wrestling match.

Suddenly the youth leapt feet-first at his opponent. The move looked suicidal, like a deer leaping into a lion's jaws. The older man braced to catch his prey. A second before impact, the boy curled his body into a tight ball. The grab that had been aimed for his outstretched leg closed on empty air and the two collided. Both fell, but the youth rolled and sprang to his feet while his opponent still scrambled to regain his footing. A spinning kick sent the older man back to the ground, and an outstretched hand touched one of the water channels. The two instantly ceased their contest. They faced each other, both panting, and bowed. Despite the sudden calm, Ander still felt the kei straining like a guitar string pulled too tight.

The fighters gathered at the northern edge of the arena where a trail entered the forest. Each took a simple black robe from a pile and slipped it on before vanishing among the palms.

Thane leaned close to Ander. "Let's follow. You feel the kei?"

Ander nodded. "Yes, and I don't like it. My teeth ache."

"Still, they touched the kei somehow. We have to learn how they did it." They waited until the last fighter entered the forest, then followed. The trail soon turned toward Skarn. The group was relaxed now, joking and talking about their plans for the evening.

Blue evening shadow had settled over Skarn. Sand drifted in the streets and shooting stars streaked across the sky with razor sharpness. The fighters wove through narrow streets, passing brothels and taverns without slowing. Ander and Thane followed at a discreet distance.

Shortly they arrived at a bathhouse. A courtyard containing a garden and fountain separated two structures, one for men and one for women. Thick earthen walls, painted white, supported domed roofs riddled with large round openings. Steam from warm pools beneath the domes swirled through the openings and wafted away on the evening's cool breeze.

The fighters entered the men's bathhouse, and a few minutes later Ander and Thane followed. They undressed in an antechamber and left their clothes with an attendant, then entered a circular room beneath the dome.

Though small by the standards of Izmir's cities, Skarn's bathhouse possessed an exotic charm. The pool was large enough to hold fifty without crowding. Blue tiles in shadows from palest aquamarine to deep violet covered the room's walls, and the domed ceiling was covered with tiny glass mosaics that gleamed with gold. Oil lamps filled the space with wavering light, and a boy wearing a brown robe sat in an alcove playing a shepherd's tune on a flute. The fighters were at the far end of the pool and were using long sponges to scrape dust and sweat from their bodies. A dozen other bathers lounged in the water.

A hush fell as Ander and Thane stepped out of shadow and walked to the pool's edge. Even the boy playing the flute stopped to look. Ander's shyness surged and he blushed crimson, an old habit he had been unable to break. Even with eyes downcast he could feel the scrutiny they were receiving. He knew how startling Thane's strapping body and handsome features could be, and felt sure everyone must be enraptured by the mage's beauty.

A sudden jolt, felt through the kei, made him look up. His gaze was drawn irresistibly across the pool to the fighters, to the boy who had bested the others. The youth was watching them with an intensity that bordered on the physical. The others seemed indifferent to their presence.

Thane put a hand on Ander's back, nudging him toward the pool. "Their champion seems to have an eye for boys," he whispered. "I wonder which of us he wants?"

Ander gulped, feeling butterflies in his stomach as they walked over round stones to the edge of the pool. He eased into the lukewarm water and dunked his head while Thane fetched a scrubbing sponge and then joined him in the pool. The mage brushed wet hair back from Ander's eyes, then started scrubbing his chest with the rough sponge.

"He's still watching us," Ander said, looking over Thane's shoulder. "Though he's trying to hide it."

Thane turned and glanced at the youth. The boy blushed and turned away, his body taut. The mage returned his attention to Ander and smiled knowingly. "Not hard to guess what's on his mind. Luck is with us for once. Let's try talking to him."

Ander nodded, feeling his heart beat faster. Strangers had always made him feel awkward. Even with Thane, whose earthy warmth could melt anyone's reserve, the thought of flirting with a stranger left him tongue-tied. "What . . . what will we say?"

"Leave it to me," Thane said. He put his sponge on the pool's edge and gestured for Ander to follow.

The boy who had been watching them started to look alarmed as they crossed the waist-deep pool. *He's as nervous as I am*, Ander realized with a start. A surge of empathy filled him. Ever since adolescence, amorous overtures had made him feel bewildered and defensive. But even if the boy was a kindred spirit, there was no denying the desire in his eyes.

All ten fighters fell silent as Thane approached with Ander in his wake. They were an impressive group, but the boy who had won the evening's match stood out. Broad shoulders tapered to narrow hips, and his slender build emphasized his torso's cleanly etched muscle and his strong arms. Widely spaced lavender eyes highlighted features both masculine and sensual. Curly black hair, cut short on the sides but longer on top, sparkled with water droplets. His stance was poised yet somehow diffident. He reminded Ander of a colt, vibrant but skittish.

Thane raised a hand in greeting and gave the bathers a friendly smile. "Sorry to bother you," he said. "But my friend and I just arrived in Skarn. We're hoping someone can tell us where musicians might find work. We need to earn some coin for supplies before continuing our journey."

The oldest of the group gave him a surly glare. "Ask someone else. We're not interested in trivial pleasures."

Thane's smile faltered. "Apologies, sir. We didn't mean to offend." He lowered his hand. "Could you suggest someone—"

"No. Our concerns are elsewhere."

The rebuff stung, and Ander blushed. He touched Thane's arm and nodded toward the far side of the pool, indicating his desire to leave. Thane sighed and turned.

"Wait." The softly spoken word came from the youth who had been watching them. "Try Fayed's gaming den, on the street of potters." The youth was breathing hard, and the yearning in his eyes was almost desperate.

"Thank you," Ander said. "Which way is it—"

"Ask somebody else," the group's elder said sharply. "We don't mix with your kind."

"They're travelers," the comely youth objected. "They don't know—"

"Don't argue, Dannel!" He looked exasperated. "Of all people, *you* should know it's best to stay away from them."

Ander blinked, wondering what they were talking about and hoping the argument didn't escalate. Everyone in the bathhouse had turned to watch.

"Don't lecture me, Zevon! There's no rule that we be rude to strangers. I was only—"

"Don't let your victory tonight go to your head. You're a good fighter, Dannel, but you're still weak. Do you *like* making a fool of yourself?"

The youth's face flamed. He threw his sponge to the side, splattering water against the blue tile walls, then stepped toward Ander and inclined his head.

"I'm sorry," he said. "Don't judge Skarn by oafs like Zevon. I'll show you the way to Fayed's place, if you'd like."

"Dannel . . . " The note of threat in Zevon's voice was unmistakable. The other fighters stirred restlessly, casting hostile glances at Thane and Ander.

Ander's heart thudded. He could see how difficult it was for the youth to defy his elder. "Thanks for your help," he said. "May fortune reward your kindness."

Without another word, Dannel went to the pool's edge and hopped out in a graceful vault. Thane and Ander followed, leaving the muttering group of fighters behind. They retrieved their clothes from the attendant, then made introductions and dressed quickly, sharing an unspoken agreement to get away from the bathhouse before Zevon decided to continue the argument.

Leaving the thick-walled bathhouse was like stepping from summer into autumn. Desert air cooled quickly at night and the sky had become black velvet filled with a blazing glory of stars.

Dannel didn't seem to mind the cold, though he was dressed only in a loincloth and lightweight robe. He looked at Ander with an enigmatic expression. "Fayed's place isn't far," he said. "He . . . he has good food, if you're hungry."

"Would you join us for a meal?" Thane asked as they started down the narrow street. "We'd like to hear about Skarn."

Dannel smiled, shy but excited, and ducked his head in agreement. He was breathtaking when he smiled.

As promised, the gaming den wasn't far. Dannel stopped in front of a mud-brick building with a wooden sign shaped like dice above the door. When they entered the smell of smoke and wine greeted them along with shouts of gamblers.

"It'll be quieter out back," Dannel said. "It's not often used at night." He led them through a low-ceilinged room where men threw dice and wagered on cockfights. They passed a tiled hearth, large enough to roast a whole boar on a spit, then passed through an arch to a courtyard. A wall enclosed a small orchard of olive and pomegranate trees, along with a few unoccupied tables. The mud-brick wall still held heat from the day's sun and sheltered them from the breeze.

Dannel gestured toward a table, looking flustered. Ander ached in sympathy with the youth's awkwardness. "It seems your friends didn't like us," he said. "It was good of you to help us anyway. We're grateful."

Dannel flashed a nervous smile as they settled around the table. "You're welcome . . . Ander." His lavender eyes were all desire. "Zevon's wrong to stay away from travelers, I think. He's not interested in anything outside Skarn. I can't understand it."

"What about you?" Thane asked. "Have you traveled?"

Dannel's face clouded and he hunched his shoulders. "What do you want to eat? Fayed makes the best roasted peppers in Skarn, filled with rice and chestnuts and spices. That's what I have when I come here. Though I don't often eat away from . . . I've only had it a few times."

"That sounds good," Thane said. "We'd be honored if you'd be our guest. It's the least we can do to repay your kindness."

Relief swept Dannel's face, unhindered by any attempt at concealment. Ander almost wanted to laugh. At last, he had met someone with even less guile than himself. And apparently less money as well.

The proprietor arrived to take their order, bringing a pitcher of water and three mugs. After he left Ander raised his mug. "To new friends." They drank to the toast and Dannel seemed more at ease.

"You're musicians?" Dannel asked. "Minstrels are always popular in Skarn."

"I play the guitar," Ander said. "And Thane is a better singer than most." He paused, watching Dannel closely. "He knows many ballads. And love songs. They're beautiful."

Dannel gulped and put down his mug. The moon had risen and it bathed him in silver light. Black curls tumbled over his forehead unnoticed. The idea of Thane singing love songs plainly captured his imagination. Thane smiled seductively, playing his part at enchanting the handsome youth.

Ander's cock hardened as he felt the weak-kneed sensation of keenly anticipated pleasure. Though he and Thane had shared lovemaking with others many times, this was the first time they had seduced someone together.

Dannel's body was taut with need. *Is he too shy to ask us?* Ander wondered. It seemed doubtful such a comely youth would be inexperienced at love, but Ander understood how difficult it could be to admit interest. Or maybe the custom in Skarn required the visitor to make the overture; Ander had heard tales of such places. The youth's reticence made him all the more attractive.

After taking a deep breath Dannel nodded. "I'd like to hear your songs," he told Thane. He gulped. "Do you . . . do you ever sing them for Ander?" His blush revealed what he was thinking.

Ander smiled at the halting question. He leaned across the table and lowered his voice. "We're lovers, yes. And you, Dannel? Do you have a special friend?"

The boy seemed at a loss for words, fascinated and wary at the same time. Despite his awesome fighting skills, he seemed vulnerable.

Wanting to soothe, Ander reached forward and touched the youth's right hand. Dannel surged to his feet, knocking his chair over. He looked at Ander wildly, panting like a stag ready to bolt.

"I . . . I'm sorry," Ander stammered. "We're from the west, I'm ignorant of your ways. I . . . I thought you might like to share more than a meal with us. I apologize for giving offense."

"We'll leave if you'd like," Thane said. "Or we can talk of other things. Believe me, we would never impose on you."

Dannel let his breath out slowly. He bent down and righted his chair, then took his seat at the table. He looked desperately unhappy.

"Zevon was right," he said, his voice thick. "I should know better. There's no hope for me."

Thane handed him a water goblet. "You've done nothing wrong," he said. "We misunderstood, that's all. It's a mistake travelers often make."

Dannel took a drink, then put the mug down and clasped his hands. His eyes remained downcast. "No," he whispered. "You . . . you understood what I want. I could see that you're lovers. I wanted to warm my heart by getting near. Wanted to see if I could get close enough to feel some of what you share." He took a shuddering breath, his young face a mask of misery. "I'm a weak fool, like Zevon says."

"I don't understand," Ander said. "There's no weakness in wanting love."

Dannel looked up, forlorn, and pointed to a small stone on the lobe of his left ear. "Have you ever seen one of these?"

Ander leaned closer. The earring looked like a black pebble, pitted with many tiny holes, mounted in a silvery setting. Any symbolic significance it held was indiscernible. If anything, the ornament was modest to the point of being drab.

"I've never seen one like it," Ander said, not wanting to offend. "What does it mean?"

"It means I'm indentured to the Torii Guardians. Practically a slave."

"Slaves in Skarn aren't allowed to make love?" Ander asked, incredulous. "How would anyone even know?"

Dannel's hand clenched into fists. "Torii Guardians *can't*," he said bitterly. "The firestone prevents it."

"How?" Ander asked, curiosity overwhelming discretion.

Dannel grimaced. "Take my word for it."

"Why not take the earring off, then?"

"You can't do that, either. The hierophants use a spell to affix it. Only the hierophants can remove it. Otherwise the Guardian dies."

Thane peered intently at the earring. "Would you let me touch it? I've encountered sorcery before, in my travels, but never anything like this. Maybe I can help."

Surprise filled the boy's face, followed by doubt. While it was impossible not to notice Thane's keen mind, he still looked more like a lusty young laborer than a scholar. After a few moments Dannel shrugged. "Go ahead."

Thane reached forward with his right hand, moving slowly as

if feeling the air for currents. Puzzlement flickered across his face. He lifted his hand higher and touched the dark stone with an outstretched finger. Blue-white light flashed and he jerked his hand away like it had been bitten.

Dannel rocked back in his chair, nostrils flaring. "What happened? What did you do?"

Thane blinked, looking at the fighter with burning curiosity. "I was trying to feel for a spell or a cantrip. The stone holds a spell, a complex one. And more power than I expected." He nodded thoughtfully. "Yes, it would easily kill you if you meddled with it."

Dannel looked near to panic. "How much *do* you know about sorcery?" he whispered. "Are you a hierophant?"

Thane shook his head. "I don't even know what a hierophant is. But I've studied many strange things and heard of even stranger. That's why Ander and I travel, to seek knowledge."

Dannel didn't appear mollified. "Why did the firestone lash out at you? It's never done that before."

"I don't know. As I said, I've encountered magic before, the spell might have responded to that. Maybe I can help, if you tell me more."

Dannel looked skeptical. His robe had fallen open at the top and his broad chest rose and fell with rapid breaths. "How do I know—"

"Wait," Ander said. The proprietor entered the courtyard carrying a tray of stuffed peppers. They waited until they were served and the man left before Dannel spoke again.

"Why would you help me?" he asked. "You felt what the firestone can do. It's dangerous."

"*Life* is dangerous," Thane replied. "And besides, I don't like slavery." His expression hardened. "I know what it's like."

Dannel looked amazed. "You're a freedman?"

"Not exactly," Ander said. "He was born a serf. He defied his shire's landlord and fled. He's lucky he's alive."

Dannel shook his head and took a bite from his stuffed pepper. He chewed in silence while looking at Thane thoughtfully. Ander could tell the youth's feelings toward them had shifted. They shared a bond in addition to desire.

After a few bites the fighter put down his food. "What do you want to know?" he asked softly.

Thane leaned forward, ignoring his meal. "These hierophants, are they mages or sorcerers?"

"They're priests who know ancient secrets. Some people call them wizards."

"You said you're some kind of guardian. Do you know any of these secrets?"

Dannel snorted. "Torii Guardians keep watch over the places where secrets are kept. We protect the hierophants when they leave the citadel, do what we're told. We're not given secrets."

"But you *guard* secrets," Ander said. "You know where they're hidden?"

Dannel shrugged. "That's hardly a mystery. The citadel's library is huge. Some scrolls are so ancient nobody even knows their age. The Guardians defend the citadel, you could never get in. And everyone knows the Torii Gates are in the Forbidden Lands."

"The Forbidden Lands?" Thane asked. "Where's that?"

Dannel pointed east. "High in the Khepera Mountains. A few days travel. The Torii Gates are in a remote valley. You have to know the right paths and passes, but of course only the hierophants and Guardians can go there. There's a pilgrimage every year."

"What are these Torii Gates?"

Dannel eyed his dinner as if he regretted inviting Thane's questions. "Huge gates, carved into a mountain. I've never gone through them. There are hundreds of stories, but only the hierophants have entered the mountain. Only they really know what's beyond the Gates, and they reveal nothing. Everybody else is guessing. The hierophants give us a sleeping potion before they start working magic at the Gates." He grimaced. "Makes you feel terrible when you wake up. Like you've run for three hours."

"I'd like to see those Gates," Thane said, a determined gleam in his eye. "I've felt something here, a power. These Gates might be the path to it."

Dannel shook his head. "You're not listening. They're in the *Forbidden* Lands. Your life is forfeit if you go there."

Ander sighed. Telling Thane something was impossible only piqued his interest. "Were you born into these Torii Guardians?" he asked, hoping Thane would remember his meal and not press their guest too hard.

It was the wrong question to ask. Dannel's features filled with unhappiness. He pushed his plate away as if he'd lost his appetite and looked down, his tightly clenched fists resting on the tabletop. At last he looked up and met Ander's gaze. "No." His voice was strained. "I wasn't born to it. Nobody is. My parents indentured me to the temple when I was ten. They . . . they wanted money more than they wanted me."

"I'm sorry," Ander said softly. The boy's pain made him ache.

"I don't understand how any parent could do that."

Dannel rubbed angrily at his eyes. "They made excuses. Said it's not really slavery since Torii Guardians are freed when we turn thirty, if we meet our bond. They said it's a sacrifice I had to make for the rest of the family." He laughed bitterly. "Thirty! I don't think I can stand nine more years like this!"

Thane raised an eyebrow. "I'm surprised they free you at thirty. Did they tell you why?"

"It's obvious. When you get that old you can't defeat younger opponents. Your flame cools."

"Your flame?" Ander asked. "I don't understand."

"It's why we can't have sex," Dannel replied. "The hierophants say that making love weakens a fighter. When the flame of desire fades, so does your strength."

Thane looked fascinated. "I wonder . . . certain crystals and minerals can channel anima, the energy of life. This firestone you wear might be more than a simple shackle. It might be drawing anima from you, what you call your flame."

Dannel shifted nervously. "How much do you know about sorcery, anyway?"

Ander understood the youth's reaction. Most sorcerers wielded power ruthlessly and were rightly feared. Only Thane and his band of mages pursued a different path, using anima drawn from pleasure to weave reality's hidden fabric.

Thane leaned forward, his eyes shining with conviction. "We should go to the Torii Gates," he insisted. "If my guess is right, the hierophants have been lying to you. They could be using anima drawn from the firestone to work their magic. The key to your freedom might be there, Dannel, if we can learn how the firestone works."

The fighter gaped, hope warring with doubt on his face. At last he shook his head. "No. You don't know what you're asking. You were lucky when you escaped your shire, but luck wouldn't help you in the Forbidden Lands. You'd die."

"Don't judge Thane too quickly," Ander said. "He knows more than you'd expect. You want your freedom, anybody can see it. Maybe we can help."

"Freedom." Dannel shivered. "You can't know how much I want it."

"Then give us a chance. I trust Thane with my life. You can trust him too."

Dannel reached out, his hand stopping an inch short of Ander's, his eyes filled with yearning. "I found what I sought tonight. I can feel what it would be like to have a lover."

"Will you show us the way?" Thane asked again.

Dannel sighed deeply, then stood. "I'm sorry." His voice was thick with unhappiness. "Leading you to your deaths would be a poor reward for your kindness. You have each other. Be grateful for that and forget about me."

"Wait!" Ander stood, but the fighter turned and fled back into the gaming room.

"Should we follow him?" Ander asked, knowing in his heart it would be futile.

Thane shook his head sadly. "We have no claim on him, and wouldn't want one. He has too little freedom as it is."

Moonlight bathed the orchard in pale light, making the leaves shimmer with silver. Ander's heart ached for the lonely fighter, but he knew Thane was right.

5

SKORRI WAS baffled. "Is he a eunuch, then? How else could you keep from having sex?"

Thane sighed patiently and shook his head. "He didn't say how it works," he repeated. "Just that the firestone won't let him have sex. And that he's been stuck with it since he was ten. He *wants* to make love, but can't."

Skorri scowled and rode in silence, ignoring the basalt pillars laced with white crystal and black obsidian that towered beside the trail like petrified giants. The idea of forced celibacy had horrified the randy blond.

"Wait up," Ander called from behind. "There's someone behind us."

Thane twisted to look. A hundred feet back, Ander had brought his horse to a halt and was staring west. Skarn was a smudge in the distance. A plume of dust was rising where the trail from Skarn entered the foothills.

"Whoever it is, he's moving fast," Ander called.

"Ride ahead and tell Erik to wait for us," Thane told Skorri. The blond nodded and spurred his horse ahead, where his partner was scouting the trail. Thane turned and backtracked. Shielding his eyes against the hot sun, he looked where Ander was pointing. Dust and boulders obscured the view, but he caught glimpses of a rider galloping up the trail at breakneck speed.

"Only one," Ander said. "And he's not trying to hide."

The rider rounded a corner and pounded into view again. This time Thane got a better look at him. "I think it's Dannel!"

Ander squinted, then slowly nodded. "You're right. But why? Last night he thought this journey was folly."

"We'll know soon enough." He drank from his water skin, then handed it to Ander before waving at Skorri and Erik. The pair started back down the trail. Once together they dismounted and found shade beneath an upward-tilted slab.

Thirty minutes later, Dannel rode into the rock-strewn field where they waited. He reined in his horse and approached at a trot. His black leathers were soaked with sweat.

Thane walked forward to greet him. "I didn't expect to see you again. I hope you're not going to try stopping us."

The youth wiped his brow, pushing wet curls out of his eyes. His gaze flickered across the rest of the group, lingering a moment on the hunting bow Erik held at the ready, then returned to Thane.

He looked somber, even frightened, but not threatening.

"I tried stopping you last night," he said at last. "I failed. You and your friends might be fools, but I can't fault your courage."

"Why are you here, then? Did you change your mind about coming with us?"

Dannel dismounted while the others clustered around. Erik watched the young guardian warily, and Skorri scrutinized the fighter with morbid fascination.

"Well?" Thane asked again.

Dannel looked embarrassed, but stood firm. "I dreamed about you last night," he said at last. "You and Ander. I kept remembering how you made me feel. It *hurt*; I couldn't think about anything else. Then the news this morning made me wonder whether you truly might be able to help me." He sighed. "I'm not explaining this well. Maybe *I'm* the one who's crazy."

"What news?" Thane asked.

"The hierophants met with a visitor last night. A traveler from Izmir. That's where you're from, isn't it? I can tell by your accent."

Thane stiffened, but nodded. There was no use trying to deny it.

"They called the Guardians together after morning exercise," Dannel continued. "We're to watch for someone with gray eyes. A youth fine enough to warm the bed of royalty, they said. There's a prize for his capture." He paused, watching Thane closely. "For *your* capture?"

Thane's stomach knotted, but Dannel wouldn't be telling him this if he meant harm. "You're not here to hunt a bounty," he said. "But you still haven't said what you *are* seeking."

Dannel looked at his feet, his body tense. When he looked up he was determined. "You fled your master, even though you knew it might mean your death. Last night, I saw my own cowardice. I've never tried to escape. They bought my obedience with a bribe. But I can't stand it any longer."

"I couldn't stand it either!" Skorri blurted. "You might as well be *dead* if you can't—"

Erik's kick to Skorri's shin interrupted the outburst, but Dannel still blushed scarlet. Ander held out the water skin as a kind of peace offering. Dannel took a long drink before handing it back.

"I'll show you the way to the Torii Gates. Maybe you can free me from the firestone. If you can't, your friend is right. I might as well be dead. At least I'll die fighting for freedom, not serving my masters."

Thane saw the determination in Dannel's stance, and the way his gaze lingered every time he looked at Ander. Newfound resolve might have led to Dannel's decision, but desire was the heat that forged the resolve.

"We're grateful for your help," Thane said. "Welcome to our band. These two are Erik and Skorri." Dannel bowed, but didn't offer the customary handclasp. His aversion to touching had apparently not changed.

"Apologize," Erik whispered to Skorri. The blond rolled his eyes, but cleared his throat and dipped his head. "I'm sorry. I can't imagine what it must be like. I mean, doesn't it make you crazy, not to—"

"That's enough," Erik said, clamping a hand over Skorri's mouth and giving Dannel a nod. "He means well. It's just that he's always horny."

A smile tugged at Dannel's lips, and the tension went out of his stance. "Then we have something in common. No offense taken." He turned to Thane. "We should be away. Whispers about gray-eyed boys are already filling Skarn and the reward is generous. No one would dare search in the Forbidden Lands, but these hills won't be safe."

Given the danger that would already be spilling out from Skarn, they rode as far as they could before night fell and the trail grew too treacherous. Stars glittered like jewels in the depths by the time they made camp beside a dry creek bed. Aspens lined the banks, drinking from an aquifer that dampened the soil even though no water flowed. They shared their rations, then spread their bedrolls near the campfire.

Despite their exhausting ride and the rapidly cooling night, Dannel insisted on going to a clearing to exercise and stretch. The others sat around the fire and watched in bemused admiration.

"How does he *do* that?" Skorri asked. "Not even acrobats can bend that far."

"He's been training since he was ten," Thane said as he watched the young warrior balance on one foot with the other leg held straight out, his foot higher than his head.

"Where does he get the strength?" Erik asked. "He must be as tired as us."

Thane leaned over and rubbed the hunter's crotch. "Think how much energy *you'd* have, if you never had sex. But there's something more, a power in him."

"You still think it's because of that firestone?" Ander asked.

"Probably. But the stone's still a mystery. We've always used crystals to work magic. Whatever the firestone is, it's not a crystal."

"How are you going to find out?" Skorri asked. "If he can't have sex, you can't use the art to learn about it."

Thane nodded, watching the disciplined youth move smoothly through his exercises. "He doesn't even like being touched. The lack of love has made him wary, I think. Being touched torments him with hints of what he can't have."

"Then maybe we should do without too," Ander said. "We don't want to make him feel any worse than he already does."

Skorri groaned. "For how long? It makes my stomach ache to think about it."

Erik cuffed his partner's shoulder. "We know what's aching, minx, and it isn't your stomach."

"Ander's right," Thane said. "And besides, he's not an initiate. We can't let him learn of the art until we're sure of him. Sex will have to wait, at least when Dannel's around."

"Ohhh," Skorri moaned, wrapping his arms around himself and rolling onto his side. "My stomach!"

Thane sighed and picked up a stick to prod the logs in the fire. Embers flew into the black sky. It was going to be a long journey.

Three days of hard riding brought them to a pass between two crags that speared the sky like a bull's horns. The mountains were unlike anything Thane had seen before, jagged shards of rock forming a forest of spears. He rode ahead of the others as they approached the pass, drawn by the mystery ahead.

Dannel's description of the hierophants' sorcery had yielded more questions than answers. The hierophants claimed to possess ancient secrets and guarded them jealously, but much of their knowledge had been lost when fire swept their temple's library many generations past. Annual pilgrimages to the Torii Gates were more than a ritual; they were expeditions to recover lost powers. According to Dannel, the attempts mostly met with failure.

The smell of water flavored the air as Thane neared the pass. His horse smelled it too and scrambled up the steep path with renewed energy. They reached the crest and cool air washed over the mage like balm.

A valley spread before him like rolling green waves, shocking after days of arid rock. Springs gushed from fissures in the barrier wall separating forest from desert, streaming in rivulets to a glittering lake. Brilliantly feathered birds soared above pines and cedars. Their caws and songs filled the air. Thane stared in wonder as the others caught up.

"The Valley of the Gates," Dannel said as he reached Thane's side. "Only hierophants and Guardians have seen it, for as long as anyone remembers. We're at the heart of the Forbidden Lands." He wiped his forehead on a sleeve, streaking dirt in the sweat. "The Guardians tend gardens and orchards each year during the pilgrimage, but mostly it's wild."

Skorri reached the crest and whooped. "Water!" He pointed at the lake. "Last one in has to groom the horses!" A moment later he was racing down the slope toward the verdant forest.

Thane gave chase, galloping through pines and untended orchards, intoxicated by the fragrant air. He reached the lake at the same time as Skorri. They jumped from their saddles and peeled off their shirts while running to the water's edge. Excited shouts from behind spurred them on. They paused briefly on the soft pine needles lining the beach to pull off boots and pants, then raced into the lake.

Thane dived, long and shallow, as soon as he was thigh deep. The lake's waters were clear as a sheet of ice and nearly as cold. He came up gasping, his skin tingling. Dannel's laughter carried easily across the water.

"I tried to warn you," the fighter said. He pointed to the waterfalls cascading down the barrier wall. "The water comes from under the ground. It's a stranger to the sun."

"Doesn't matter," Thane called back as he treaded water. "Diving in is *still* the best—" He yelped as Skorri came up from beneath and grabbed his legs. He went under, sputtering bubbles as the blond groped him beneath the water.

Though Skorri had the advantage of surprise and was slippery as an eel, Thane managed to get a hold on him before running out of air. He kicked to the surface with the squirming youth squeezed against his chest. The muscular boy was shockingly warm compared to the frigid water. They both took gasping breaths when they broke surface, then Skorri twisted around and licked the tip of Thane's nose.

"Let me go, Thane. I want to help Erik wash."

Laughing, Thane released the blond and watched him swim off to attack his partner.

Ander and Dannel had reached the lake last and were wading into the water side by side. They were a striking pair. It was hard to tell which of them was the more beguiling.

Despite his stubborn refusal to attempt intimacy, Dannel wasn't shy about his body and had no reason for modesty. His lean build served to emphasize broad shoulders and a pendulous cock, and his innocent features would have inspired any artist. Ander's kindness toward him during the journey had produced a gratitude that was almost painful to behold. It was plain the youth had been starved in spirit, even while his body was being honed to deadly perfection.

Thane reached shallow water and waded to where Ander and Dannel were standing in thigh-deep water. Shouts and splashes from nearby marked an encounter combining equal parts of wrestling, bathing and foreplay.

Ander nodded toward the rowdy boys. "Doesn't look like the water has cooled Skorri off any."

Thane snorted and looked over his shoulder at the playful lovers a few yards away. They were totally immersed in the excitement of the moment, enjoying the water and each other's strenuous grappling with wild abandon. Both were hard, their rigid cocks waving as they laughed and tumbled in shallow water.

Thane glanced at Dannel, who had turned to look at Skorri and Erik as well. The fighter was transfixed. A blush spread across his face and chest, and his lips were parted as if he had frozen in mid-speech. His engorged cock speared up from his crotch like a smooth horn of pale ivory. It was as long as Thane's and nearly as thick, but looked even larger on Dannel's slim frame. Ander was watching their new companion with wide eyes, obviously impressed.

"Frisky, aren't they?" Thane said.

Dannel jumped and turned away from the frolicking youths. He put a hand over his genitals but couldn't completely cover the rampant cock. He looked terrified.

"There's nothing you need to hide," Thane said. "You know us better than that."

Dannel turned aside, shielding himself with both hands. "Stay away," he said, his voice thick. "I can't help it, leave me alone!"

Ander moved closer and held his hands out, palms up, in a placating gesture. "Let us help, Dannel. You can trust us. We only want—"

"Got you!" Skorri whooped as he grabbed Ander around the waist in a wet bear hug. Ander staggered, arms flailing, as the blond tried to topple him. In two short steps he stumbled into Dannel. His outstretched hand brushed the startled youth's hip.

Dannel jumped back and shouted, a cry half ecstasy and half despair. His cock fountained, splattering Ander and Skorri with hot cum. He tried to cover his cock again, his body swaying as his knees started to buckle, but couldn't conceal the copious ejaculation. Semen squeezed out between his fingers and smeared his flat belly.

Vertigo swept Thane at the moment of Dannel's sudden climax, as if he had jumped off a cliff and his stomach hadn't caught up with his body. An intense surge of desire left him aching hard. Shimmering waves of distorting light seemed to radiate from the fighter like ripples when a stone drops into still water.

Dannel moaned, his slimy hands pressed over his genitals, and knelt in the cold water. Humiliation burned on his face.

"What happened?" Ander asked. He was blinking, a dazed expression on his face, his rampant cock thrusting up from his crotch.

Dannel turned away and moaned. He looked like he wanted to sink beneath the water and never be seen again.

Thane gulped, trying to clear the hot lust that still clouded his mind. Amazement at what had transpired soon prevailed over his body's demands. He knelt in the water next to Dannel, even though the distraught youth cringed at his presence.

"Are you all right?" Thane asked. "All I could sense was pleasure. Was it different for you?"

"Leave me alone," Dannel moaned.

"No." Thane's voice was firm. "You've got to tell me what happened, Dannel. Magic was involved. Strong magic. Is this why you can't make love?"

Dannel met Thane's gaze. His eyes brimmed with tears. "You don't understand what it's like," he said, his voice anguished. "We feel desire as much as anyone. But nobody can touch us when the need burns hot. If they do . . ." His voice caught and he looked down again, his face blazing.

"Everyone in Skarn knows about this, don't they?" Thane asked softly. "Is that why you wanted to talk with travelers?"

"They think it's a joke," Dannel said bitterly. "Everyone laughs, taunts us. They don't care how it makes us feel."

"But being touched only makes you cum if you're hard? Does touching you anywhere make it happen?"

Dannel shook his head, sullen eyes downcast. "Only between the waist and knees. Skin has to touch skin. The hierophants curse us enough to steal love, no more."

Thane put an arm around Dannel's shoulders. The youth shivered, looking surprised and panicked, but the mage held him tight. "It's all right. What was done to you isn't your fault. Let us try to help." The boy still trembled, but Thane felt the tension start to leave his shoulders.

"Do you really think you can?"
"I don't know yet," Thane confessed. "There are secrets to learn, but we're in the right place to find them."
Skorri approached, looking sheepish. "I'm sorry," he said. "It was an accident. I didn't know—"
"I didn't *want* you to know," Dannel said. He stood and touched Skorri's hand. "You didn't laugh. Thank you."
Skorri beamed, his sunny disposition quickly returning. "Your seed hit me from ten feet away! I haven't seen anybody cum that hard since Erik and Ander—"
Erik came up behind his partner and shook his shoulder. "Save the stories," the hunter suggested. "He has enough on his mind right now."
"We all do," Thane said. "This place has power. You can almost touch the kei even without using the art. It's time to find out why."

The Valley of the Gates carved a broad crescent through the landscape. The crescent's outer edge, separating the valley from desert, was a daunting crown of saw-tooth peaks. The inside curve was like the soaring wall of a fortified city. It loomed over them as they rode out of the forest and entered a broad stone courtyard at the cliff's base. Wilderness suddenly yielded to imperial majesty.
The Torii Gates were huge. Two columns like obelisks were carved from living rock, twin pylons rising at least eighty feet above the courtyard. Two crosspieces shaped like flattened pyramids, the lower of the two inverted like a reflection, connected them at the top.
Clear water poured from holes at the base of each column and flowed away in channels that fanned out from the gate like the sun's rays. Two hundred feet of rock on each side of the gate had been chiseled smooth and then carved with densely packed symbols. Stylized birds, plants, people, snakes and a myriad of other pictures were mingled with curlicues, geometric shapes and elongated faces of indeterminate sex. A huge passage lined with basalt blocks, filling the space framed by the gate, led straight into the cliff.
Cool wind blew from the cavernous opening as they approached. Thane felt a deep rumble, too low to be heard as a sound. His horse whinnied and he patted its neck to calm it. He shared the animal's sentiment; the sense of implacable power emanating from the portal was fearsome. They came to a halt twenty feet from the yawning opening.
"I've never been inside," Dannel said. Resentment colored his

voice. "The hierophants spend most of their time in there during the pilgrimage, but we're forbidden to enter. They say we're not strong enough to face what's inside."

Thane looked at the Torii Gates thoughtfully, craning his neck to peer into shadowed vaults high overhead. "How do you know it's dangerous, if you've never been inside?"

Dannel reddened. "They warned us often enough. And even some of the hierophants die when they go inside. At least, some who enter never come out. We're never told what happened to them."

Thane extended a hand as if grasping for a message hidden in the cool breeze. He frowned, concentrating, then shook his head. "If there's a cantrip here, I can't sense it. Power and strangeness, yes. But not a trap. I'll try going in."

"Wait!" Ander said. "Let me go first."

"Or one of us," Erik added. "There's no reason—"

Thane raised a hand. "If there *is* a cantrip inside, I'm more likely to sense it than any of you. Trust me." He nudged his horse forward, approaching the rectangle of darkness with more trepidation than he allowed his friends to see. Dannel looked sick with worry, but didn't try to stop him.

Crossing from sunlight into the shadowed passage was like stepping through a door from summer into the chill of early winter. Damp air smelled of moss. The sense of hidden power blossomed, making his hackles rise. Nothing happened, so he waved for his friends to follow. The clatter of horses' hooves on the stone floor echoed eerily in the darkness.

"It's like a cave," Ander muttered. "I don't like caves."

"It only seems like a cave because of the darkness," Thane replied. He halted his horse and felt again for tremors in the kei. If there was a trap waiting to spring, it was undetectable. "I think we can risk a telos light," he said.

He twisted around in his saddle to face Ander. "Want to help?" Ander's smile was almost lost in the darkness, but the mage felt a surge of gratitude through their bond. His young lover yearned to feel needed and Thane welcomed any chance to bolster his confidence.

They leaned toward each other and clasped hands. A tingling sensation flowed between them as Ander concentrated on sharing his anima with Thane. The mage accepted the energy and let it flow through his body. Ander's essence, fresh and permeated with lusty eagerness, lifted his spirits.

Releasing Ander and raising his right hand overhead, Thane let the energy flow through his arm and coalesce inside his clenched fist as his mind wove the spell to hold it. After a few seconds golden light seeped through his fingers. He opened his hand to reveal a radiant globe, the size of a walnut, floating in midair. Green streaks pulsed through the golden orb in time with his heartbeat. He started forward again, the telos light trailing along overhead as if connected to him by an invisible tether.

The corridor maintained its original dimensions as they went deeper, as high and wide as the Torii Gates themselves. Soon the telos light revealed the same mysterious glyphs as were displayed outside. The carvings inside the gallery were smaller than those outside and shined with vivid colors. The ancient symbols extended as far as they could see as the gallery penetrated deeper through solid rock.

Thane felt like they were riding through a vast painting. He turned to Dannel. "Do you know what any of this means? It looks like writing, but I've never seen anything like it."

Dannel looked away from the telos light, which he had been watching with open fascination. "It's true. I knew you were a mage, I *believed* it, but seeing it with my own eyes is different somehow."

"The writing," Thane prodded. "Can you read it?"

Dannel shook his head. "No, but I've seen it before. The hierophants' library at the temple has thousands of scrolls and parchments. We're forbidden to touch them. But sometimes they forget and leave something out where you can look at it. Anybody can see what some of the pictures are, but I don't know what they mean."

"Another puzzle to solve," Thane said as he prodded his horse forward. Soon the mosaic floor began descending at a gentle slope. The low thrum grew louder, filling their ears and vibrating in their bones. Though there was still no sign of danger, Thane's heart raced and a sense of pressure filled his head.

Ander moved up to ride beside him. "Is it wise to move this fast?" he asked, keeping his voice low.

"You feel it too, don't you?" Thane replied. "We're near something."

Ander shivered, sending a tremor of apprehension through their bond. "I'm new to the art, but I know there are strange things in the kei. I've never felt such power. I feel like an ant surrounded by elephants."

"At least the elephants aren't looking for us. Perhaps we're beneath the notice of whatever dwells here."

"Something ahead," Erik warned. The hunter had the keenest eyes of all the initiates, and always kept a careful lookout.

Thane peered down the lofty gallery, straining to see beyond the pool of illumination shed by the telos light. At first he saw only blackness. Then, faintly, a deep red glow emerged from the darkness. It pulsed slowly, seeming to resonate with the deep rumble that filled the stone realm.

His throat dry, Thane reached up and snatched the telos light out of the air. It vanished when his fingers closed around it and the corridor plunged into darkness.

The distant red glow grew more distinct. Erik gasped, and in moments Thane saw it too. The glyphs covering the walls were glowing as well. A rainbow of faint colors and twisting shapes seemed to swim around him. A sense of order and purpose permeated the ethereal writing, but it was implacably alien and disorienting.

Thane moved ahead, using the red pulsations as a guide. He rode slowly, as if in a dream. The enigmatic symbols seemed to almost make sense; he sensed a pattern and strained to hear the concealed message. Time blurred and stretched. While his mind still danced with the illuminated symbols soaring around them, they reached an arch separating the gallery from a vast circular chamber.

Heat rippled across them, like passing through a sheet of water, as they left the corridor and entered the next room. The thrum of power became a physical presence, a pressure against the skin like wind. The source stood before them.

The chamber they had entered was round, with a high ceiling shaped like a shallow inverted bowl. In the center, a hundred feet distant, a square stone block thirty feet high rested atop a stepped platform. Its surface was inlaid with glyphs formed from precious metals and was encrusted with sparkling jewels that gleamed from within. A circular opening filled the side of the block facing the door, and the opening seemed bottomless. It held a black void broken only by a vibrant red spot throbbing like the heart of some unearthly beast.

Thane dismounted and faintly heard the others do the same. He couldn't look away from the opening in the stone block; it drew him like a lodestone draws a compass. Walking forward as if in a trance, he felt himself become more attuned to the force emanating from the object. Voices filled his mind, songs and chants in a tongue that seemed hauntingly familiar. He moved closer.

Ander was saying something, but Thane barely noticed. The

gems embedded in the huge stone artifact were glittering like stars. The red light in the opening started to swirl, sending out gold streamers in curved arms that seemed to beckon. He lifted his right hand toward it, felt a tingling sensation creep from his palm down his arm. A smell like cloves beguiled him.

The voices behind him grew louder, yet seemed distant and insignificant. The stone block shimmered. It was like a vision in the kei even though the object's physical reality was massive and undeniable. He walked to the base of the stepped platform and craned his neck to look up at the hypnotic spinning pattern within the opening. Red and gold light bathed his face. He felt like he was being sucked into an infinitely deep whirlpool.

There was shouting and someone grabbed his shoulder. He ignored it. The chorus of voices singing in his mind was starting to make sense. Their message was vitally important, he could feel it to his core. He climbed the platform's first step.

A coruscating burst of color filled his vision, as if a thousand fireworks exploded around him. He felt a violent impact, and then darkness claimed him.

6

"THANE! SAY something!" Ander rolled aside and looked at the mage, who lay motionless where Ander had knocked him. Squirming lines of ochre light still zigzagged across his body like tiny lightning bolts. Ander put a hand against his chest and felt a faint heartbeat.

Erik knelt at his side and held a finger beneath Thane's nose. "He's still breathing," the hunter said. He gestured to the side with his head. "Look at Dannel."

Ander looked up. Dannel stood motionless before the huge circular opening, his body like a statue lit by a fiery sunset. Light still spun inside the stone block like a whirlpool of magma. At least Dannel wasn't walking into the maelstrom the way Thane had. Skorri stood by the fighter's side, shaking his shoulder and murmuring urgently in his ear.

"We have to get Thane out of here," Ander said. "Help me get him onto a horse." The two of them lifted the mage's limp body over his horse's saddle. "Can you make a telos light?" Ander asked.

Erik nodded. "Not as bright or as fast as Thane, but I can do it."

"Go ahead and make one. I'll help Skorri get Dannel mounted." He turned and went to Skorri's side.

"He doesn't hear or see us," Skorri said anxiously. "His eyes aren't moving at all."

Ander looked closely. The young guardian stared at the stone artifact with glazed eyes, as if enraptured. A glint of light caught Ander's eye and he moved to Dannel's side. The drab lump of rock at the boy's ear pulsed a dull red.

They both peered at the firestone, which no longer seemed as misnamed as Ander had first thought. *He must be in thrall to the stone. How can we release him?* At a loss, he extended a finger and touched the firestone. A numbing jolt shot up his arm and he staggered back. Dannel grunted like he had been punched in the belly and started to crumple. Skorri caught him and eased him to the floor. The fighter shook his head, looking dazed, but sat up by himself.

Ander's arm tingled with a thousand pinpricks as feeling returned. He flexed his fingers to make sure they were working, then crouched beside Dannel. "Can you ride? We have to leave *now*."

"I . . . I think so." Dannel struggled to his feet and managed to stand, though he looked ready to topple at any moment. Skorri helped him mount. By then Erik had created his telos light, a pale blue sphere hardly larger than a grape. He took the reins to Ander's horse and started back the way they had come. Ander walked beside Thane's horse and kept close watch on his still partner.

Their retreat through the gallery was as hasty as they could manage without spilling Thane. Erik's light wasn't bright enough to illuminate more than the area immediately around them; they followed along one of the monumental walls. The intricate glyphs now seemed more threatening than intriguing. The rumble of power still reverberated through rock like the tread of a ponderous beast on their trail.

At last a tall rectangle of light formed in the darkness ahead of them. It grew to colossal proportions as they approached, and filled with sky. Ander kept a hand on Thane's shoulder, hoping the unconscious mage might somehow sense relief through their bond.

They crossed the plaza outside the Torii Gates and stopped at a grove of cedars on the other side before sliding Thane from his horse. They laid him in dappled shade and clustered around him.

Ander touched Thane's cheek. The skin felt cool and the mage's shallow breaths barely lifted his chest. Ander frowned, trying to remember the healing lore he had heard while growing up at Lady Tayanita's House of Companionship. "Skorri, fetch your oils."

The blond dug through his saddlebags and returned with his small leather case of oils and elixirs. Ander opened the case and removed a vial of amber fluid. He twisted the cork out and sniffed. His nose wrinkled at a pungent smell like hot peppers. "This might work," he said. He raised Thane's head with his other hand and waved the vial under the mage's nose.

Thane snorted and his eyes fluttered open. He turned his head away from the vial and coughed weakly.

Ander handed the vial back to Skorri, then helped Thane sit up. He felt Thane's disorientation through their bond, and knew the mage could sense his overwhelming relief.

Thane's bewilderment made him look even younger than Erik and Skorri. He turned back to Ander and blinked. "I'm cold," he whispered, shivering.

"You'll be all right," Ander said, leaning over and holding him tightly. The mage stirred against him, responding to his warmth. Ander kindled their bond, sharing anima until he felt his lover's strength returning.

Soon Thane was standing and looking at the Torii Gates. Curiosity had replaced his confusion. "I remember entering the chamber," he said. "The copper dome like the desert sky. And something in the middle, calling to me." He frowned and shook his head. "Then I was back out here."

Ander described the stone block, the vortex that swirled within it, the effect on Dannel. Thane remembered none of it.

Ander could tell the mage was already planning another foray. A difficult challenge only kindled his determination. "Don't do anything hasty," he advised, although he knew Thane would find the mystery irresistible. "You were lucky you weren't hurt. And look at Dannel." He nodded to the side, where Dannel sat on the ground with his legs pulled against his chest and his face pressed against his knees. "Whatever happened, he took it hard. He hasn't said a word since we got out of there."

Thane flinched. "I've neglected him. Too damned distracted." In a moment his eyes widened. "Maybe he knows something about what happened." He looked around. "Where are Erik and Skorri? I should ask what they saw, too."

"They crept off as soon as they saw you were all right. I think they're, um, probably busy right now."

Thane's smirk showed his agreement. "At least *they* weren't affected. Come on, let's talk with Dannel."

Dannel didn't stir as they approached. They sat cross-legged in front of him and waited, giving the youth time to collect himself.

A minute passed, then two. At last Dannel sighed. "I'm sorry," he said without looking up. His voice was muffled and small. "I didn't want any of you to get hurt."

"No harm was done," Thane said. "You have nothing to feel bad about."

Dannel moaned and pressed his face tighter against his knees. "I'm a freak. I'll never escape the firestone."

"Give Thane a chance," Ander said. "We just got here. He'll figure it out, you'll see."

"He'll die, as I warned. You should leave now. While you can."

Ander snorted. "If you think what happened today is enough to chase Thane off, you have a lot to learn." He leaned forward and touched one of Dannel's knees. "Open your eyes," he urged. "We're all right. Thane's ready to work on the problem. Maybe he can free you from the stone. He needs your help."

A few seconds passed in silence, then Dannel lifted his head and looked at Thane. He looked chagrined. "'You're more of a fighter than I am. You never give up, do you?"

Ander grinned and cuffed the boy's shoulder. "*Now* you're starting to understand him. Anyway, why should we give up? We might have learned something in there. Why did the magic only touch you and Thane?"

"A good question," the mage said. "We must have something in common, something the rest of you don't have."

Ander nodded, his curiosity piqued. "The biggest difference for *you* is your power, the strength of your anima. And your experience with magic."

"But *I'm* not a mage," Dannel said. "I don't have any powers."

"I'm not so sure," Thane said. "I've always felt something around you. At first I thought it was just the firestone, there's certainly magic in it. But the stone holds no anima. I think it draws all its power from *you*."

Dannel looked confused. "I don't understand. Will any of this help free me from the firestone?"

"It might." Thane's eyebrows pulled down as he thought, then he seemed to reach a decision. "The time has come. To learn more, you'll have to learn about magic."

Ander was startled. Dannel had no hope of learning sex magic, at least not while he was in the firestone's sway. He began to wonder if Thane had escaped unscathed after all. His expression must have betrayed his doubts.

"It's not as crazy as it sounds," Thane said. "We use the art to touch the kei, but we know it's not the *only* way to do it. Look at the zamindar's sorcerers. They use pain for the same end."

Ander was stunned. "What are you saying? Even if Dannel were willing, none of us would ever use blood magic!"

"Of course not," Thane agreed. "What I mean is, if there are two ways to reach the kei, maybe there are more. You said Dannel was entranced by whatever's in there. I was too."

Realization dawned in Ander's eyes. "You're the strongest mage, closer to the kei than the rest of us. You think Dannel's close to the kei too, but in a different way?"

"The firestone is no ordinary talisman, I'm sure of that much. And I've wondered about Dannel's training. His strength and stamina suit a fighter, but they're the same qualities we look for in initiates. The hierophants might be using fighting to conceal the training's *real* purpose."

Dannel had been listening intently, his frustrated scowl fading as Thane's voice grew more hopeful. "What's the kei?" he asked. "I've never heard of it."

Thane turned deadly serious. "You've already thrown your lot in with us, I know. But before you can become an initiate you have to do even more. Will you join our fight to bring down the zamindar? And swear on your life to never reveal what we teach you?"

Dannel was equally solemn. "I swear it." He glanced at Ander and colored. "You're the best friends I've ever had. Whatever aid I can offer, I pledge to give it. You have my word."

"One more thing," Thane said. "You'll have to trust us. Learning the art is hard for anyone. For you it will be even harder. Will you try what we tell you, even if it seems impossible?"

Dannel held his head high. "I'm flawed, but I'm not a coward. I'll do as you ask or die trying."

Thane stood and the others followed. He clasped forearms with Dannel and held him strongly. "I accept your pledge. The path won't be easy, but we'll walk it together." He released Dannel and gave him a wry smile. "Ander was surprised when I offered you initiation. Have you guessed the nature of the sorcery we practice?"

"What's to guess? I suppose it's like the hierophants' magic. Spells and rituals, bits and pieces of ancient knowledge, meditation and chants. That's the only kind of wizardry I've heard of."

"It's, um, a bit different than that," Ander said. He scuffed at dirt with the toe of a boot, wondering how to break the news. "Actually, it's a lot different."

Dannel shrugged. "I heard what Thane said, about how there's more than one way to touch this kei you speak of. That the imperial sorcerers in Izmir use pain, but you don't. Even if there *is* pain, I'm willing to do what's needed. I'm a fighter. I'm not afraid to face danger."

Ander took a deep breath. "As Thane said, learning the art will be harder for you than for most. You see, the art uses botanical secrets Thane has discovered, and special minerals and, um, . . . sex."

Dannel gaped, looking at Ander as if he had sprouted horns. After a few moments he shut his mouth and gulped, blushing crimson.

"But . . . but I can't . . ."

Thane gripped him by both shoulders. "You can't have sex *now*, because of the firestone. I'm hoping we can find a way to use the art to defeat the firestone. I warned you it wouldn't be easy. Trust us, and start to learn."

Without giving the fighter a chance to answer, Thane slid his arms around Dannel's back and held him in a firm embrace. The boy shivered and moaned softly as Thane drew their lips together. He went slowly, allowing the youth's panic to pass, before consummating the kiss.

Ander watched, fascinated, as his partner welcomed the new initiate into the art. Though Dannel was physically two years older than the mage and a deadly warrior, it was clear who was dominant. Soon the stiffness left Dannel's neck and shoulders. He hesitantly lifted his arms and returned Thane's embrace.

The mage let the embrace linger until Dannel was trembling. At last he broke the kiss and pulled back. "Welcome, Dannel. I'm glad you've joined us."

Dannel looked dazed. He touched his lips briefly, as if amazed by the new sensation, then smiled hesitantly.

"My turn," Ander said. He held his arms wide in invitation.

Thane's lesson had not been ignored. Dannel took a deep breath and stepped forward. Though diffident, his resolve was plain. He put his arms around Ander and carefully pulled him close. His breath was hot on Ander's cheek. "I feel like I'm dreaming," he whispered. "Please, Ander. Don't let me fail."

"Trust us," Ander repeated. "If anyone can help, it's Thane." He hugged Dannel fiercely. "Now quit worrying and kiss me!"

Dannel closed his eyes and let his lips brush Ander's. He shivered with excitement, breaking the kiss after a few seconds and pressing their cheeks together. When he calmed and turned his gaze back to Ander, his eyes were filled with undisguised wonder. They kissed again, timidly at first. Ander responded warmly, gently welcoming the boy's timorous exploration. As he felt Dannel's confidence grow, he opened his mouth and let the tip of his tongue graze the youth's sensitive lips.

Dannel moaned and gathered Ander tightly against his body. Both were hard, cocks straining against the confinement of their leathers. The kiss deepened as Dannel's hesitancy melted in the heat of desire. Ander submitted to the youth's pent-up longing. Now that the feared threshold had been crossed, Dannel kissed with fervent single-mindedness.

At last Ander pulled back. "You learn fast. Are you *sure* you're new to love?"

"I've dreamed of it for years. It's even better than I imagined!"

Ander smiled seductively and let a hand slide along the fighter's lean torso. Dannel's eyes widened and he licked his lips nervously. "Don't worry," Ander said in a husky voice. "I remember what you said. No skin against skin, between your waist and knees. But there's still lots of *other* skin."

A shudder ran through Dannel's body as Ander slid a hand under his shirt. The flesh was warm and smooth; the youth's muscles quivered in response to Ander's light caress.

Thane stepped close and put an arm around Dannel's shoulders while Ander continued his gentle exploration. "We need to learn more about the firestone's spell," he said. "It manifests when you try to make love. So that's when we'll have a chance to study it."

"I have an idea," Ander said. He was gazing into Dannel's lavender eyes, gauging the effect of his caresses. The heaving chest beneath his fingers showed his efforts were appreciated. "Sometimes people bring a virgin to Lady Tayanita's house. It's usually a friend who was brought up as a follower of Ashtaroth, but who broke free of the sect. They're deathly nervous about sex. Kind of like Dannel."

"How do companions help them?" Thane asked. "We're always testing experienced lovers when we look for possible initiates. We haven't had any practice with virgins."

"Lady Tayanita says the main problem virgins have is that they're anxious. They're not sure what to expect, what to do. Watching two companions demonstrate their skills can ease their minds."

A blush crept up Dannel's neck. "I don't think that will make me less tense," he said, his voice thick.

"It's worth a try," Ander said. He pulled his hand from beneath Dannel's shirt and cupped the boy's crotch. The long mound of leather-covered flesh felt hard as iron. "To use the art, your body has to bear more pleasure than you've ever imagined. And that means your *mind* has to master it."

"I'll . . . try," Dannel said, squirming as Ander traced the length of his cock.

"We'll help you," Thane said. "Let's go find Skorri and Erik. They're probably fucking anyway, you might as well see what you can learn."

"They won't mind?" Dannel looked doubtful.

Thane grinned and thumped him on the back. "Huh! They've been sneaking around the last few days only because we didn't want to trouble *you*. They're about as shy as a thunderclap."

It took only a few minutes to find the young lovers. They had found a bower in a stand of oaks, a small clearing with filtered sunlight where a bed of moss covered the forest floor. They were sitting face to face in the middle of the glade, nude, their legs wrapped around each other's hips. Erik was gently fondling Skorri's stiff cock while the blond puffed on a small clay pipe. Wisps of bluish smoke hovered around them. Their boots and leathers were piled to the side, along with an open case of elixirs.

"Keeping in practice, I see," Thane said as he emerged from behind the thick oaks. Ander and Dannel waited in the shadows.

Skorri coughed, then put the pipe down and gave Thane a sheepish grin. "We thought everyone else was going to rest a while. And besides, we were both so horny."

Thane returned the grin and crouched beside the youths. "When *aren't* you horny?" He reached between them and stroked Erik's erection. "I've made Dannel an initiate. He doesn't know anything about sex, but watching you two might be a good way for him to start learning. Would you mind?"

Erik laughed. "You know the answer. Where is he?"

Thane waved for Ander and Dannel to join them, and they emerged from the forest.

The fighter stared at the nude youths with wide eyes. He gulped and looked up, his face flushed. "Thane, uh, he and Ander think I should start learning about magic. By watching you while you're, uh, . . ."

Skorri fixed him with a seductive gaze. "Only watch? You'd learn more if you join us."

"He's not ready for that," Ander said as he knelt beside the lovers. "Thane needs to study the firestone's spell and Dannel needs to learn about love." He took Dannel's hand and tugged the embarrassed youth to his knees. "Watch. Your turn comes soon."

Erik and Skorri pulled tighter together, until their balls and the bellies of their cocks touched. Then Erik, in a gesture of unmistakable invitation, closed his eyes and parted his lips. The invitation was accepted without hesitation. Skorri put a hand behind his partner's head and brought their lips together. The kiss lingered as tongues explored. The young lovers were completely absorbed with one another, as if they were alone in the forest. Without breaking the kiss, Erik slid his hands to Skorri's waist and leaned forward, lowering the blond onto his back. Lithe bodies arched, hard muscle forming clean lines beneath honey-brown skin, as the lovers shifted into a passionate embrace.

Thane peeled off his shirt and tossed it aside. "You too," he told Ander and Dannel. "Dannel needs to learn the feel of a friend's hand." The new initiate shivered but complied with the instructions. His broad chest moved with rapid breaths and his nipples stood out in hard nubs.

Erik soon released his partner and moved to a crouch at Skorri's side. His lips brushed taut flesh with feathery kisses as he teased the boy's body. Moving to a nipple, he lapped at the brown nub while the fingers of his right hand brushed the length of Skorri's cock with delicate strokes.

Ander leaned against Dannel's side and put an arm around his waist. Beads of sweat glistened on the fighter's brow, and his powerful muscles bunched beneath Ander's arm. The boy trembled with anticipation.

Erik moved around to straddle Skorri head to toe, his legs straddling the blond's head. He held Skorri's penis upright with one hand and licked around the crown of the glans. Dappled light played over their hard bodies, making them seem like wild creatures of the forest.

Skorri's hands slid along Erik's lean body from muscle-sheathed ribs to slender hips. The blond tilted his head back and Erik's long cock disappeared down his throat with practiced ease. The hunter reciprocated, engulfing Skorri's slightly curved shaft in his throat with a single smooth slide.

Ander shivered. He knew how good Erik's mouth felt on a straining cock. His bond with Skorri, though weak, already tingled with a pleasurable itch. He could imagine how Dannel felt at the sight of the frisky lovers. It was time to overcome his reticence.

"Touch them," he murmured. "They won't mind."

"I can't," Dannel said, his voice strained. "I'm not ready."

"There's nothing to fear. You can touch others. It's the other way around that sets off the firestone. You've been touching me. Did that make you cum?"

"Uh, no." He squirmed, clearly uncomfortable with his erection's confinement. "But I'm close."

"Try," Thane urged. He was sitting on the other side of Erik and Skorri, observing Dannel intently. "Take as much time as you want, but try. Keep touching Ander and go from there. Wait until you're ready."

Ander released Dannel and reached forward to touch the slippery shaft of Skorri's cock. His fingers trailed Erik's lips up and down the rigid organ. Dannel watched, enthralled, but didn't move.

After a few more strokes Erik let the blond's erection slip out of his mouth and rolled onto his side, leaving his cock engulfed in his partner's suckling mouth. Skorri turned his head and continued sucking, not missing a stroke. While the irrepressible blond could be carefree to the point of giddiness, he was diligent when making love.

Ander wrapped his fingers around Skorri's slick penis and held it in a light grip, pulling it away from the blond's flat belly. With one finger he spread the slippery precum oozing from its tip over the dusky glans. The contact strengthened his bond with Skorri;

he felt slippery caresses along his own engorged cock, tantalizing and intense. The blond's arousal, never far from the surface, surged through their link. He felt Dannel's hand on his back, strong and steady.

"Good," Thane said. "Touch Ander, watch what he does. He'll lead you well."

Encouraged, Ander bent down and slid his lips over Skorri's slippery cockhead. Wet pleasure engulfed his own aching cock. He wrapped his lips around the flared crown and tugged, feeling the soft pressure as if lips circled his own penis. After a few moments he slid his lips down the smooth shaft until his nose pressed into Skorri's balls and all seven inches of the shaft were enclosed in the hot, wet tunnel of his throat. Skorri moaned softly, deep in his chest. Ander appreciated the sentiment; his own cock throbbed in magically linked resonance with the boy's pleasure.

"Ummm," Erik hummed as he watched through half-shut eyes, propped up on an elbow. "I feel it too, Ander. Through Skorri. Like you're both sucking me at once." His body flexed slowly as he slid his long cock in and out of Skorri's attentive mouth.

Ander shared the young hunter's rapture. Skorri's lithe body arched beneath him, the muscles sheathing his abdomen forming hard symmetrical curves. As he began a slow glide back up the shaft he felt Dannel's hand move to his throat. The fighter leaned close, rapt. Soon his fingertips shifted to Ander's cheek, then to his lips. At last he touched Skorri's cock.

Ander felt a jolt, like a climax but without the release of ejaculation. Dannel moaned softly and pulled his hand away. Relinquishing Skorri's cock, Ander sat upright and turned to the fighter.

"What happened when you touched him? Did you cum?"

"I . . . I don't know. I mean, no, but it felt like I did!"

Thane rocked forward onto his knees, fascinated. "Somehow you can touch the kei, or come close to it, just from touching. It's like you formed a bond without using the art." He picked up the case of elixirs Skorri and Erik had opened and removed a vial, then handed it to Dannel. "Here's some jocasta oil. Put it on your cock. It'll help you keep control."

Dannel accepted the vial, holding it like a deadly viper. His embarrassment was painful to witness.

"Don't be shy," Ander said. "We're *all* hard, who wouldn't be? You have to stop worrying so much about sex."

"We'll strip too," Thane said. "That might make it easier for you." He tugged off his boots, then stood and unfastened his belt and trousers. His leathers slid down to reveal strong legs and a perfectly proportioned cock that curved up with virile bravura. Ander did the same, hoping that Thane was right about putting Dannel at ease. The young fighter watched him as if dazed.

"Your turn," Ander said as he kicked his trousers aside and plucked the vial from Dannel's hand.

Dannel took a deep breath, then rocked back and pulled his boots off. His hands were shaking. Then he stood, his cock making a long mound beneath his soft brown leathers. A sweaty sheen covered his lean body. He slowly unbuckled his belt and unfastened his trousers. A small wriggle of his hips sent the leathers snaking to the ground.

Though he blushed crimson, Dannel held his head high and didn't try to conceal his upthrust phallus. The smooth column of hard flesh had nearly uniform thickness its full length, and the dusky purple glans was slick with precum. It swayed provocatively as he shifted his weight from foot to foot.

Skorri had turned to watch, briefly relinquishing Erik's cock. He looked genuinely impressed. "As fair as Ander, and as sexy as Thane! Look at him, Erik!"

"You're right," Ander agreed. "But remember, we're trying not to make him nervous."

Skorri gave the fighter another sultry gaze, then tugged on Erik's leg to urge the hunter back into a straddle. "Come on, Erik, let's show him some more!"

The randy boys slid into action, moving with perfect coordination. Devotion to each other's pleasure inspired their lovemaking. Dannel sat on his haunches beside them, his cock spearing up past his navel.

Ander glanced at Thane. The mage was studying Dannel closely. Despite his arousal, there was a task to complete and Ander knew he wouldn't allow his own body's demands to interfere with the work at hand.

Ander removed the cork from the vial of jocasta oil he was holding. Mint fragrance wafted out as he handed the vial to Dannel. "I wish I could do it for you," he said, suddenly feeling shy. "You won't need much, it's *very* slippery. Be careful. It will help your self-control but it doesn't lessen sensation."

Dannel accepted the vial and poured a quarter of the oil into the palm of his other hand. He met Ander's gaze briefly as he returned the vial, his expression unguarded. Uncertainty and embarrassment were still there, but hope as well. He spread the clear oil over his cock, his body trembling as slick fluid lubricated the contact between hand and hard phallus.

"Lift Skorri's legs," Ander said as he touched Erik's shoulder. "I'll make him slippery for you."

Erik hummed in agreement, not letting Skorri's penis escape from his caressing lips. He hooked an arm behind one of Skorri's knees and then the other, his powerful shoulders bulging as he pulled the blond's hips off the ground. Skorri wiggled his toes in anticipation.

"First watch," Ander said to Dannel. "Then you can try."

Forming his fingers into a funnel, Ander poured half the remaining oil into his palm and then channeled it into the crack of Skorri's upturned ass. The blond spread his legs further apart and the oil trickled down to the rosette of his ass. Ander spread the slick fluid with his fingertip, stroking silky flesh as he applied more lubricant and pressing gently until the tip of his index finger slipped inside the ring of muscle. He gradually eased the finger in further, twisting gently to spread lubricant evenly. Erik held himself motionless on straightened arms, Skorri's cock down his throat to the hilt, as Ander finally slipped his finger all the way into the boy's clenching ass. The warm glove of flesh squeezed insistently.

A soft moan made Ander turn his head. Dannel had rocked back on his heels, both arms stretched behind for support. His glistening cock lay across the hard muscles of his abdomen, precum pooling beneath the glans.

Ander let his finger slide from Skorri's ass and reached for Dannel's hand. "Now you try," he said. "The jocasta oil has had time to work. You should be fine."

Dannel rocked forward and caressed the firm globes of Skorri's buttocks. He stroked the smooth flesh with his fingertips, breathing fast, as Erik resumed sucking his partner. The young fighter was transfixed.

"That's the way," Ander said softly. He put an arm around Dannel's shoulders, taking care not to touch him below the waist. "Tickle his balls, he likes that. Don't be afraid."

Dannel's fingers drifted higher and touched the twin globes, lightly brushing the soft blond hairs. Skorri showed his appreciation by curling his body tighter and plunging his cock deeper into Erik's mouth. Dannel continued caressing the boy's scrotum, using his thumb and middle finger to trace around its base as Skorri's balls pulled up tight in their satiny sack. Self-consciousness faded as he was drawn deeper into the marvel of the blond's athletic body.

"Touch him inside," Ander suggested, his voice a whisper. "Help make him ready for Erik."

This time Dannel didn't hesitate. His fingers slid from Skorri's balls to the rosette of his ass. The sensitive flesh glistened with oil; Dannel's finger left a trace as it moved through the sheen. The opening twitched beneath his tentative explorations. Skorri moaned softly, vocalizing as best he could despite the rigid cock sliding deeply into his mouth and throat.

Slowly, Dannel slid his index finger back and forth over the winking hole. Erik shifted his arms to spread Skorri's legs wider, and the tip of Dannel's finger slipped into the well-lubricated opening.

Dannel shivered but didn't move his hand. Ander gave him a reassuring squeeze. "It's all right. See, it didn't make you cum. You can do it!"

Sweat glistened on Dannel's forehead, matting the black curls to his skin. Hesitantly, he pushed his finger in deeper. His serious expression softened, blossoming into a dazzled smile, as Skorri's ass squeezed his finger in its slippery grasp.

"Work it around a little," Ander urged. "Get used to feeling his flesh."

Dannel obliged, his eagerness tempered by extreme gentleness. Ander picked up the vial and dribbled more oil as Dannel explored inside another youth's body for the first time. The young fighter was intensely aroused, his body quivering beneath Ander's encircling arm.

"That's good," Ander said. "You have the touch of a good lover, I can tell." He put down the vial and moved his hand to rest atop Dannel's, feeling the growing confidence in the fighter's slow movements. The youth's fear of losing control was fading as the thrill of discovery overtook him.

"He's ready for Erik," Ander said. He drew Dannel's hand away from Skorri's firm ass, then handed him the vial of jocasta oil. It was a quarter full. "Why don't you try putting it on Erik? You should be able to do it now."

Dannel accepted the vial and gazed into Ander's eyes, fear replaced by trust. "If you think I can, I'll try." His eyes glowed like the last clouds before sunset, lavender rimmed with pale blue, deep and richly colorful.

Erik and Skorri released each other and rolled apart, wet cocks slapping against bellies. The hunter knelt next to Dannel. He grinned and leaned back, presenting his thick erection to the fighter.

Dannel took a deep breath, then poured the remaining oil into the palm of his right hand. He reached forward and grasped the upthrust shaft.

A jolt ran through Ander's body, a tingle that centered on his cock and rippled outward in a tide of pleasure. A gold halo pulsed into existence around the hunter's straining penis.

"What happened?" Dannel asked. He held himself motionless, his fingers still cradling Erik's shining phallus.

Thane stood to get a better view. He was fully aroused. "Your touch brought him near the kei, without even using the art. Perhaps the hierophants' sorcery isn't so different from our own after all."

"But it didn't make me cum," Dannel said softly. An ecstatic smile suffused his handsome features as he slid his hand along the hard shaft of Erik's penis, making it glisten with oil.

"Ander's right," Erik said. "You have a sweet touch."

After a few more unhurried strokes Dannel released the hunter's erection. He leaned back and gave the hunter a triumphant grin. "Now I think you're *both* ready."

Erik moved between Skorri's legs and lifted them, a hand beneath each knee. Ander reached between them and guided the hunter's cock to its target as the boy leaned up and forward. His cockhead rested briefly against the slippery hole, then slowly eased in. Erik lowered himself further, still holding Skorri's legs apart with his arms, and moved his hands to the blond's shoulders.

The two boys clung together while Skorri adjusted to his lover's entry. While both were enthusiastic initiates, sharing pleasure joyously with other mages, their own lovemaking had never lost its striking tenderness. The two years they had spent protecting each other after being exiled from their village in punishment for their forbidden love had forged an unshakable bond. Dannel watched solemnly, as if he sensed the devotion between the youths.

Erik lowered his head and kissed Skorri. Then, without breaking the kiss, he began to shift his hips back and forth. His strokes were leisurely and long. The flared crown of his glans barely emerged from Skorri's clenching hole before he reversed direction and the oily shaft eased in again to the hilt. The hunter's broad back rippled with the interplay of hard muscles as he fucked.

"Your turn will come," Ander murmured. He took Dannel's hand and squeezed it, then pulled him close to the lovers. "Feel them, imagine what it's like. Get ready for when you can try it yourself."

Dannel let his hand rest on one of Erik's buttocks. The firm muscle bunched beneath his fingers, as solid as the rest of the fighter's strapping body.

"Try touching his cock," Ander urged. "Feel how hard Skorri makes him."

Dannel's hand trembled as Ander guided it down. His fingers grazed the hunter's scrotum and paused to stroke the soft brown hairs that dusted the skin. After another gentle tug, his fingers slid into contact with the base of Erik's shaft.

Ander gasped as an unexpected wave of pleasure washed over him and ghostly echoes of lovemaking teased his body. His cock twitched and drooled, a heartbeat away from orgasm.

Dannel appeared equally close to the brink. Sweat beaded his forehead and his breath rushed through parted lips. But his fingers kept contact with the base of Erik's penis and moved along with the hunter's slow fucking. Astonishment filled his face. "I can feel them," he whispered. "Feel what Erik feels."

"I can feel some of it too," Ander said. "Just from touching *you*."

Thane moved to Dannel's side, his eyes wide. "You're a conduit for anima! I've never seen anything like it." He leaned closer, tilting his head to get a closer look. "Your earring is glowing, too. A pale green. Has that ever happened before?"

Dannel licked his lips, looking like he was having trouble paying attention to the mage's questions. "It's too much," he gasped. "It's going to make me cum."

Ander tightened his grip on the fighter's hand and pulled it away from the young lovers. Dannel slumped like a sail that had lost its wind. He looked stupefied.

"The firestone," Thane repeated. "Have you ever heard of one glowing?"

Dannel shook himself, then faced the mage. "No. But I've never felt anything like this before, either. Does this tell you how the firestone's spell works?"

Thane chewed his lip thoughtfully. "We're closer," he said after a pause. "It's like a puzzle. The more pieces we have, the better our chance of seeing a pattern. Let's keep going." His smile flashed, a lightning change in expression. "Besides, I doubt Erik and Skorri want to stop now."

"We don't!" Skorri agreed. "Don't think it, Thane!" Erik growled, a rutting animal sound more emphatic than words.

Grinning, Ander took Dannel's hand and tugged him over so he knelt by Skorri's side. "Try feeling Skorri's cock," he suggested. "See if you can share his feelings, like you did Erik's."

Skorri looked at them through half-closed eyes. "Better hurry. We haven't fucked for so long, I don't think we can make it last."

Ander laughed and tousled the boy's blond curls. "I don't believe it," he said. "You've just been fucking discreetly."

Skorri grinned, not denying it. Erik shifted to his knees and lifted his torso upright, spreading his partner's legs wide and arching his back as he continued fucking with slow strokes. His cock was a sleek column of flesh, smooth and slick with oil, gliding back and forth inside his partner's welcoming body. He moved his hips from side to side, varying the angle of his thrusts and rubbing his cockhead against the spot that gave Skorri the greatest pleasure. The blond's lips parted with a soft gasp.

"I know that look," Ander said, giving Skorri's nose a tweak. "He *is* close." He reached for Dannel's hand and guided it to the blond's cock. The fighter extended his fingers and let the rigid penis lay across his palm.

Dannel's mouth fell open as Skorri's cock throbbed in his light grip. "I . . . I . . ." Suddenly his nostrils flared and he wrapped his fingers around the boy's stiff penis. Erik and Skorri both gasped, ecstasy filling their faces. Skorri's cock spasmed and sprayed jet after jet of semen across his smooth chest. Erik's hips moved in short thrusts as he shared the shattering climax that had overtaken his partner.

At last Dannel pulled back, looking stunned. Cum dripped from his fingers in thick white strands. He looked at it with wonderment. "I felt them," he whispered. "Like Erik was inside me." He licked his lips and a smile slowly blossomed. "It was *wonderful*."

Skorri opened his eyes and gave the young fighter a dazzling smile. Erik's cock was still inside him. "We felt *your* pleasure, too. Did it make you cum?"

Dannel grinned fiercely. "Almost. But whatever happened, it didn't trigger the firestone's spell. The oil Thane gave me must have worked." He rocked back on his haunches, making his long cock slap up against the washboard muscles of his abdomen. "Maybe there's hope for me after all."

"You can fuck me if you want," Skorri offered. "You're big, but so is Erik, and we're both slick."

Ander rubbed Dannel on the back. "Might as well see what happens. If nothing else, you won't be a virgin any longer."

Dannel blushed, quivering with excitement. "You're sure? I mean . . . I've never . . ."

"Ander's right," Thane said. "The firestone's spell is designed to prevent sex. We should find out what real sex makes it do."

"It's decided," Erik agreed. "Move beside me, so you can slide in as soon as I'm out. It'll be best for Skorri that way." He pushed Skorri's legs forward, along his sides. Ander took hold of one and

Thane grasped the other, flanking the lissome boy like attendants. Dannel watched, dazed, then slowly put his hand on his own cock and added Skorri's cum to the slippery oil that already covered his shaft.

As soon as Dannel was at his side, close but not touching, Erik leaned forward and extended his arms to hold himself above Skorri's body. He lowered his head and kissed his partner, then slowly withdrew his engorged cock from the boy's well-lubricated ass. Cum smeared his phallus and oozed from Skorri's ass. He pressed full length against his partner, sharing another tender kiss, then moved aside to make room between the blond's splayed legs.

Dannel moved into position carefully, making sure Skorri's legs didn't touch him below the waist. He leaned forward and supported himself with one arm, using his other hand to press his cock down. Now that the moment had arrived he hesitated, as if fearing the experience he had been denied all his life.

"Do it," Ander said. "It's time. You're done with waiting."

The young Torii Guardian took a deep breath, then rocked his hips forward and guided his cock the last inch to Skorri's ass.

As his glans touched the slippery hole, Dannel bellowed like a man caught in an avalanche. His cock slid smoothly into Skorri as his body curled in a contraction.

Ander gasped as an intense orgasm seized him. He clutched Skorri's leg as his cock spat semen against his chest and face. The sensation was overwhelming, making his body jerk time and again as he ejaculated. A groan made him look up to see Thane's muscular body in the throes of uncontrollable ecstasy, his cum fountaining high into the air.

Dannel had collapsed on top of Skorri and wrapped the boy in a fierce hug. His hips hunched back and forth as he pumped his seed into the young blond. His breath rasped like a runner at the end of a race. A red aura surrounded them both, and a blue symbol shimmered on Dannel's back like a ghostly tattoo.

Ander fell back, dizzy from the wrenching orgasm. Dannel and Skorri remained entwined. Their convulsing bodies showed no sign of escaping pleasure's grip.

"He's under the spell's power," Thane said. "Help me get them apart."

They pried Dannel's arms from around the dazed blond and pulled him back while Erik pulled from the waist. Dannel moaned softly as his twitching cock withdrew from its slimy sheath. The spell had affected Skorri as well; he had climaxed again and fresh cum smeared his belly.

The two youths came to their senses as soon as they were separated. Dannel rubbed his eyes, then reached out and touched Skorri's arm. "Are you all right?" he asked.

Skorri, still panting, was staring at the fighter in awe. "It felt like we were going to keep coming forever!" He blinked as he recalled the experience. "Can you teach Erik and me how to do that?"

Thane tugged one of the blond's toes. "We have to master the firestone's spell first. *Then* you can help him catch up on the tumbles he's missed. But we saw something that might help." He turned back to Dannel.

"There's something on your back, a marking that appeared when you were coming. A circle with glyphs inside it, like the ones inside the Torii Gates. Do you know anything about it?"

Dannel shook his head. "The hierophants give us a sleeping potion when they use spells on us, to protect their secrets. I didn't even know I *have* a mark." He reached behind his back with one hand and felt around. "Is it still there? I don't feel anything."

"No," Thane said. "But think about what it means. There's some kind of link between the Gates, the firestone and the Torii Guardians. I still think you might be *more* than a fighter. There's a stronger power in you than your masters have let you know. More than they'd share with any slave, even a warrior."

Dannel shivered, looking lost and a little frightened. "If I'm not a fighter, then what am I? I've never been anything *other* than a fighter."

"It's a mistake to let others tell you who and what you are," Thane answered. "You need to discover that for yourself. I wager what you find will surprise us all."

7

DANNEL SHOOK his head in disbelief. "I've been trained to *fight*. That's all. How could the Torii Guardians be used for magic?"

Thane shrugged. "I'm not sure. But magic is mainly a method for using anima. Maybe they use you to store it, or channel it." He sprang to his feet and went to the pile of clothes heaped nearby. "Don't worry about what happened with Skorri," he said. "No harm was done, and it gave me an idea. Something that might help control the firestone's spell." He slipped his shirt over his head, then gave Dannel a wolfish grin. "And you've finally shared pleasure with another, at least briefly. How did you like it?"

A shy smile dispelled Dannel's anxious expression like the sun banishing storm clouds. "I'll never forget it," he said softly. His gaze shifted to Skorri and the smile widened. "I'll be dreaming about you, Skorri. I know it."

The blond grinned back as he reached for his pants. "Only if Thane *lets* you sleep. He never rests. Just ask Ander." Though he was teasing, the observation was mostly accurate.

"Who can rest when there's so much to do?" Thane said as he stepped into his leathers. "And anyway, who can think of resting this early in the day?" He fastened his belt, then picked up his boots. "Dannel, you mentioned gardens. Would you show me? There are lots of plants here. I'm sure we can find some useful ones."

"What about us?" Ander asked as he dressed.

"The three of you should go back through the Gates. None of you had problems like Dannel and me. Explore more carefully, on foot, see if we missed anything. We didn't really get a good look the first time."

The eager nod in reply made Thane smile. Ander's avid curiosity was one of the traits he loved most. "Let's meet by the lake an hour before sunset," he said. They finished dressing and parted company to pursue their separate tasks.

Dannel seemed subdued as he led the way through the forest, back toward the lake. Thane allowed him the refuge of silence. The young fighter had gone through a lot, and the mage wasn't surprised he was still sorting it out.

After a few minutes Dannel lifted his gaze from the trail. "I haven't thanked you," he said. "I'm sorry. I keep thinking about Skorri, how it felt. After wondering all these years, and now finally to know. But it was still only a hint of what love is like."

"It's a beginning," Thane replied. "Love usually doesn't come easy."

A hint of bitterness tinged Dannel's frown. "Harder for some than others. How old are you, Thane? Not even *my* age, probably. Yet you and Ander must have been together for years."

The mage's grim silence caught Dannel by surprise.

"I'm sorry. I shouldn't be complaining. You've been a friend. What do *I* know about love? I'm probably being stupid."

Thane could tell Dannel felt badly, but couldn't bring himself to explain. The years of grief following Lucian's death had left scars that even Ander couldn't heal quickly. Memory still stung like a barbed lash.

They arrived at a grove of apple trees, just starting to bud. "Tell me about these groves," Thane said, his voice tight. "Who tends them?"

Dannel looked relieved at the change of subject. "The Guardians. The hierophants spend twenty days beyond the Gates before making us drink their sleeping potions. We spend the time tending crops." He waved his arm, encompassing the nearly wild trees with the gesture. "It keeps us busy and gives us something fresh to eat. Besides, we need the food. The hierophants keep the caravans small. They don't want anybody but priests and Guardians to know exactly where the Gates are."

They wandered into the grove. The smell of rotting apples left on the ground after the last harvest was thick and sweet. He felt a pang, remembering the countless hours he had spent tending gardens for Lord Tolmin and at his own estate. The leisurely pleasures of gardening now seemed an impossible luxury. "Do you grow anything besides food crops?" he asked. "Most of what we use for the art is less common."

Dannel pointed to the right. "There's another garden over that way. The hierophants tend it themselves. We're forbidden to enter it, but I've never seen them bring food out."

Thane's slouch disappeared. "That sounds promising. Let's take a look."

Dannel led the way down a trail of rounded stones. They crossed a meadow where root crops were already beginning to break through the ground, then passed through a stand of pines. When they emerged they encountered a wall eight feet high made of stone blocks that fit together with meticulous precision. The entrance gate was twice as high as the wall and looked like a miniature version of the Torii Gates, two tapering columns with flattened pyramidal crosspieces. They paused outside the gate.

Dannel regarded the gate nervously. "I'll go first," he volunteered. "There might be dangers. No Guardian has ever defied the hierophants and tried to enter."

Thane put a hand on the fighter's shoulder. "If there's a cantrip, you'd not know until it's too late. I'll be careful." He stepped next to the gate and put a hand on one of the pillars. The stone was rough, like a coconut shell, and held heat from the sun. He closed his eyes and concentrated as he ran his hand over the gray rock. A sense of ancient patience seeped from the stone.

"No danger," Thane said. "At least not that I can sense." He craned his neck to look at the massive lintel overhead. It must have weighed tons, yet seemed strangely insubstantial against the background of clouds. A shiver ran along his spine. Whoever had created this place understood the world, and dealt with it, in a way unlike anything he had previously experienced. He took a deep breath and let his hand fall away from the pillar. "Damn the hierophants and their threats. Time to break another of your shackles. Let's see what your former masters were hiding."

They entered the sequestered garden side by side. Tall zebra grass filled the area immediately inside the gate, striped blades and feather-like flowers obscuring what lay beyond. Thane brushed foliage aside and penetrated deeper, every sense straining. The seven-foot high grass soon thinned. A fieldstone courtyard lay before them.

Thoughts of cantrips evaporated as the hierophants' garden came into view. Thane felt like he was dreaming. The first plant to seize his attention was a bush six feet high with heart-shaped leaves, green on one side and shiny as mirrors on the other. Sun reflecting from the leaves made the plant blaze, an impression magnified by flowers with bright red petals surrounding orange and gold florets.

Another plant bore puffballs the size of peaches on long stalks. Faint clouds of colored pollen wafted from the spiky balls and left streaks in the air as a breeze stirred the foliage. Scents of lavender and honeysuckle teased Thane's nose as they passed through the mist.

A sound like soft laughter emerged from the depths of a squat plant with broad leaves that curled into cones. Bees buzzed in and out of the cones, attending to the plant as if summoned by a mirthful jester.

Scores of marvels drew Thane's gaze from bed to bed. Half the plants he had never seen before. He felt dizzy, dazzled by the garden's wonders. A light touch on his arm reminded him of his companion.

"Do you know these plants?" Dannel asked.

"Only some of them. This place is a treasure trove!" His eyes shone as he surveyed the extensive collection. Botany was one of the few things that could make him forget his worries, if only briefly.

Dannel looked skeptical. "You really think *plants* can defeat the firestone?"

"When we're done with them, yes." Thane pointed to dwarf pine with long bluish needles on their left. "That one, for a start. We'll harvest the small cones, make sure not to take the large ones. You grind them up between smooth stones, then add cold water to make a paste, and then strain it through a cloth. Then you mix it, very slowly, with oil squeezed from apricot pits, or if you don't have apricots you can—"

"I believe you," Dannel said hurriedly. "What do you want me to do?"

Thane went over to the pine and parted some needles to expose the cones. "Twist them off like this," he said, demonstrating. "Fill your pockets. We'll need a lot of them."

Dannel began to harvest the small cones, less deftly than the mage but with increasing speed as he developed the knack for twisting at the right point.

"You have nimble hands," Thane commented as he watched the fighter's rapid improvement. "Did you do work like this in Skarn?"

"Some," Dannel said, scowling as he continued working. "We did whatever the hierophants told us to do. Torii Guardians aren't officially slaves, but that's what it amounts to."

"Tell me what it was like," Thane suggested. "Maybe it will help me understand how their magic works."

Dannel sighed as he stuffed a handful of cones into a pocket. "I don't want you to think I'm a complainer."

"I know better. And I'd really like to know."

Dannel resumed twisting cones off the pine. At first he was silent, as if trying to decide where to begin. Thane felt a pang of guilt, recognizing the fighter's struggle with painful memories. Finally the boy began his tale.

"I was taken to the temple on my tenth birthday. You can't be indentured until you're that old. My parents, they . . . they . . ." He paused and cleared his throat. He yanked sharply at one of the cones, making the whole branch shake, then continued in a firmer voice. "They were well paid. I haven't seen them since then, or my brothers and sisters. They used the money to leave Skarn. They didn't even tell me where they were going."

"The temple," Thane reminded gently.

Dannel nodded. "New boys have to fast when they enter the temple. Three days with nothing but water, and they don't start counting the days until you stop asking for food. They put you in a dark little room with small openings in one wall. Big enough to reach through, no more. On the other side of the wall is a table filled with food cooked for the hierophants' own table. Roasted meats, fresh bread, ripe fruit, honey. They make sure everything is just beyond your reach."

"Senseless cruelty," Thane said, anger rising. "I've seen it often, and can never understand it."

"The hierophants are merciless, but they always have a purpose. It's the same lesson they taught us every day of our lives. Do what you're told, endure, and you'll be rewarded in the end. They use food for the lesson when you're a child. To prepare you."

Thane felt a knot in his stomach. "For the firestone's curse. It keeps something out of reach until you satisfy your indenture."

"Yes. Most Guardians learn the lesson well. Those who don't have short lives." His expression was bleak.

"Do the Guardians have tasks besides guarding the temple and its priests?" Thane asked.

"Many. Guardians do whatever work needs doing. And there are *many* daily exercises. They even pay us a little, so our families can pretend it's not true slavery. It's less of a disgrace to indenture a boy than to sell him into slavery. And of those offered for indenture, the priests only take one in a hundred." A frown crossed his face. "I could never understand it. They tell you being a Torii Guardian is an honor, but then treat you like a mongrel dog."

"It *is* strange. But they have a reason for making children starve, so maybe they have reasons for the rest. I wonder if hardship is part of what gives you power."

Dannel's frown deepened to a scowl. "Do we *have* to talk about this? Today has changed my life, and I'd rather not think about the past. At least not right now."

"Forgive me. I was thoughtless." Thane bowed his head in apology. "I used to be even worse. Terrible, really. It's a wonder my friends were so patient. Ander has helped a lot, but when we're apart my old ways return."

Dannel stopped working and gave Thane a puzzled gaze. "Your old ways? How long have you been a mage?"

Thane sighed, knowing he couldn't put it off any longer. He stuffed pinecones in a pocket and gestured for Dannel to follow. They followed a flagstone trail deeper into the garden. Silence stretched while Thane pondered the fighter's question. As much as he disliked thinking of his past, Dannel was now an initiate and had to hear the story. The need didn't make the task any easier.

The path meandered through a marshy area filled with papyrus reeds ranging from six to ten feet high. It soon emerged beside a pond, partially covered with green slime, where water lilies bloomed in a riot of color. A flat stone embankment five feet wide circled the pond. *As good a place for it as any*, he decided.

"Look at it," Thane said. "Did they create it for beauty, or only for the sake of growing the plants?"

Dannel shrugged. "Both, perhaps?" He knelt and ran his hand over the yellow stone blocks. "Smooth. Made for resting or meditation, I'd guess."

Thane bent to feel the stone. It was warm beneath his fingertips and smooth as polished wood. He sat and crossed his legs, smelling the mossy stones and letting the calm that filled the garden seep into his bones. Dannel settled next to him. They watched the pond in silence for a few minutes, hearing only the buzz of bees and occasional rustling of reeds as a zephyr passed.

At last Thane turned to his companion. "We're more alike than you know," he said. "My parents were serfs. Our family worked the same land for generations, always in debt to the squire. I don't know if it's the same here, but in Izmir serfs who leave the land without first paying their debts forfeit their lives."

"I remember Ander saying you ran away from your master," Dannel said. "I guess that makes us alike, at least some. But you were a serf. You must have spent most of your time farming, not fighting."

"I started out farming along with everybody else. When I got older the squire decided to give me schooling along with his own children."

Dannel lifted an eyebrow. "Since when do squires let serfs into their manors?"

Thane shrugged. "I had a reputation in the village for being clever, and he thought he could use me. At first I didn't understand what he was doing. I was just happy to discover a world beyond the fields. But soon I saw how he cared less about his serfs than his cattle. I began to plead with him, then to argue."

Dannel shook his head in disbelief. "I know what would happen to a Torii Guardian who tried that. Did you fare any better?"

A pained squint was answer enough. "He treated me like a head-strong horse, tried to break me. It took me a few weeks to recover from the beating. Then I ran away. I'd just turned sixteen. I knew if I defied him again he'd kill me."

"Did Ander run away with you?"

"This was before I met Ander. I went to Chanture and made some friends. One of them got me a job in an aristocrat's household. Lord Tolmin was like a father to me, showed me how to look at the world with an open mind. He loves plants and taught me some of their secrets." He paused, his reluctance plain. At last he continued in a soft voice.

"That's when I met Lucian. We fell in love and everything changed. We started using some of what I learned about botany, looking for ways to give each other even greater pleasure. Finally we touched the kei. It was a complete surprise. We kept exploring and what we learned became the art."

Dannel's brow creased. "Are Ander and Lucian *both* your lovers, then? I understand about using sex to work magic, but I know you and Ander share far more than pleasure."

Thane took a deep breath, let it out slowly. "Ander . . . you're right, he means more to me than anyone. Lucian died ten years ago. I never stopped loving him, but Ander has filled the place in my heart that was empty. It's . . . a long story."

"Ten years?" Dannel looked dubious. "You're not making sense. You said you ran away when you were sixteen and didn't meet Lucian until after that. You're no older than me."

"It's time you know one of our greatest secrets. The art uses anima, the force of life itself. It *creates* anima. Once you master the art you stop aging. Lucian and I mastered it when we were nineteen. Not long before he died in the zamindar's torture chambers." Thane's eyes stung and he looked away. The surge of memories, lost love and bitter grief, felt as sharp as ever.

Dannel stared at Thane in silence, doubt slowly transforming into sympathy as Thane's pain-filled sincerity sank in. At last he nodded. "After what I've seen the last few days, I believe you. In a way, it makes it easier to believe you're a real mage."

"Let's get back to work," Thane said, surging to his feet. "It's not good to think about the past too long."

Dannel scrambled to keep up as Thane plunged back into the garden as if fleeing a demon. They followed a narrow stone path, dodging branches bristling with long thorns. The trail opened on another courtyard, this one surrounded by purple star-shaped flowers that were beginning to open. Thane slowed as the exotic blooms tugged at his attention. A scent like roasting cloves tickled his nose. Then he noticed a tree to their right, its red bark peeling in curly strips. He stopped and grabbed Dannel's arm, the past forgotten.

"Look, a raffia tree! A useful plant. It could help us get around the firestone's spell. Let's collect some bark."

"Whatever you say," Dannel agreed. Thane had already released him and was weaving through foliage toward the tree. Small white buds had formed on the tree's branches and gave off a sweet fragrance like cider.

"Peel off strips of bark," Thane said, demonstrating. "You cut it into little pieces and scald it, then filter the pulp out and boil off most of the water. What's left is like syrup, but it dissolves in lubricant oils."

"What would it do? Make me less sensitive?"

"Not exactly," Thane answered as he peeled translucent bark from the tree's trunk. "Remember what happened when you touched Erik and Skorri? How you felt their pleasure?"

A hot flush rushed up Dannel's face as he nodded. "I'm not likely to forget *that*. Ever."

"I think the firestone makes you a channel, a place where anima flows strong and easy. But if you're anointed with raffia oil we can draw some of the anima off. Pleasure will still be there but you'll have a better chance to control it. It can grow slowly, the way your body was meant to feel it."

"How much do we need?" Dannel asked as he started stripping bark from one of the tree's spidery branches.

"A ball about six inches across should do it. The tree seems big enough, there should be plenty."

They worked side by side in companionable silence, falling into an easy rhythm. The sun was warm on Thane's back and it felt good to have plants under his hands again. He could almost feel the placid life in the great tree, its place as a connection between the soil and the sun. As always, the routine of physical labor calmed him.

He glanced sidelong at Dannel as he worked. The young fighter toiled without complaint despite the sweat beading his forehead and staining his leather shirt. An unconscious frown tugged at the boy's mouth. It wasn't hard to imagine his anxiety; he had risked everything on a desperate gamble, only to learn that success depended on a skill he'd never had a chance to master. Especially for a warrior, powerlessness would be hard.

Thane pondered the fighter's situation, and soon remembered

Ander's happiness two months ago when Skorri had asked to learn music. Though he was too modest to boast, Ander was proud of his skill with the guitar and took joy in sharing what he knew. It had given him a sense of belonging and a chance to prove his worth. An idea formed, so obvious Thane wondered why he hadn't thought of it before.

"What's it like, doing your exercises without a fighting partner?" he asked. He kept peeling bark from the raffia tree, giving Dannel only a brief glance. "I'm impressed by your discipline."

Dannel didn't look up. "Some exercises can be done alone. But there are limits to what you can do without an adversary. There's nothing I can do about it."

"Maybe there is. You have ways of fighting I've never seen before. It could come in useful. Remember those nightblades in Chanture we told you about?"

Dannel looked up and grinned, as eager as Skorri before a tumble. "Would you like me to teach you? I've taught others, at the temple in Skarn."

"I'd be honored if you would. And grateful. It would be a great gift."

Dannel looked so pleased it almost made Thane laugh, but he kept a straight face. His words were true, even if he had more than one reason for them.

"Would you like to start this afternoon?" Dannel asked. "It would be best to begin before eating."

"You're the master, when it comes to warrior's skills."

"We'll start slow," Dannel said, returning to his work with new enthusiasm. "You have to learn how to train without getting hurt. Knowing how to fall—"

"*There* you are." Erik stood where the path entered the courtyard, having approached without making a sound. "It's hard to track in here. Too many stone paths and strange scents."

Thane looked up, surprised at the hunter's arrival. "Done already?"

"We found something. A door of some kind, maybe. Ander had a strange feeling when we passed it, something in the kei too small for Skorri or me to notice. We thought you should be there before we try opening it."

Thane's eyes went wide. "A door? In the chamber that ensnared Dannel and me?"

"A little before then, in the gallery. Come see." He turned and started back down the path, even more economical with words than usual. It was a sure sign of tension. Thane wasted no time following, with Dannel close behind.

By the time they reached the Torii Gates the sun had dropped halfway to the horizon. The white stone flanking the Gates glowed a dull orange and the glyphs seemed carved from fire. Shimmering heat waves coming off the plaza made the Gates appear to waver, as if the imposing portal was the figment of a fevered dream. As soon as they passed the threshold the afternoon heat vanished. Inside the Gates was cool as a crypt.

Far ahead, a faint golden haze broke the inky darkness. As they approached the glow resolved into two telos lights hovering a few yards above the stone floor. Ander and Skorri were on their hands and knees, each casting a double shadow, brushing sand aside to clear a section of the floor. The cleared area was even more ornately decorated than the walls. Intricate mosaics formed geometric patterns that wove together like a tapestry. Blue and green tiles dominated, with red and gold pieces forming most of the lines. Like the glyphs on the walls, the patterns seemed more than merely ornamental.

"Take a look at this," Ander said, beckoning as Thane entered the double circle of light. "I felt something when we walked past, a chill. We stopped and Erik noticed a line in the sand. See?" He pointed to an area where the sand was undisturbed. A nearly imperceptible indentation continued into the cleared area, lining up with an edge in the tile pattern. "It makes a rectangle," Ander continued. "About five feet wide and seven feet long. The strange feeling is there when you stand inside it, but vanishes if you step outside."

Thane moved to Ander's side. His lover's suspicions were confirmed as soon as he stepped across the line. A cool sensation rippled through him, leaving a weak tingle in its wake.

Surprised recognition flickered across Thane's face. "Water. This is how it feels if you enter the kei when a river's nearby. But why would we feel it *here*?"

Dannel shifted uneasily. "Flowing water is sacred to the hierophants. It's a part of many rituals. Even in ceremonial combat."

Thane dropped to his knees, brushing sand aside where it had not yet been cleared. "Let's get this cleaned off. Maybe seeing the whole pattern will reveal something."

A patch of floor around the rectangle was soon swept bare. Thane conjured another light globe, brighter than the others combined, then stood back to examine the pattern from a distance. After a few moments he shook his head. "I don't see any difference in the pattern inside and outside the box. Where would they conceal a latch? Under a loose tile?"

"Maybe it's not a door at all?" Ander suggested.

"What *else* could it be?" Thane stomped on the tiles inside the rectangle, but the dull thump was no different from the sound outside the thinly etched lines. The light globe he had created began to sizzle, throwing off glinting red sparks, a reflection of his frustration.

"Maybe it's a trap," Erik suggested.

"I don't think so." Thane stomped again, harder. The thud of boots striking tile reverberated off the high walls. "If it's a trap, it's not working. No, I think it's a door. There *must* be a way to open it!"

Ander moved to Thane's side and put a hand against the small of his back. "Maybe we're looking at this wrong," he said. "Maybe it's a door and the latch is in front of us, but we're just not seeing it."

Thane stopped his restless investigation. "What do you mean? There's nothing to see except tiles and four grooves in the floor."

"That's all *most* would see. But only mages can sense the kei. Maybe you have to use magic to open the door."

Thane blinked, feeling like a fool. Ander only grinned at him.

"You're right," Thane said. "I didn't stop to remember that sorcerers built this place." He took Ander's hand and gave it a squeeze. "Would you help me explore? You're more sensitive to the kei than any of us imagined."

Ander's grin widened into a dazzling smile. "What do you want me to do? I'll do anything."

The pulse of affection through their bond was enough to make Thane's heart melt. It still amazed him that Ander offered such unconditional devotion. He resolved, for the thousandth time, to set aside more time for his beloved. But it would have to wait; a mystery still remained. He put his hands on Ander's shoulders and held him at arm's length, basking in the happy youth's masculine beauty for a few moments before returning to the task.

"We'll start by sharing anima without fully joining. We might need to act quickly if the door opens."

Ander nodded, his eyes half closing in a seductive gaze. "As you say. The rest can wait until tonight."

Thane grinned in return, feeling Ander's randy anticipation through their link and answering it with his own. He could already tell the night's lovemaking would be memorable. He slid his hands around Ander and tugged up the boy's shirt.

Ander raised his arms and shimmied out of the leather garment.

His smooth skin gleamed in the soft glow of the telos light. He pulled Thane's shirt off before reaching down and pressing a hand against the bulge at the mage's crotch.

The soft pressure made Thane ache and wish all else could wait. Instead he held Ander against his chest and kissed him gently. He felt the boy's erection straining against his own, felt the strong heartbeat against his chest. They exchanged a fierce hug before Thane forced himself to return to their task.

"You know what to do," he said as they moved to the center of the rectangle. "Share your strength, let me know if you sense anything. Especially if you think it might be a cantrip."

Ander nodded, then moved behind Thane and put his arms around the mage's waist with fingers splayed against his slatted ribs. While the limited contact wouldn't provide as deep a bond as sex, the technique was far safer if something should go wrong and they needed to act quickly.

Thane slowed his breathing and leaned back, letting Ander brace him. He cleared his mind and focused on the chilly tingle that lurked on the edge of his awareness like a wolf in a dark forest. It was a cool magic, not filled with agony like the sorcery used by the zamindar's mages or pleasure in the manner of the art. The prevailing sensation was of cool remoteness, vast as an ocean but moving with relentless purpose.

A strange combination of sensations began to fill his body. He could feel Ander's strong embrace, accompanied by a steady flow of anima that warmed his skin where they touched. Thin lines of amber light outlined Ander's hands. As their bond strengthened the bands of light began to shimmer outward across Thane's muscular torso. Lines of ribs and muscle lifted and glowed with golden accents as he breathed. Gradually his perception of the gallery faded. He closed his eyes and let the faint sensation grow.

At first all he sensed was water, a mighty river flowing through dark caverns. He shivered at its coldness; ages had passed since these waters last sparkled beneath the sun's warming rays. Whether he was sensing a real river, or his mind was conjuring water as a substitute for some cold and ancient mystery in the kei, was impossible to know. All he could do was open himself to the experience and see where it led.

Thane drew on the anima flowing freely through his bond with Ander and surrendered himself to the frigid waters. Touching them magically was enough to raise goose bumps, but he knew the cause was psychic rather than physical. He ignored the discomfort and allowed his mind to move with the dreamlike current as it picked up speed.

Soon he felt as if his body rushed headlong through narrow chasms, carried by a force as irresistible as a tidal wave. The sense of pressure was occasionally broken by heart-stopping moments of weightlessness as he felt himself hurtled over invisible waterfalls in pitch-black chasms. He swayed, barely aware of Ander's strong embrace keeping him on his feet. The sorcery had sucked him in like a vortex and was rapidly becoming more real than the physical world. It carried him on a wave of power, filling him with equal parts terror and elation.

Dimly, he heard the whisper of Ander's voice in the back of his mind. The tone was insistent and anxious. Though it was nearly impossible to turn his attention from the weighty tugs and jerks that seemed to grip him, Ander's voice wouldn't relent. *Down*, it seemed to say. *Look beneath the waters.*

Confused by the propulsive forces that made him feel like a cork on storm-tossed waves, it took him several seconds to even decide what direction was *down*. At last he decided that down might mean the direction of his feet, regardless of his disoriented sense. He bent his head forward until the back of his neck strained.

At first he saw nothing but the same inky blackness. He began to feel real fear. This sorcery was immensely strong and physical. It was a force to struggle against, not a puzzle to unravel like most spells.

Heeding the urgent tone in Ander's barely heard words, he continued to search the darkness. Finally a swirling gray patch separated from the black. He concentrated on it, trying to force clarity to emerge from murky gray clouds spinning like a whirlpool beneath him.

Touch it, Ander's voice urged. Thane hesitated, wondering if he would be able to extricate himself from whatever force was manifesting from the void. Then, trusting in Ander, he visualized himself moving toward the vortex. He extended a hand forward. The world seemed to spin until the gray cloud swirled directly in front of him.

A jolt tugged him as powerful suction grabbed his hand. The gray vortex sharpened into a cleanly defined circle with black streamers ripping across its edges and vanishing into what looked like a tube of silver light. Perception of distances was meaningless in the blackness; the object was far smaller than he had thought. The circle that had seemed large and distant was no larger than a plum and hovered within arm's reach.

Suction pulled his hand toward the circle. His palm slapped

against it and a cold ring like metal pressed against his skin.

A deep rumble filled his ears and strong currents buffeted his body. Vibrations made him tingle from the soles of his feet to the top of his head.

He felt a strong jerk, then a bruising fall. Blackness cleared from his eyes and he found himself lying on the floor with Ander on top of him. Ander scrambled to his feet and dragged Thane with him.

"Look!" he shouted, his voice echoing in the high gallery. "It's opening!"

Thane joined the others around the rectangle where he and Ander had been standing. The whole section of floor had already sunk a foot beneath the level of the surrounding tiles. It continued to drop at a slow pace, the only sound a distant rumble that was more felt than heard.

"That wasn't like any spell *I've* ever felt," Thane said. He gave Ander's arm a squeeze. "Thanks. I wouldn't have found the key without your help."

Ander beamed. "You were too distracted. I could feel some of what you felt. It almost made me sick."

Thane peered into the deepening shaft, now two feet deep. "Do you know what we did?"

Ander chewed his lower lip a moment, then nodded. "I remembered what you said about the spell feeling like water. And what Dannel said about flowing water being sacred to the hierophants. So I started thinking about water."

Thane smiled, impressed and pleased at Ander's rational approach to the world. The youth's inquisitive mind was equal to his flawless body.

"So you were thinking about water. What did you look for in the kei?"

"Well, I remembered what Katy told me about providing water to the buildings at the Lyceum. She showed me one of the valves she built, the new one for the greenhouse. You just *start* to turn it, and the force of water from the hot springs turns it the rest of the way. So I decided maybe you were sensing real water, and there might be a valve to control it. One you turn with magic."

Dannel was nodding his head vigorously. "The hierophants use water for lots of things. Milling grain, drawing water from deep wells, that kind of thing. They use a machine they call a hydraulikos to make flowing water turn wheels and pull ropes."

"Look," Thane said, pointing to a spot on the side of the shaft being exposed by the receding floor. "A niche. It looks like there's something in it."

"A metal rod," Erik said as he leaned over the edge and peered into the dark recess. The section of floor continued to sink. "There's another," the hunter said, pointing to a spot that was coming into view a foot to the right and a little lower than the first niche.

They continued watching as the mosaics on the dropping floor grew tiny and were finally lost in darkness. Thane summoned his telos light from overhead and willed it downward. The shaft's stone sides were smooth as a fresh coat of snow and straight as a rule. Whoever carved the shaft had possessed supreme skill in working stone. Soon the shaft was twelve feet deep, and the floor still continued to retreat.

Thane reached down and gripped the metal bar in the highest niche. Cold iron an inch thick fit his hand comfortably. He tugged and twisted, but the rod was immovable. "A ladder of sorts," he guessed. "It seems safe."

A zephyr of dry air gusted up the shaft, pungent like hot peppers being cooked. Thane pulled back, his heart pounding. Nosing around secret places built by sorcerers was dangerous business, a lesson he had learned from painful experience.

Dannel moaned softly. "I know that smell. I've smelled it at the temple, at the door to the hierophants' library."

No harm appeared to come from the sere breeze. Thane leaned over the pit and forced the telos light to sink lower.

Black space now surrounded the recessed mosaic floor on three sides. It continued to grow as the floor withdrew, and then gradually brightened as light from the telos light began to reflect from more distant walls. Soon there was a soft thump and the floor stopped moving. Thane made a quick decision. "I'm going down."

"Not without me," Ander said. "You might need help if the passage closes again."

"And you might need a fighter," Dannel said. "I'll go too."

"All right," Thane agreed. "Erik and Skorri, you stay up here. Shout if the passage starts closing." Without waiting for confirmation, he slid onto his front and spun around so the lower half of his body dangled in the shaft. His feet quickly located niches and he started climbing down.

The shaft continued for twenty feet before penetrating the ceiling at the end of a tall corridor. Niches in the corridor's wall provided footholds and handholds for another ten feet.

Thane reached the bottom, standing once again on the mosaic floor from the gallery above. Jumping the last three feet, he spun in the air and landed in a crouch. The telos light hovered near the ceiling, casting golden light over stone walls that sloped outward from top to bottom. As in the hall above, the walls were covered with glyphs. They glistened in a rainbow of colors, glowing softly as if responding to the anima in the telos light. Thane moved aside as Ander and then Dannel joined him. Nothing else stirred in the passage, but there was a soft sound like a slowly modulating chant in the distance.

Ander cocked his head and listened intently a few moments. "Not an animal," he said. "Whatever's making the sound isn't taking breaths."

"And I don't feel danger in the kei," Thane said. "Let's explore." He paused to look up the shaft and wave at Skorri and Erik, then turned and started down the passage.

Thane took the lead, his caution balanced by feverish excitement. The corridor sloped down, gently at first, then steeply, though the ceiling remained at its original height and the passage grew no wider. Soon the floor turned to steps. They emerged from a narrow doorway, fifty feet high, into a huge cylindrical chamber. Its curved walls were covered with countless small glass tiles like mirrors. The tiles blazed with the colors of sunrise as the telos light floated into the room.

The peppery smell they had noticed when the corridor was unsealed grew stronger, the humming louder. As they started across the chamber whispers swirled around them like snowflakes gusting through a mountain pass. Dannel crouched warily, balanced on the balls of his feet, ready to strike.

Ander cupped his hands behind his ears and turned his head back and forth, trying to locate the faint voices. As the echoes of their footsteps faded away, astonished recognition filled his face. "It's Skorri! Not shouting, just talking to Erik."

Thane strained, his hearing not as keen as Ander's musician's ear, but soon heard the whispers transform into faint words. It was definitely Skorri; the lusty blond was giving his partner an enthusiastic account of how Dannel's spurting cock had felt as it slid into another boy for the first time.

Dannel rose from his fighting stance, blushing scarlet. Thane broke into a grin and thumped the fighter on the back. "Modesty doesn't last long around us. I would have told you, but it would only have made you more nervous."

"I'm not nervous," Dannel muttered. He didn't look like he was convincing even himself.

Thane walked further into the room. As he approached the center of the chamber the whispers grew louder, until it sounded like he was standing next to Skorri and Erik. The effect was uncanny.

"Whoever built this was a genius," Ander said, moving to Thane's side. He pointed around the chamber, drawing Thane's attention to inconspicuous slit openings scattered among the mirrored tiles. "There must be channels through the rock, designed to make sounds carry."

"That means anybody down here heard us coming," Dannel added. "We should be careful."

"A little further," Thane said. He continued directly across the circular floor from the point where they had entered. A pitch-black doorway, twice as wide at the bottom as the top, was the chamber's only other large opening. The peppery scent strengthened, carried by a gentle breeze flowing from the dark opening. He stepped through the portal, his telos light hovering above his right shoulder. Ander and Dannel crowded behind him.

Thane's throat went dry as his eyes adjusted to a new perspective. They stood at the top of a steeply inclined ramp leading from the midpoint on a wall into a vast crypt. A forest of thick pillars, bulging at the base and fluted at the top, supported a ceiling fifty feet above the level where he stood. Large marble blocks placed between the bases of the pillars were filled with thousands of niches, and the end of a scroll protruded from each niche.

Thane realized he had been holding his breath, and slowly let it out. The air inside the crypt was thick with spice.

"What is it?" Ander asked in an awed voice.

"Secrets," Thane answered. "Enough for ten lifetimes." He felt giddy and uncertain. *Where to begin?*

8

HUGE PILLARS receded into darkness like a nightmare forest. Ander shivered, longing for sunlight. He felt trapped and could sense the huge weight of rock above them. The chamber's vastness made it better than a cave, but not by much. He glanced at Thane, who seemed unusually subdued. Ander shared the sentiment. The ancients who had built this place possessed skills that Izmir and other western kingdoms never dreamed of.

Ander wrestled his dread of caves into submission and stepped onto the ramp. Lady Tayanita had always told him that fear is best confronted quickly, and she was rarely wrong. "Coming?" he asked, sounding far more confident than he felt. "We don't want to make Erik and Skorri wait too long."

Thane shook himself, as if emerging from a trance, and moved to Ander's side. "I suppose this was built by men," he said. "But I'm not sure they were men like us."

"There are legends," Dannel said. He spoke softly, apparently not immune to the intimidating architecture. "The hierophants whisper about another race. Powerful and old, from a place beyond any maps. I always thought it was vainglory. Now . . . I'm not so sure."

"True or not, it seems nobody's here now," Thane said. He started down the long ramp.

Ander was about to follow when he noticed a faint pulse of blue light around Dannel. He stopped, eyes narrowed, and looked more closely.

"What?" the fighter asked, looking at Ander suspiciously.

Another pulse of faint light haloed Dannel's head. This time Ander saw a flash in the firestone, like the blink of a firefly.

"The firestone," Ander said, pointing at Dannel's ear. "It's flickering."

Dannel scowled while Thane turned around and examined the earring. Ander felt a pang of sympathy. The new initiate's deepest desire was to win freedom from the firestone, but instead it remained the focus of his life.

"It's responding to something in here," Thane said. "Like a talisman." He touched it lightly, prompting another flash of light. "Do you feel anything when it does that?"

"No." Dannel looked uncomfortable, turning his head away from Thane's touch.

"Be sure to tell me if you *do* feel anything," Thane said. He clasped Dannel's shoulder and gave it a squeeze. "Don't worry. We're making progress."

Dannel ventured a feeble smile. "I hope you're right. It's just . . . I can't help remembering all the stories. We should keep our guard up."

"Good advice. We'll heed it." They continued down the ramp, keeping close. Rows of pillars marched off at their sides, fading into the darkness.

When they reached the floor Ander looked back the way they had come. The far end of the ramp looked tiny, like the sharp end of a wedge, where it touched the wall high above. He felt as if they had entered another world. Not allowing time for fears to overtake him, he walked over to the nearest marble block and removed one of the scrolls from its niche. The parchment felt dusty as he unrolled a few inches, and the spicy scent that permeated the room's air tickled his nose. Thane moved to his side, the telos light trailing overhead, and peered over his shoulder at the scroll.

The text looked like worm tracks to Ander, twisting across each other in a tight tangle of lines and loops surrounded by dots in various patterns. He turned the scroll over, thinking he was perhaps holding it upside down and hoping it would make more sense the other way.

"You had it right the first time," Thane said. He took the scroll and righted it, then unrolled another foot of text.

"You can understand it?" Ander asked, feeling a familiar jolt of surprise at his lover's abilities.

"Not really," Thane confessed. "It looks something like Ionian manuscripts I've seen in Lord Tolmin's library. But it's only a similarity. I can't translate it." He angled the parchment toward Dannel. "Do you have any better luck with it?"

Even in the dim light, the fighter's embarrassment was plain. "Our training doesn't include reading," he said, his voice strained.

"That's all right," Ander said, touching the youth's arm lightly. "You'll have time to learn, now that you've escaped your indenture."

The fighter gave Ander a grateful look, then reached for the scroll. "I've seen marks like this at the temple in Skarn. They're carved around doorways, and on ceremonial staffs." He seemed to flinch as he held the scroll in one hand and touched the writhing text with the other. "They use the staffs in rituals. And to punish disobedience."

"It might be a code," Ander suggested. "Normal writing, but with the parts moved around."

"Maybe," Thane agreed. He took the scroll back from Dannel and rolled it up, then started pulling more documents from their niches. "Let's take these outside. This isn't a good place to study them."

Ander greeted the suggestion with relief. They collected an assortment of scrolls from a dozen nearby repositories. The tightly rolled documents were surprisingly heavy.

"How are we going to climb the shaft with these?" Ander asked as they started ascending the ramp. "Erik and Skorri will need a rope if we're going to hoist them up."

"You'll see," Thane said, a sly smile on his lips. "I'm beginning to get ideas about this place."

Their retreat from the ancient library was far faster than their cautious exploration had been, but none too fast for Ander. They heard whispered endearments between Skorri and Erik as they crossed the cylindrical chamber; apparently the youths had turned to each other's fervent attentions to pass the time while awaiting their comrades' return. Strange hums and drifting notes like songs on the wind, echoing through narrow airshafts, pursued them down the long corridor. Ander found himself breathing fast as the end of the corridor appeared in the golden glow of Thane's light.

Skorri and Erik heard them coming and shouted excitedly. The three explorers returned the calls, not trying to answer the torrent of questions. When they reached the bottom of the shaft Thane placed his collection of scrolls on the floor and gestured for the others to add theirs to the pile.

"What's that?" Skorri asked, leaning so far over the shaft Ander feared he'd tumble down. "It smells."

"Stand back," Thane called up the shaft. "I'm going to try something." He pulled Dannel and Ander close, so they all stood on the section of floor that had dropped from the upper gallery. "I was wondering why they'd build a door that opens straight down. Not very practical. But now I think I understand how they used it. Watch." He closed his eyes but maintained his firm grip on his friends.

Ander felt a surge of power through their link as the mage reached out with his mind. A nearly inaudible hum raised in pitch, and a soft breeze caressed his cheek. It carried the scent of water. A moment later he felt a deep rumble beneath his feet and the floor began to lift. Thane's eyes opened. His pleased smile reminded Ander of the boyish spirit that still filled his lover's heart.

"No harder than creating a telos light," Thane said. "The power is already there, all you have to do is know where to find it and how to direct it. I wonder what other tricks they built into this place?"

They huddled closer as the floor lifted them into the shaft that penetrated the ceiling. It was ascending faster than it had dropped, though not by much. The deep vibration beneath their feet conveyed a sense of great weight, as if a column of solid stone was rising from the earth to bring the ornately tiled floor back to its original position.

Skorri and Erik watched with wide eyes and open mouths as their comrades rose from below like statues growing from the stone floor. They clamored to try the mechanism themselves, but Thane was intent on getting to work and persuaded them to wait for the next foray. By the time they reached the Torii Gates the sun was low in the sky and cicadas were starting their drone in the forest.

"There's a lodging hall on the other side of the lake," Dannel said, squinting as his eyes adjusted to the sun. "It's where the Guardians stay during pilgrimages. It's best to be inside at night. There are lions in the mountains, and they come into the valley to hunt."

"Good," Thane said. "I was worrying about keeping these scrolls dry. Let's get started."

They retrieved their horses and followed a shaded trail around the lake. Sunlight glinting off the water and the forest's sweet fragrance soon banished Ander's thoughts of underground oppression. His companions were in high spirits; even Dannel had shed his seriousness for the moment. Their adventure beneath the ground appeared a success and hope was in the air. Soon they arrived at what Dannel called the Guardian's Hall, a large building of rough-hewn logs located in a clearing near the lake. The building lacked windows, having only a door at each end. They dismounted and left their horses in a stable on the other side of the clearing, then went inside.

It took Ander's eyes a few seconds to adjust to the dim light inside the hall. The roof was some thirty feet high, supported by parallel rows of tree trunks that ran from the wood plank floor to massive joists overhead. A smoke hole was cut in the middle of the wood shingle roof. Afternoon light streamed through the hole, dancing with motes, illuminating a long trestle table flanked with benches. Stones lined a rectangular fire pit sunk two feet deeper than the surrounding floor, and sleeping benches lined the building's long walls. Leaf debris had drifted through the smoke hole, but otherwise the hall was reasonably clean.

"Nothing fancy, but it's only used for meals and sleeping," Dannel said. "There's a sweat lodge and washhouse not far from here, an exercise yard, a shed for firewood. Fishing's good, and there's a garden nearby."

"Where do the hierophants stay during pilgrimages?" Ander asked.

"In their tents, pitched at the courtyard before the Torii Gates. With us standing guard in case hungry animals come visiting."

Skorri was peering around the rustic hall with interest. "It's a lot like Tapray," he said, referring to the sparsely populated lands in the northwest where he and Erik had grown up. "Except the halls there are round. And not so clean."

"Why don't you and Erik tend to the horses," Thane suggested. "Dannel and Ander can try catching some fish while I start preparing the raffia bark. With luck it'll be ready tomorrow."

After helping haul saddlebags inside, Dannel and Ander took fish spears and wicker baskets from a stack near the door and started for the lake. Evening was settling over the valley. The setting sun painted clouds with fiery hues of red and purple, and reflections in the lake turned the water into a marbled expanse of rosy colors. Flat rocks had been placed among the shallows as platforms for spear fishing. Speckled trout darted through the water, their violet mantles making them hard to spot among the cloud reflections.

"Have you spear fished before?" Dannel asked as he tugged his shirt off. He tossed it on the bank, then started across the rocks until he reached a broad stone a dozen yards from the shore.

"No," Ander said. "I'm from Pella. The river there runs fast and deep. We fished with traps and nets."

"It's not hard. Try to spear them through the sides. Then you can pin the fish to the bottom by pushing your spear upright and forcing it into the mud. Watch first. And take your shirt off if you want to keep it dry."

Dannel stood motionless, feet wide apart, holding his spear with one hand at the end and the other hand near the middle, angling the prongs down sharply.

Ander did not have to wait long. In less than a minute Dannel's spear flashed down. He leaned into it and pushed it upright, then looked at Ander and grinned. "See? Nothing to it." He reached into the cold water to grab the fish, then jerked the spear out of the mud and held up his prize. The trout flapped vigorously, like a pennant in the breeze.

Ander took off his shirt and mimicked the way Dannel had stood, trying to feel the balance of his fourteen-foot willow spear with its hardwood prongs lashed to the end.

"Feet wider apart," Dannel said.

Ander complied, and found he was able to lean further over the water. He kept as still as he could, waiting for a fish to pass within his spear's reach, quivering with anticipation and staring at the water intently. At last a fish swam into the passage between the rock he was standing on and the next. He jabbed with the spear and staggered forward a step, barely catching his balance before tumbling into the water. The trout darted away untouched, further away than he had thought.

"Try again," Dannel said. "It takes practice."

Ander licked his lips and resumed his stance, feeling awkward. The water played tricks with light and distances but he thought he could adjust for it. Muscles began to feel the strain as time passed and tension increased. *Where did all the fish go? Did I warn them off?* He stared harder, leaning closer to the water. Warm flesh suddenly touched his right hand. He jerked back and twisted his head. Dannel stood behind him. The fighter had moved as silently as Erik on a hunt.

"You need to relax," Dannel said. He stood behind Ander, reaching around him and grasping the spear so their hands were side by side. His broad chest pressed against Ander's back, his breath was warm on Ander's cheek. "You're tense, it will make you rush. Hold the spear with me and see how I time it."

Ander turned his attention back to the water. The warm press of Dannel's body against his back, as intimate as an embrace, was a surprise. He pushed the thought aside and focused on how the youth shifted the spear's angle, how he radiated a sense of calm, and tried to imitate him. Time seemed to slow. A fish swam past, but Dannel didn't even tense. Ander took a deep breath and began to sense the slow beat of Dannel's heart. *It's like music*, he thought. *The pauses are as important as striking the right notes*. Quiet joy filled him as the new perspective settled in. His muscles relaxed.

"Good," Dannel whispered. "Stay like that."

Soon another fish approached the rock where they stood. Ander remained calm, grasping the spear lightly with Dannel's hands next to his own. He followed the fighter's movements when the swift plunge finally came, feeling the rightness of the timing and the easy economy of motion. As they leaned forward to pin the fish, Dannel's left arm wrapped around his chest to compensate for the weight behind him. The embrace was fleeting.

"Yours to fetch," Dannel said, releasing both Ander and the spear. "Keep it pinned until you've grabbed it."

Ander retrieved the fish, not minding the cold water in the least. "You're a good teacher," he said as he held up the trout.

Dannel turned to hop back to the rock where he had left his spear, but Ander could easily see the reason for his hasty retreat. The youth was powerfully aroused. Yielding to physical contact had not come easily to him.

"We need to finish before it gets dark," Dannel said. He picked up his spear and turned away from Ander. In moments he caught another fish.

Ander devoted his attention to fishing. By the time the sun touched the ridge surrounding the valley they had enough trout for a hearty dinner. They carried their catch to a sluiceway built of ancient stone blocks and started to clean the fish.

Dannel worked with downcast eyes, and the silence grew strained. Ander could see the tight set of his jaw, the bunching of muscle in his broad shoulders. The contrast with his earlier ease was stark. They finished their work and washed their hands, taking their time and watching the sunset's fading glory.

At last Ander couldn't stand his companion's discomfort any longer. "You shouldn't be embarrassed, you know," he said softly. "I understand how you feel. I used to be shy myself. But nobody in Thane's band thinks twice about somebody getting hard. It happens all the time."

Dannel turned, at last meeting Ander's gaze. He swallowed, then nodded. "I . . . it's just that . . ." He took a shuddering breath and put down the shirt he had been drying his hands on. He rocked back and sat cross-legged, looking down.

Ander felt only sympathy for the youth's awkwardness. Until becoming an initiate at the Lyceum, he had felt the same anxiety around people he didn't know well. It had kept him from becoming a companion despite the constant inquiries and generous offers Lady Tayanita had received from customers who craved his attentions.

"You'll get over it, I promise," Ander said. "You already know what Skorri and Erik are like. They're irresistible and always horny. They won't let your modesty linger. And wait until you meet my friends Sorel and Nicolai, back in Izmir. Two stallions, only a year older than you and they already know more about love than the most experienced companion in the kingdom. And then there's Thane." Ander smiled, his expression filled with tenderness. "Making love with Thane is like touching the sun, the stars. You'll be changed forever. *I* was."

Dannel was watching him with wide eyes. "You . . . you

wouldn't mind? If Thane and I were together?"

Ander grinned again, radiant. "Love is what we're all about, Dannel. It's what binds us together, what makes the art possible. It forges bonds between us and makes us closer than you've ever been with *anyone*. You can't imagine how lucky you are to have found Thane."

Dannel gazed at Ander as if entranced. At last he licked his lips. "Thane said he was going to prepare the bark we collected today. To make an oil that might help overcome the firestone's spell. Do you think he'll want me to use it with . . . with one of you?"

"I suppose so. How else would we know if it's working?"

Dannel took a deep breath, looking briefly toward the heavens as if seeking inspiration. His sensual features were more beautiful than ever in the soft light of dusk. When he lowered his gaze from the skies a trick of the light made his eyes glisten with unnatural intensity. "You've told me of your friends' prowess. What about you, Ander? Would Thane mind . . . ?"

For a moment his old reticence surged, an echo of the doubt he heard in Dannel's voice. Then he remembered how Thane had eased his fears when he first arrived at the Lyceum. And there was no denying Dannel's appeal. Few companions in Izmir could have matched the boy's beauty, and the innocence of his unspoken question spoke of a sensitive spirit hiding beneath the wary reserve.

"You have nothing to fear," Ander repeated. "Thane rejoices in love. And he knows my heart." He reached forward and touched Dannel's cheek, a fleeting caress. "Would you share a kiss with me, Dannel? Only if you want to."

The yearning in the youth's eyes left no question of his answer. Ander moved to his side. Dannel watched him as if unable to move, eyes wide and nostrils flaring. Slowly, Ander touched his lips to Dannel's. The handsome boy trembled. Ander gently put a hand behind his head, enmeshing fingers in the heavy black curls. Dannel's soft moan was almost a whimper. His lips parted and pressed against Ander's with virile eagerness. Ander felt the hesitant touch of Dannel's hand on the bare skin of his torso.

Ander took the light caress as a sign the youth was ready for more. He leaned forward without breaking the kiss and eased Dannel onto his back. The boy was shaking, but his arm slid around Ander and held him tightly. Ander moved his other hand behind Dannel's head and cradled it as their lips and bodies pressed together urgently. At last he felt the tension ebb from the fighter's strong embrace. He broke the kiss and lifted his head to meet Dannel's gaze.

"Are you all right?" Ander asked. "You wanted to, didn't you?"

"Yes," Dannel whispered. His lavender eyes were wide with wonder, and his heart hammered beneath Ander's chest. "Can we share another?"

Ander answered by renewing the kiss. Hesitancy was forgotten as Dannel's confidence grew. Ander moved his right hand to the youth's chest. The skin was hot, the muscle beneath it solid. His hand slid lower, caressing the lean torso and drifting lightly over Dannel's ribs. The boy moaned again, clinging to Ander even more strongly.

Ander broke the kiss enough to speak. "Don't fear," he murmured, continuing to nuzzle his companion all the while. "I'll stop whenever you want."

Dannel nodded, breathing hard. The trust in his eyes was like a child's, coming from his core.

Ander kissed him on the cheek, fleetingly, and brought their lips together again. Their tongues began to explore, first Ander's and then Dannel's as his inhibitions burned away. Ander's right hand shifted lower. He felt hard muscle contract as the boy's washboard abdomen tightened. One finger dipped into the tight navel and stroked it gently. Dannel's body curled from the ground where he lay, partially covered by Ander, but there was no protest. Instead, his tongue slipped into Ander's mouth and began to explore with fevered intensity.

At last Ander's hand moved lower, until it rested against the soft leather at Dannel's groin. A long mound stretched the pants tight beneath his fingers. He rubbed it gently, moving his hand in small circles, as the youth squirmed against him. The garment prevented his touch from triggering the firestone's spell and overpowering Dannel's body, but it seemed the youth's own passions were likely to have the same result at any moment. Reluctantly, Ander pulled away. Dannel gasped as they broke contact.

"A good start," Ander said. He bumped his nose playfully against Dannel's, then rolled to the side. Night was falling and the air was cooling quickly as the last traces of sunset faded. "Soon we'll do more. Thane can defeat the spell that binds you, don't doubt it."

"I don't know what to think," Dannel said, pushing himself upright. "I've never been happier, or more confused. Or hornier."

"You're going to fit right in," Ander assured him, grinning. He slipped his shirt over his head, then picked up his wicker basket and spear. "Let's see if they've got a fire started. I'm ready for dinner."

Smoke was curling from the vent in the lodge's roof by the time they returned. Warmth enveloped them when they went inside.

Erik and Skorri were collecting hot coals from the fire, and Thane was using the trestle table to prepare ingredients for the oil he hoped would dissipate the firestone's energy. Earthenware dishes were strewn about, filled with shredded bark and bits of other plants, and the mage was using a knife to cut slits in a water skin to use as a filter.

Thane looked up and waved happily when he saw Ander. "This will be easier than I thought," he said. "There are cooking pots and tools I can use. There's even a hatchet, it's perfect for chopping up raffia bark. See?" He picked up a wooden bowl and proudly displayed a pile of fine brown splinters.

"We were lucky too," Ander said, holding up his basket of fish. "Dannel taught me how to spear fish."

"Erik could have taught you that," Skorri said. "He can even catch fish with his bare hands." Erik ruffled his partner's golden curls and smiled, but said nothing. He looked relaxed and content beside the log fire, like a sleek cat. Ander joined them at the fire pit and helped them spread the coals. A pile of small stones was already on hand, perfect for layering on the coals to make a rock broiler.

Dannel placed his basket by the fire, then went to watch Thane. "Can I help?" he asked.

"Almost done. I've been thinking about this, though. Dispelling the anima might not be enough. You respond so quickly to the spell, you might cum before we can dissipate the power. We're more likely to succeed if we can slow your reactions."

Dannel sat across the table from the mage, putting his elbows on the table and leaning forward. "How? Wine makes you slow, but we don't have any wine or even ale."

"Other things work too," Thane said. "Dream smoke leaves, juice squeezed from certain berries, even some spells. We don't have many supplies, but we've got enough to make an elixir."

"When can we try? Soon, I hope."

Thane laughed. "I don't blame you. You've been celibate *far* too long."

The smell of sizzling fish soon seized their attention. They gathered around the fire, sharing fish and nuts, and passing around a water skin. The fare was rustic, but to Ander nothing had ever tasted better. The distance from home faded from his mind and contentment filled him. Thane's happiness warmed him more than any fine meal or luxurious surroundings.

After they had eaten their fill they threw a few more logs on the fire and watched flames dance. Ander brought out his guitar and played old ballads from Pella, slow and melodic tunes, dispensing with the bravura techniques that dazzled audiences. Erik, who was sitting behind Skorri with his arms wrapped loosely around his partner's chest, began to sing softly. His clear voice was perfectly true to pitch, masculine yet gentle in tone. Ander's heart squeezed at the beauty of the boy's sensitive singing. Though he could have performed in the finest courts, Ander knew the thought would never have entered Erik's head. The hunter's spirit belonged in the forest, not in palaces. Skorri nestled in his lover's arms while Thane and Dannel listened with faraway looks on their faces.

Ander played as long as Erik would sing, but as time passed the fire ebbed and Skorri nodded off. Erik held him tenderly, falling silent and gazing into the fire, once again a silent creature of the woods.

Ander laid his guitar aside and reached for Thane's hand. No words were needed. They retired to one of the sleeping benches along the wall and curled together beneath a shared blanket. Dannel stretched out where he was, near the fire, and Erik continued to hold his slumbering partner. Sleep claimed Ander quickly.

9

A BIRDCALL WAKENED Ander from pleasant dreams. He stretched, warm beneath his blanket, then started when he realized Thane wasn't at his side. He yawned and opened his eyes.

The mage was sitting at the trestle table with a scroll unrolled before him. A golden sphere hung above him and cast soft light over the tabletop and parchment. Ander slid off the bench and joined him at the table. "Been up long?" he asked. He noticed that Erik and Skorri were still sleeping soundly, but Dannel was absent.

"Oh . . . a few hours, I guess. I woke up with an idea about this language and had to try it out."

A corner of Ander's mouth quirked in a half smile, but he said nothing. He had quickly grown accustomed to Thane's rigorous work habits. There was a time when the mage had immersed himself in work to escape grief. Now, though deep wounds caused by Lucian's death had begun to heal, the exhausting habits remained. The mage's keen mind could not rest for long.

"Well?" Ander asked. "Any luck?" He rubbed the back of Thane's neck gently, feeling the tension stored there. He suspected his partner had worked most of the night.

Thane gave a contented moan and rolled his head back and forth as the massage loosened tight muscles. "I can't be sure," he said. He pointed at a row of symbols inscribed across the scroll, including several jagged dots that suggested stars. "I noticed these symbols and started wondering if they refer to seasons or calendars. If they do, I could look for patterns. From there I could start guessing words, try to piece things together."

Ander shook his head, marveling at his lover's optimism as much as his resourcefulness. "Does it? Fit together, I mean?"

Thane twisted his head to look over his shoulder, giving Ander a tired smile. "Some of it, maybe. I think this one's about the moon's phases. Other patterns are part of a numbering system. It looks complicated."

A door opened on the far wall and Dannel entered. He was breathing hard and his shirtless torso dripped with sweat. He waved, then took a drink from a water skin.

"He says we'll need to start exercising before dawn too," Thane said. "Learning his way of fighting is going to take a lot of work."

"I expected that," Ander said. "Last night was the first time I've seen him miss an exercise since we started this journey."

"And I paid for it this morning," Dannel said as he joined them at the table. His smooth skin glistened under the telos light. "At least we can use the sweat lodge and washhouse while we're here. I'm going to go start a fire and wash off. There's a water reservoir over the fire. It should be good and hot in an hour if you want to use it."

"That's a good idea," Thane said as he rolled up the scroll he was working on. He went over to the fire pit and picked up a clay pot with a piece of leather tied over the top. "The raffia oil finished distilling last night. We can try it this morning. It'll work best if you and your partner are warm and relaxed. Have you decided who you'd like to try it with?"

Dannel opened and closed his mouth a few times, then cleared his throat. "What, um, what exactly do I need to do?"

Thane's wolfish grin was not reassuring. "Don't worry, you're not ready for anything complicated. The first step is for you and a partner to try forming a bond. The bond will help him dispel your anima. And if the bond is good enough, he can feel when you start to lose control and keep it from happening. That's what I hope, anyway. You should try this in a trance state the first time."

"A trance? How can I have sex while in a trance?"

"Your task is to forge a bond and control the firestone. The trance will help with that. The rest of us will take care of giving you and your partner pleasure. Any of us would be honored to be your first, but you should choose for yourself."

Dannel swallowed hard and glanced at Ander. He blushed and looked at his feet, but not before Ander saw the unspoken plea.

"Would you like me to show you what comes after the kiss?" Ander asked.

"Yes," Dannel said, nearly inaudible. "I'd like that."

"A perfect choice," Thane said cheerfully. "Ander's sensitive and forms bonds more quickly than most." He carried the clay pot over to the table and untied the cord that held the leather cover in place. A rich aroma, like sandalwood and eucalyptus, wafted out. The mage took a careful whiff, then put the cover back on. "It's ready. Come back after you finish in the washhouse and we'll have some breakfast. You'll want to rest before we start."

Dannel nodded, giving Ander a grateful look, then turned and quickly left the hall. Thane watched him go, then put an arm around Ander's shoulders. "It must be hard, after going without love all your life. Do you think we're rushing him?"

Ander leaned against Thane and returned the hug. "He's nervous, but desperate to get on with it. And remember, you said he might hold the key to solving the mystery of this place and its power. Don't forget the zamindar and his reward. Time is a luxury we don't have."

During breakfast, Skorri decided the best way to prepare Dannel for his experience was to tell him everything he knew about pleasuring Ander. A few months ago the bawdy observations would have left Ander paralyzed with embarrassment, but as an initiate at the Lyceum he had learned to approach lovemaking as an art and a voyage of discovery. He took the intimate suggestions in the friendly manner in which they were intended. Besides, Skorri knew what he was talking about.

Dannel's reaction to the blond's suggestions was more complicated. His red cheeks showed how unaccustomed he was to candid talk about sex, but his heated glances at Ander revealed intense interest in the information. He was soon squirming, breakfast forgotten, his erection awkwardly confined by his leather trousers. Embarrassed or not, he sizzled with desire.

When the meal was finished Thane handed Ander the pot of refined raffia oil, then turned to Dannel. "We'll give you time to get accustomed to the oil before we join you at the sweat lodge. It'll be easier for you to start forming a bond with Ander if there aren't distractions. But don't try anything beyond touching until we get there. The oil alone won't be enough to defeat the firestone."

"I'll remember," Dannel said as he stood. Now that the moment had arrived he looked painfully nervous, but the long mound at his crotch showed that fear couldn't conquer his body's demands.

"Give us half an hour," Ander said. He and Dannel left the hall, accompanied by Skorri's last-minute salacious advice.

A short hike through the awakening forest brought them to a small clearing at the base of a hillside. A stream flowed from a spring halfway up the slope and spilled into a stone trough where it was captured and channeled to a reservoir. Beneath the reservoir stood a log building that extended from the clearing into the hill itself. Smoke curled from a stone chimney.

"You'll like this," Dannel said as they approached the building. He pointed to the reservoir on the hillside. "It's lined with slate and catches the sun's heat. Then the water flows over a stone channel in the washhouse, heated by a fire beneath. By the time you use it for washing, it's hardly cold at all."

"I wish we'd had that in Pella," Ander said diplomatically. He resisted the temptation to tell Dannel about the hot springs beneath Thane's manor, where the luxury of hot water could be had at any time of the day or night. Instead he admired the ingenuity that made creature comforts possible in such a remote place.

Dannel opened the door to an antechamber lined with wooden benches. "We leave our clothes here. The inner room is for bathing and sweating. It's inside the hill, an old cave that was enlarged. I put some stones in the steam pit after washing, so it should be warm now." He took a deep breath and closed the door, all the while watching Ander nervously. "I . . . I guess we'd better get started."

Ander laughed as he put the jar of oil on one of the benches. "Don't try to tell me you're suddenly reluctant. I've spent enough time with randy boys to know better. I hope Skorri didn't embarrass you too much."

Dannel's serious expression didn't change. "I'm ready. You can't know how much this means to me. But what if we fail?"

Ander took the fighter's hands in a firm clasp. "If this fails we'll try something else. Defeating the firestone won't be easy, but we'll find a way."

"I'm glad you're the first to try," Dannel said, pulling him closer. Their clasp turned into an embrace.

Dannel's reticence had passed along with the night. Wrapping his arms around Ander's back, he pulled their bodies together and initiated a deep kiss.

Even accustomed to passionate kisses as Ander had grown, Dannel's intensity was dazzling. He explored Ander's lips and mouth with fierce concentration, as if engraving every moment of the experience in his memory for eternity. Ander submitted to the virile youth's passion without reservation. He returned the hug and pressed his body against the young warrior. The kiss left him breathless.

"We'd best begin," Ander said when Dannel finally gave him a chance to speak. "They'll be here soon. We need to begin forging a bond before they arrive."

Dannel released him and stepped back, his hungry gaze never wavering. "I don't understand these bonds. How do they work?"

Ander sat on a bench to pull his boots off, and Dannel did the same. "Thane isn't sure, but he thinks the kei somehow connects everything. Like a river that flows through the whole world, the stars, even time. He thinks the world is *much* more complicated than our eyes can see. Maybe more complicated than we can ever understand. But that won't stop him from trying." Ander kicked his boots under the bench, then loosened the drawstrings and pulled his shirt over his head. Muscle rippled as he tugged, his honey colored skin already glistening with a sheen of sweat in the warm room.

"The bonds," Dannel reminded him. "What *are* they?"

Ander stood and unfastened his belt. A shimmy sent his pants to a heap around his feet. He gave Dannel a sultry grin, pleasantly aware of the avid attention his sleek body was receiving. Dannel had taken his shirt off but not his pants. Ander reached over and patted the mound at the youth's crotch, making him blush.

"A bond is what can happen when you're sensitive enough to what your partner is feeling. You sense his reactions, imagine how he feels. The closer you grow, the more you can feel." He paused, looking thoughtful. "Maybe you have a hint what it's like from your training. When you fight, do you ever start to know what your opponent is doing or feeling?"

Dannel nodded. "If he's hurt, I can tell what he feels. Even feel it myself, a little."

"With a bond, the art allows something much closer. Touch your partner and it's like touching yourself. Lick his cock and it's as if you're licking your own. Fuck him and—"

"I understand." The blush spread down Dannel's neck to his chest. Ander touched the youth's right arm and traced the hard curve of muscle, tracing it to the sensitive skin near Dannel's armpit. The boy gulped and started to sway.

"You'll like it," Ander said softly. "Since I'll be able to feel what you feel, I can go as slowly as you need. That's why the art works. You can feel your lover's sensations, make pleasure grow without making him cum. Perception grows with the pleasure until you can even sense the kei. Without the bond, sex can't increase awareness enough to reach other realms."

Dannel quivered beneath Ander's gentle hands, but stood his ground. His hands moved down Ander's sides, following the taper from broad chest to slender hips, until coming to rest on firm mounds of buttocks. His fingers pressed into the solid flesh, cradling the muscular globes. Ander's rigid cock rubbed against the mound at his crotch.

"Let's begin," Ander urged. "I'm as eager as you. But leave your leathers on until the oil has had a chance to work."

Anticipation filled the young fighter's features. Almond shaped eyes and high cheekbones reminded Ander of Leif, his first lover, and the warrior's lavender gaze promised erotic mysteries. The youth's skin glowed with the flush of arousal as he turned and led the way into the next room. Ander picked up the jar of oil and followed.

A small fire in a stone oven illuminated the inner room. A pile of rocks rested on top of the oven, absorbing heat. The back two-thirds of the chamber was carved from solid rock. Water flowed from a stone spout near the oven and into a basin carved from a boulder before overflowing and disappearing through a cleft at the back of the cave. A steam pit next to a wall contained a bed of pine needles and several hot stones Dannel had placed in it earlier. The air was pleasantly warm and humid.

Ander put the clay jar near the fire, then dipped his fingers in and scooped up some oil. He started with Dannel's right hand and forearm, giving him time to adjust to the oil's slippery feel. The fighter shivered, despite the room's wet heat, as Ander oiled his flesh. "You too," Ander said. "The bond has to work both ways, each sensing what the other feels."

They stood face to face, Ander nude and Dannel clad only in brown leather pants, as their journey of discovery began. Ander used the raffia oil liberally, stroking solid biceps and strong shoulders before sliding his hand around his companion to trace wide shoulder blades and tapering muscles of the back. The fighter returned the caresses, his callused hands applying oil and stroking Ander from neck to buttocks.

At first the glide of oiled hands against taut flesh felt like ordinary foreplay—though Ander was sure nobody would ever regard a tumble with Dannel as ordinary. The impression did not last long. As the oil's ingredients started to take effect a mild tingle tickled Ander's fingertips, like brushing a cat's fur on a dry day. The sensation had a sharply erotic edge; Dannel was tense with lust. As his fingers caressed one of Dannel's nipples the charge intensified and a pleasurable echo twinged his own flesh.

"It's started," Ander murmured. "The oil's working. Can you feel it too?"

Dannel's hand trembled as it stroked Ander's side. "Yes," he whispered. His eyes were half-closed, his broad chest rose and fell with deep breaths.

The bond was already strong enough for Ander to sense the ache of Dannel's hard cock in his leathers. His own penis twitched in response. The blending of sensations, constricting clothing and the freedom of nakedness at the same time, was strange even for an initiate like Ander. For Dannel it must have been bewildering. But the bond's effect was also a tool. Ander seized it.

"We don't have much time," he said. "We should try to strengthen the bond before the others get here."

Dannel tensed, then nodded. While his fear of failure was easy to see, Ander also felt his trust.

Closing his eyes, Ander pressed against Dannel. Their chests touched, skin moving against skin. Ander felt his companion's heart beating rapidly and strongly. "Easy," he said as he brought his arms around the fighter's back. "Remember, I'll wait until you're ready." He felt Dannel relax a bit, but the youth still quivered like a stag poised on the brink of flight, his hands resting lightly on Ander's hips.

The sights and sounds of the sweat lodge faded as Ander concentrated on the muscular body he held. Gradually awareness of his own sensations faded. He began to feel ghostly hands pressed against his back, an echo of Dannel's feelings. He squeezed harder and felt the corresponding pressure of strong hands against the small of his back. Dannel remained silent, his anticipation palpable.

Ander moved his hands lower. When they were within an inch of Dannel's leathers a dizzying surge of pleasure swept him from head to foot. His cock ached and precum slicked the spot where his glans pressed against the mound at the front of Dannel's pants. The fighter moaned softly, part warning and part excitement.

"I felt it too," Ander confirmed. "Try to sense what *I'm* feeling. Use it to anchor yourself. I know it's confusing, but try."

Dannel's heart hammered, but he pressed his cheek against Ander's and nodded.

Ander waited a few seconds and then moved his hands to Dannel's waist, level with his navel. He waited until he sensed the youth calm. A spark sprang into existence inside him, a fiery point of surprise and delight. He smiled and opened his eyes. Dannel had found the bond.

Almost imperceptibly, Ander edged his hands lower, into the area proscribed by the firestone's spell. The spark within him flared. Streamers of pleasure shot through his body like lightning and converged on his cock. He stiffened, nearly overcome by the shared sensation as he struggled to accept and dissipate the searing power. His knees started to buckle. The look of panic in Dannel's eyes was alarming. Failure now would dash the fighter's hopes for perhaps the last time. Desperately, Ander blanked his mind and let the spike of anima fill him. He felt like a vibrating bell, radiating with invisible ripples of energy. The wave of pleasure passed without cresting.

Dannel staggered back, the firestone at his ear sparkled like a diamond in the sun. Ander grasped his forearm. "Are you all right?"

Dannel gave him a dazed nod. "I . . . I didn't cum," he said, a look of wonder spreading across his face.

"I know." Ander couldn't help grinning. Dannel still had a lot to learn about bonds. "The anima you released was far more than one person could master. Even for two, it was a close thing."

"It worked then?" Dannel straightened and wonder filled his features. "You can defeat the firestone?"

"We've made a start," Ander acknowledged. "The bond was strong enough to let me draw part of the anima away. It's *only* a start, though. We'll need a much stronger bond to truly control the firestone's power."

Approaching voices marked the arrival of their comrades. The sweat lodge's outer door swung open and Thane entered with Erik and Skorri close behind, all three carrying baskets. They crossed the antechamber and entered the back room, looking around curiously.

Ander explained their progress at forging a bond while Erik and Skorri pulled blankets from their baskets and spread them on the middle of the floor. Thane listened intently, touching Dannel's earring gingerly as the stone continued to pulse with fiery sparks.

"You've made a fine start," the mage said. "Now we'll deepen the bond and see if your combined strength can master the firestone." He rummaged through the basket he had brought and extracted a glass vial containing pale orange liquid. After shaking the vial vigorously, making it turn cloudy, he handed it to Dannel. "Trances are a normal part of learning the art. They help you focus and forget distractions. Don't worry, you won't need them after you've learned how to forge bonds."

Dannel held the murky vial in front of his eyes and looked at it closely. "How much do I drink?"

"Half," Thane said. "The rest is for Ander. You'll both need to be in a trance for this to work. It will take a few minutes."

A scent like yeast spiced with jasmine wafted out when Dannel twisted the cork from the vial. He tilted his head back and sipped slowly, careful to take only half, then replaced the cork and gave the vial to Ander. "Tastes good," he said. "Feels good too." He stretched sensuously as his body reacted to the potent elixir. His eyes became deep black pools as his pupils expanded, lavender irises shrinking to thin rings. He turned to Ander and gave him an inviting gaze.

Ander drank his share and then pulled the fighter into an embrace. This time they kissed without hesitation. Whatever else it was doing, the elixir had loosened Dannel's inhibitions. Hesitancy had already given way to lust.

Ander slid his hands down Dannel's side until he felt the newly forged bond kindle and ignite, burning like a welcoming watch fire in an unseen realm beyond the bounds of ordinary experience. A warm sensation filled him, like returning to a place once known intimately but long forgotten, when Dannel found the bond. Their experiences flowed and merged as the elixir started to take effect. The press of skin against skin, of lips and tongues engaged in mutual exploration, seemed all consuming.

Ander slid his hands down until his fingers slid beneath the waist of Dannel's leathers. The jolt of pleasure was as intense as before, but this time they were prepared. Time slowed as sensation echoed between them through the strengthening bond. Ander kept his hands in place while the wave crested, then broke their kiss.

"Keep going," Dannel urged in a husky whisper. "It's working!"

Ander nodded, mute with the strain of controlling the anima surging between them. He could feel the fighter leaning on him through the bond, drawing on his strength and restraint, and shared the boy's euphoria at the victory they had achieved.The elixir was already making him light-headed.

Wasting no time, he unfastened Dannel's leathers. They slid down and pooled at his feet. The boy's cock sprang free and rubbed Ander's torso, smearing it with precum. Dannel trembled, poised just short of release.

Thane's murmured approval encouraged Ander to explore further. As his hands slid down Dannel's hips the firestone assaulted his senses like the tide against a seawall, wave after wave, relentless. But the intensity of each wave remained constant. Between the two of them, the onslaught was barely controllable.

They clung together in a tight embrace. Ander felt the hard nubs of Dannel's nipples against his chest, felt the press of the youth's rampant cock against his own. He parted his lips and yielded to Dannel's probing tongue, basking in the euphoria streaming through their bond.

Gentle hands on his shoulders pulled him back. Opening his eyes, he first saw Erik standing behind Dannel with his hands resting on the fighter's shoulders. He glanced over his own shoulder and saw Skorri's smiling face. The young blond looked flushed and aroused by the magic they were about to attempt.

Dannel was swaying. The elixir was hitting him hard, and Ander could feel lethargy stealing into his own limbs. He felt disoriented once separated from the anchor of Dannel's body.

Thane moved close and peered into his eyes. "You're both entering the trance. Lie down next to each other, focus on strengthening your bond. We'll take care of the rest."

Ander and Dannel settled on the floor side by side, their only touch a handclasp. In moments the elixir's effects overtook them. A feeling of lightness swept through Ander. He blinked slowly, feeling as if he were floating free of his body. Lassitude filled him. He basked in the sensation, momentarily forgetting what he and Dannel had embarked upon. All his awareness focused on his throbbing erection and the beautiful youth lying at his side. Dannel's head was turned toward him, and his expression was filled with amazed joy.

Ander shivered as Thane's fingertips lightly traced the muscles of his chest and abdomen. His skin tingled, the way it did when standing near a manifestation of energy from the kei. Erik and Skorri knelt at Dannel's side and began to caress the youth's torso with oiled fingers. Ander felt feathery echoes of their fingers dance across his own flesh.

"Don't try to speak," Thane said softly. "Keep your minds on the bond. As your pleasure grows, so will the anima. Don't be surprised by it. Help each other control it." He poured raffia oil over his hands, then reached down and held Ander's straining cock across the palm of his left hand. The fingers of his right hand moved delicately along the underside of the shaft, tracing it with clear oil and precum.

Bolts of pleasure raced from Ander's phallus through the rest of his body. Through a haze of lust he saw that Erik was pleasuring Dannel with the same caresses. Power coruscated through the bond as the firestone's spell flooded Dannel's body with anima. The fighter's eyes rolled back, showing only white. Ander clasped the boy's hand fiercely to give him an anchor, something to help prevent being swept away by the aching sweetness Thane and Erik were coaxing from their cocks.

Thane gave him a moment's respite, pressing his cock upward, then to one side and the other. The skin covering the shaft tugged at the cockhead with each movement. After a moment of gently squeezing the thick shaft Thane eased it back down. It twitched spasmodically against the tight muscles of Ander's belly. Thane placed one hand beneath the glans, with his thumb and index finger forming a loop around the crown. He pulled with short gentle pulses, tugging at the sensitive flesh, as he traced over and around Ander's balls with the fingers of his other hand. Ander gasped, his muscles tightening and lifting his pelvis up from the cushion. Erik matched Thane's actions, masturbating Dannel's cock with excruciating delicacy.

"You're doing fine," Thane encouraged. "Keep building your bond. Help each other as the pleasure grows."

The mage tightened his finger and thumb around the corona of Ander's cock, rotating them in the slick coating of oil. Then he squeezed the shaft of Ander's penis, still rotating his hand as it slid over the edge of the glans.

Ander's body jerked as a searing bolt of ecstasy shot through his cock. His penis spewed a thick jet of cream into Thane's waiting palm. The second blast was as strong as the first. It splattered his cheek as Thane's hand moved up and down the length of his cock, smearing it with cum and lubricant.

Ander's body shook. He was dimly aware of Dannel thrashing at his side, of the handclasp they shared and the aching strain on their bond. Ten times his cock spat, his balls pulled up tight and hard, as Thane coaxed semen from his distended cock. He felt Dannel's ecstasy at the slippery glide of Erik's hand along the fighter's rigid phallus.

Unleashed anima spiraled and within moments the youths touched the kei. Something stirred. Within a heartbeat it blossomed and exploded from the kei into the ordinary world. Ander's eyes rolled back as he succumbed to overwhelming power.

10

A JOLT KNOCKED Thane off balance. He toppled backward as an angry red cloud three feet across shimmered into existence at the back of the cave. It pulsed and twisted like a fireball, dazzling yellow fissures erupting and twisting across its surface.

Ander and Dannel were motionless, their eyes open but unfocused. Banshee wails echoed down the valley from the direction of the Torii Gates. The short hairs on the back of Thane's neck stirred as he thought for the first time that the true function of the Gates might be to keep something *in* instead of keeping intruders *out*. Something powerful had awakened when Dannel and Ander touched the kei.

"Go see what's happening at the Gates," he told Erik and Skorri. "Keep out of sight. And watch each other's backs. I'll look after Ander and Dannel." The boys nodded and ran out the door.

Ander moaned softly. As Thane leaned toward him the red cloud pulsed and spat a bolt of ochre light. The bolt hit Ander and raced across his body, then spread to Dannel's. Both youths shuddered as if under the lash, and Ander cried out weakly.

"Ander!" Thane reached for his lover's hand. When their fingers touched he was knocked back again. His arm felt like it was encased in ice.

Ander grunted like he'd been kicked, but the dazed expression faded from his eyes. "It's alive," he gasped. "It sees us now."

Thane came forward again, sweat beading his forehead. "We all have to get out of here." He extended a hand toward Ander, cautiously this time, and felt the invisible aura surrounding the youths. He moved his hand closer, ignoring pain that tore like claws. A sense of hostility emanated from the fiery cloud and it rumbled as if in warning.

"No," Ander gasped. "Too strong . . . can't free us." He grimaced as jagged lines of energy rippled over his body, tracing lines of muscle and limb, seeming to twist into arcane characters and glyphs as they flickered. Whatever magic had been unleashed from the kei was more powerful than anything Thane had ever encountered.

"I won't leave you," Thane said, though sweat poured down his face from the pain. His hand moved forward another inch.

The red cloud erupted into a spinning fury, like a small tornado. It hissed angrily and blobs of ochre light streaked down to two sticks lying on a pile near the fire. Thane ignored the fireworks and concentrated on penetrating the aura that held Ander and Dannel prisoner. He had almost mastered the pain enough to reach his companions when movement flickered at the edge of his vision. It came from the woodpile.

His heart thudded as he felt ripples moving through the kei like sharks streaking through water. He turned to the woodpile.

Two thick sticks, each a yard long, glowed with mottled blotches of shifting color. They quivered as light raced from one end to the other and back again. Thane stepped back warily. Scents of hot sulfur and metal permeated the air. The sticks began to writhe and the lights streaking along them brightened until it seemed they would burst into flame. Thane shielded his eyes against the brilliance. When it faded the two sticks were gone. Two serpents slithered off the woodpile and moved toward him.

Thane edged back. Unlike most real serpents, these creatures were not shy. They moved with determined purpose. One of them slithered between Thane and the door. The other took position in front of Dannel and Ander. It raised its head and swayed back and forth like a drunken sentry.

Ander struggled to his knees, his face white with pain. "Run," he urged, his voice barely a whisper. "What we awakened is too strong. It will kill you if you stay."

"Too late for running. I think I made it mad." Thane swallowed, feeling the dryness in his throat. Then he noticed one of the wicker baskets they had brought to the sweat lodge. It lay on its side halfway between him and the snake blocking the door. The creature started toward him with reptilian relentlessness.

Whatever had created the serpents was also guiding them; there was no time for caution. Thane dove for the basket and snatched it as he rolled to the side. The serpent streaked toward him. He brought the basket around in a desperate swing and slammed it down.

Thane's timing was perfect. The creature slammed into the basket with a heavy thud. It thrashed violently, hissing and seeking a way out, but Thane held the basket down tightly and hoped the wicker would hold.

One of the stones used for making steam was near enough for Thane to reach. He pulled it from the bed of pine needles, relieved it had cooled enough to handle without blistering his skin, while holding the basket with his other hand. He put the rock on top of the basket as the serpent guarding Ander and Dannel advanced on him.

Ander struggled to his feet, barely able to maintain his balance.

"Watch out!"

"I see it." The second snake, shiny green with golden bands encircling its body, was smaller than the first and seemed more wary.

"Run," Ander repeated. "It's poisonous, a cantrip, I can sense it."

"I'm not leaving you. Stay back, Ander. You're too weakened to fight." Thane glanced around the room, searching for weapons. One of the heftier sticks on the pile near the fire looked promising. He took a step toward it.

A golden beam speared from the red cloud and bathed Thane's face in dazzling light. He staggered, his vision swimming with afterimages. The serpent moved forward to strike.

"*No!*" Ander lurched forward, collapsing as his legs folded beneath him. His outstretched arms flailed as he fell, but he managed to grab the snake by its tail.

Thane rubbed his eyes. Through the blurred spots he saw Ander's fall. The snake lashed violently, but Ander's hands were strong from years of playing guitar and the creature could not escape. Hissing furiously, the beast whipped around. Its fangs plunged into Ander's right bicep.

Ander screamed, an incoherent cry of agony. He seemed to shimmer like a ghost. Within two heartbeats he was motionless.

At the moment of Ander's scream, Dannel jerked like a puppet whose strings had been yanked by a malicious child. He jumped to his feet, eyes wild, automatically assuming a fighting stance. He glared at the fiery red cloud with teeth bared, as if it had seared him with a brand. The manifestation was more solid now, like the crater of a volcano oozing lava through bleeding fissures.

Thane, still dazed, took a step toward Dannel and Ander.

"Stay back!" Dannel held up a hand to command Thane's obedience. He was a warrior now, despite his nakedness, all uncertainty put aside. The firestone glistened on his ear like a tiny sun. Thane stopped.

"Ander's—" Thane began.

"I know. It's an avatar and it's almost ready to strike!"

The queasy sensation of reality slipping sideways hit Thane again as forces surged in the kei. The air throbbed with potential. The mage felt as if he were standing on top of a mountain in the middle of a lightning storm.

Dannel bellowed a defiant warrior's challenge, taking three running steps and leaping for the manifestation. Few dancers could have matched his feat.

Dannel's outstretched hands reached for the fireball as if he meant to snatch it from the air. His leap was true. His fingers touched the avatar.

The sense of hostility that had permeated the sweat lodge vanished in a burst of surprise. The avatar vanished and Dannel's fingers closed around emptiness.

Thane watched in astonishment as Dannel tucked and tumbled to the floor, landing heavily on his right shoulder. He rolled to his knees and retched with dry heaves.

Ander moaned. The snake that had attacked him was gone, but he clutched at the spot where he had been bitten. Thane knelt at his side and pried his lover's fingers away from the wound. He nearly choked. Physical contact reinforced their bond, and Ander was in agony.

The gash on Ander's bicep was no ordinary snakebite. Blood seeped from two ragged punctures, but the venom was magical rather than chemical. Flesh around the wound looked as shiny as glass and rippled like a lake's surface during a storm.

Thane was still examining the injury and trying to fathom the spell when Dannel crouched at his side. The fighter's ashen face glistened with sweat. Pain showed in his face like a grim mask.

"You feel it too?" Thane asked after a glance at Dannel. "You still feel a bond with him?"

"Yes." Dannel looked miserable. "It's my fault. The hierophants warned us not to pry into their secrets. I should have heeded them."

Thane turned back to examining Ander. "Never believe people who tell you not to ask questions. You did nothing wrong." He held Ander's arm so Dannel could see the injury. "Ever see something like this before?"

Dannel leaned close, then shook his head. "No. I think an avatar attacked us. The hierophants pray to them, but I don't think they've ever really seen one."

"Why not? And what's an avatar?"

Dannel licked his lips, looking sick but determined. "It's an incarnation of a god. At least, the hierophants say they're gods. They have paintings of them. But they always spoke of waiting for their return. If they'd seen one they would have said so."

Thane's frown deepened. "We might have awakened something they never summoned in all their years of trying. We'll have to figure out what to do ourselves. Be still while I try something."

Dannel rocked back and sat with his arms wrapped around his knees, disconsolate.

Thane leaned over Ander. Their eyes met and held. Ander

looked fevered and wild, as if pain held his reason at bay. Thane brushed a lock of hair from his eyes and gently kissed his forehead. When he pulled back Ander's gaze seemed less agitated.

"Seek our bond," Thane said softly, squeezing Ander's hand. "You've learned to master pleasure. You can master pain as well. I'll help."

Ander's attempted reply was a hoarse croak, but Thane knew he had been heard and understood. His heart ached at his lover's bravery; he had taken the snakebite without the slightest hesitation and was facing his pain with the same resolve. Another spasm shook Ander's body. The mage's heartache changed to fear. There was no time to spare.

Thane sat cross-legged, then pulled Ander toward him so the youth's back slumped against his chest. He wrapped his arms around Ander's torso and closed his eyes.

Pain boiled as he focused on their bond. It seemed as if needles ran through his veins, radiating from his right arm through the rest of his body. He began to sweat, yet felt cold as ice. The spell was growing, feeding on Ander's anima, an infection of the life force itself.

Amid the pain, Thane also sensed Ander's spirit huddled in a tight defensive kernel. It pulsed weakly, but was still marked with the strains of curiosity and lyrical beauty that made it distinctively Ander. It called to him with a plaintive wail.

Joining with Ander had become nearly effortless in the past weeks, a joyous reunion rising on fountains of shared pleasure. This time the effort was a battle. The serpent's spell fought at every step. Needles of pain became daggers. They seemed to tear at him, ripping flesh to tatters, as he sought the heat of Ander's spirit. He tried to ignore the pain, but could not. Still he did not relent.

Thane's heartbeat was like thunder in his ears and he felt he was suffocating, but Ander's need drew him on until he reached the besieged core where his lover's mind sheltered.

Touching Ander's spirit was like balm on tortured flesh, but the mage had no chance to savor it. The magical attack was draining his strength at an alarming rate.

Communication was impossible, but no words were needed to understand what Ander had been enduring. Fatigue was like a crushing weight and the onslaught continued unabated. Thane opened his empathic link with Ander to its fullest. The youth's relief at his presence, mingled with desperation, gave him strength.

Now that he was at the focus of the attack Thane could see the nature of the spell more clearly. It was unlike any magic he'd previously encountered; it lacked the spark of anima that animated magic at the Lyceum, but also lacked the stench of the zamindar's blood magic. The feeling was ancient and cold, as if magic could spring from the earth itself. It was relentless as a hurricane.

Thane faced the maelstrom and sought a way to defeat it. But despite his best efforts, there was no way to dissolve the spell. No knot, no weak point, no gap in the assault could be found. He could tell Ander sensed his frustration, felt the boy's assurance begin to waver. Even an adept would succumb quickly to such an attack, and Ander was new to the magical arts.

Time had run out. Withering forces slashed at him as if he was being laid open by a lash. Blackness tinged his vision.

As consciousness started to fade he felt a vast force rise beneath him, like a whale rising beneath a swimmer. It churned with chaotic energy. At first he thought it was a new line of attack. Then he caught an echo of proud defiance and recognized the presence. *Dannel!*

Thane opened himself to the fountain of power and let it flow through him. He met the spell's whirlwind with his own torrent.

The energies struggled like two tigers, snarling and tearing into each other. To Thane's amazement, the power flowing from Dannel seemed bottomless. Drawing on it only seemed to strengthen the flow. With the realization came victory. The energy unleashed by the spell, though nearly indestructible, was not limitless. Thane encircled it and squeezed until nothing was left. The effort left him quaking and drenched with sweat.

He opened his eyes. His arms still encircled Ander, whose heart thumped beneath his hands with reassuring steadiness.

Dannel crouched at his side and watched him intently. His eyes blazed and a shimmer of golden anima still flickered around both his hands.

"What happened?" Thane asked. His voice was ragged. "I felt your help. But how?"

Dannel's gaze never left Thane's. "I had to do *something*. Ander stopped breathing, and you were turning white. You once said I was a conduit. So I put my hands on yours and hoped you'd find something that helped."

Ander moaned and stirred. His eyes flickered open and the moan became a groan. Thane kissed his neck and gave him a gentle hug. "Easy, jirí," he said softly. "We almost lost you. Do you remember what happened?"

Ander grimaced, then nodded. "I wish I didn't," he said, his voice haunted. "It's a nightmare I'll never forget." He shifted his shoulders to nestle more comfortably against Thane. "But you came for me. I knew you would."

"Dannel came too. I would have failed without him."

Ander shifted his gaze to the young fighter, curiosity battling against fatigue. "Thank you," he murmured.

Dannel shifted uneasily. "You've no need to thank me. I caused the trouble in the first place. It almost killed you."

Thane sighed. It was clear the fighter still felt blameworthy for leading them into danger. "You didn't cause the harm," he said. "You've been used by the hierophants, a tool. *Your* only decision was to fight for your freedom and your friends. And to seek knowledge, a decision that's brave and honorable." He paused, eyebrows pulled down as he thought. "A decision that pays good rewards, too. Think what we learned."

Dannel looked startled. "We nearly got you and Ander killed! Defying the firestone's curse is too dangerous, is what we learned."

Thane pressed his cheek against the side of Ander's head. The youth had nodded off, exhausted by the strain of their ordeal. The terrible fear Thane had felt at the prospect of losing him started to fade as he cradled his lover in his arms. "Any experience you survive can make you stronger," he said. "Knowledge is worth pursuing even if there's danger."

Dannel still looked unconvinced, but didn't argue.

"There was noise at the Torii Gates when you and Ander touched the kei," Thane continued. "Erik and Skorri went to investigate. They should be getting back soon, then we'll know more. You'd better get dressed. We need to leave in a hurry."

Dannel surged to his feet. "Maybe the avatar came from the other side of the Gates! Could they have opened, after the hierophants have always failed?"

Thane shifted back, gently laying Ander on his side, then rose and tossed Dannel his pants. "Your former masters are greedy. They tried to keep you ignorant, *use* you without you knowing it. I think that's why they failed."

"I don't understand," Dannel said as he pulled his leathers on.

"This place was designed by people who used magic. They used their minds to control powers most people never sense." Thane handed the fighter his shirt. "What we saw today makes me think awakening the powers here requires two things. Strong anima, like you and the other Torii Guardians have, is only half. The anima also requires a conscious mind to guide it. The priests tried to wield the firestone's power second-hand, so its power would be theirs alone. That's what I think they've been doing when they make Torii Guardians drink the sleeping potion."

Dannel stood motionless, half dressed. Thane observed him closely, watching as shock battled with dawning comprehension. He was impressed by the fighter's resilience. After a few seconds Dannel nodded.

"It explains a lot. The constant training, their interest in our health. They could have hired mercenaries for protection, but instead they spent half their time overseeing the Guardians. Pushing us, always demanding more."

"They were shaping you. They understood the need for strong life force, but were blinded to how to use it."

A fierce grin grew on Dannel's face. "They got what they deserved. Defeat at the hand of their slaves, though we didn't even know we were in a struggle."

"They're not defeated yet," Thane cautioned. "Remember, *we* don't know how to use your powers yet, either."

The sweat lodge door slammed open. Erik nearly collapsed through the door, panting hard. He gulped, fighting for breath, and grabbed Thane's shoulder. "You'd better come," he said between gasps. "See . . . for yourself."

"What happened?" Thane asked, alarmed by Erik's agitation. The young hunter was usually calm even in the face of mortal danger.

"Come look," Erik repeated, tugging Thane toward the door. "It's growing, you can even see from here now."

Thane went to the door and stepped outside. The morning light was blinding after the sweat lodge's dark recesses. He squinted in the direction Erik was pointing.

At first he thought his eyes were deceiving him. He rubbed them and looked again. This time there could be no doubting it. He shivered, filled with dread.

In the direction of the Torii Gates, a new sun blazed in the sky. It was small and low, twice the height of the tallest trees, and blood red. As he watched it continued to rise. Shimmering spears of violet light radiated to the four points of the compass, stretching across the sky as far as the eye could see. The sphere started to rotate, its arms sweeping the sky to infinity.

Thane stepped back, feeling as if all eyes in the Forbidden Lands and beyond were turned in his direction.

11

SOMEONE WAS shouting. "You don't understand. They'll *know.* They can probably even see it in Skarn!" Ander stirred, trying to ignore the noise, wishing it would go away so he could get more sleep. He couldn't remember ever having felt so tired.

"All the more reason to hurry." Ander recognized Thane's determined voice and started to pay attention. "We might not have another chance to learn what we need to know."

Ander opened his eyes and propped himself up enough to look outside. Thane was standing at the sweat lodge door, speaking with Dannel. Erik sat in the antechamber, silently watching the argument.

"Hiding is one thing." Dannel stood with arms crossed. "Defeating the hierophants and all the Torii Guardians is something else. It's not wise to invite a fight you can't win."

"Erik and Skorri can stand guard at the pass," Thane said. "We'll see them coming, having enough time to run if we need to." The mage kept looking out the door, craning his neck to peer at the sky. Curiosity stirred and Ander's drowsiness faded.

"And how will we get out of the valley?" Dannel said. "The pass is the only way. We'll need to get *away* from them, not run toward them. You won't solve any mysteries once the hierophants get their hands on you."

"We could hide in the forest. Sneak out at night." Thane was staring at the sky again, not seeming to pay much attention to the argument.

"But—"

"You might as well save your breath," Ander said. "Trying to convince Thane when his mind is made up is like trying to keep a cat out of catnip." He pushed himself up further, arms thrust behind his back. "What's everybody looking at?"

Thane left the door and returned to the inner chamber to crouch at Ander's side. "There's another manifestation outside. Something big. It's rising above the Torii Gates like a new star."

"More like a beacon," Dannel said.

Ander's heart lurched. "Is it dangerous like the last one?"

"Yes," Dannel answered.

"No," Thane said at the same time. "Well, it hasn't attacked anybody."

"So far," Dannel added.

"Let me see." Ander got to his feet. He still felt weak and standing made him dizzy. Thane helped support him until he got to the door.

Leaning against the frame, Ander squinted against the sun and looked up. Uneasiness swelled at the disorienting sight. He had encountered many strange visions while immersed in the kei, but seeing something like this in the everyday world was different. For one thing, *everyone* could see it. He understood Dannel's fears. He also understood Thane's irresistible attraction to the new mystery.

"How quickly could they get here from Skarn?" Ander asked. "If they bring extra horses and make their best time?"

"Two or three days," Dannel said. He looked at the sky and glared. "They've probably already started."

Ander turned to Thane, saw the pleading in his lover's eyes. The mage understood the danger. "You know how I feel," Ander said, putting a hand behind his partner's neck and squeezing gently. "I understand how important this is. You'll be careful, won't you?"

Thane wrapped an arm around his back, hugging tightly. "Give me one day," he said. "We're so close to success!"

Ander returned the hug, then pulled away. "How can I help?"

Thane gave him a careful appraisal. "You're still weak from the serpent's spell. For now, you should rest. I'll come back after getting a closer look at what's happening at the Gates."

"I'll go with you," Dannel said. "New powers are loose in the valley. You'll need a guard."

"Erik and I can take care of ourselves," Thane answered. He took Dannel's hand in a clasp. "I value your skills, truly. That's why I'd like you to stay with Ander while he's recovering. He's in no condition to defend himself."

Dannel looked unhappy, but nodded. "As you wish. But I share Ander's concern."

"We'll be careful," Thane promised. He gestured to Erik, who rose from the floor with fluid grace and went silently to the door. There was no doubt the young hunter would remain vigilant, regardless of how distracted the mage might become. Thane gave Ander a wave, then turned and started down the trail to the Gates.

Ander watched until they vanished into the forest. Then he sighed and closed the door. The sweat lodge felt cooler than before.

"He's brave," Dannel said. "Perhaps too brave for his own good."

Ander nodded as he returned to the inner room. He sank into the pile of blankets and pulled one around his shoulders. For a long while he sat motionless, eyes closed. Dannel settled nearby and waited. At last Ander opened his eyes and met the fighter's patient gaze. "I fear for him," he said softly. "He knows, there can be no secrets between us. I just have to accept it."

"Why won't he leave now, while we can go safely?"

"Because he's Thane. He can't give up. Giving up would kill him."

After a few moments Dannel nodded. "He's driven by his cause, yes. But he loves you, as well. He'd give his life to save you. I saw him try, this very day."

Ander nodded, wistful. "I know. Thane's hard to understand. It sometimes feels like he's at war with himself. But yes, he loves me. With all his heart."

Dannel shifted and cleared his throat, then reached to the side where his leather shirt lay. He picked it up and kneaded it between his hands.

Ander saw the tightness in the fighter's muscular shoulders. The camaraderie they had been sharing suddenly felt strained. "What is it?" he asked.

Dannel stopped worrying the shirt and looked up. Even in the dim light his blush was easy to see.

"I . . . I understand why Thane loves you." His voice was soft. "He's very fortunate."

It was Ander's turn to blush. "We're *all* lucky," he said. "At least, ever since we found each other. There have been bad times too, but it's been worth it."

Dannel sighed and stopped fidgeting with his shirt. He shook it out and started to put an arm through one of its sleeves. His forlorn expression tugged at Ander's heart.

"Wait," Ander said. "Why don't you rest with me awhile? We didn't have a chance, earlier."

Dannel froze, his uncertainty making him appear the younger of the two. He slowly put the shirt down. Desire and confusion flitted across his face.

"I'd welcome it, Dannel. But only if you want to." Ander lifted a corner of the blanket in a gesture of invitation. His lithe torso still glistened with oil and disheveled hair fell before his eyes. Though he had only been a musician in Lady Tayanita's brothel, none of the famed companions in her house had ever looked more beguiling.

Dannel gulped, lavender eyes wide. "Thane . . . he wouldn't mind?"

Ander smiled seductively, reclining and lifting the blanket

higher. "Thane would approve. I can tell you want to. You shouldn't have any problems with the firestone as long as you leave your pants on."

"All right." Dannel slid over and settled next to Ander, adjusting the blanket to cover both of them.

Ander fashioned another blanket into a pillow, then stretched against Dannel front to front. They cuddled, entwined as closely as they could manage. The fighter's handsome face was alight with wonder and arousal.

"You've never done this before, have you?" Ander asked. "Even with your clothes on."

Dannel shook his head. "Love between Torii Guardians is forbidden. And to everybody else, our curse is a joke. In Skarn I'd only be mocked for this."

Ander laughed softly, reaching between their bodies to press a hand against the hard mound at Dannel's crotch. "You've been this randy every day since you were thirteen!"

The youth squirmed as Ander's fingers teased his erection. His breathing quickened, warm on Ander's cheek. "This is different," he said. "Before, I dreamed of sex. Now I also dream of love."

Ander kept his hand at the fighter's crotch, cupping the mound, as he brought their lips together. He closed his eyes and listened to the boy's rapid breaths, felt the quivering anticipation in his wiry frame. "Learn to accept love," he said softly. "I love all my friends, each in a different way. Nobody is the same as Thane, just as nobody is like Skorri. Or like you. But I can still love all of you."

Dannel's arms wrapped around him tightly. "It may be as you say. But for now, you fill my dreams. There's so much I want to do, Ander. But the firestone still keeps us apart."

Ander stroked the fighter's back, running a hand along the hard curves of muscle. He could feel desire filling Dannel's body like a drowning man's yearning for air. An idea began to grow.

"Dannel . . . maybe we should forget the firestone. Free your heart, even if we haven't yet freed your body."

Dannel pulled his head back, quizzical. "How? I'm bound by the curse. Thane's oils let us touch, no more. We shared *something*, but it wasn't really making love."

"There are many kinds of lovemaking," Ander replied. "And there's nothing wrong with experimenting." He sat up and reached to the side, where the clay pot containing raffia oil still lay. "Sit up."

The fighter complied, though he looked more puzzled than ever. When Ander reached for the waistband of his pants he tensed.

"Don't worry," Ander said. "I won't touch you below the waist. Trust me."

Though he still looked nervous, Dannel nodded.

Ander swirled the oil in the half-full pot, his smile mischievous. "Skorri showed me this trick. You'll like it." Without waiting for assent, he hooked a finger through a belt loop on the front of Dannel's leathers and pulled the waistband away from the youth's body. His erect cock sprang out, the glans and two inches of shaft pressing against the boy's flat belly. Ander poured the remaining raffia oil over it. A copious amount flowed down, creating a slippery mess inside the soft leathers. Dannel's cock twitched, bouncing up from the taut skin beneath it, dripping with the clear lubricant. Ander gripped the shaft near its base, holding it through the leathers, and tugged it down so the pants fully covered it.

Ander put the clay pot down, keeping one hand pressed against the long mound at Dannel's crotch. He could feel the hard shaft clearly through the soft leather. The young warrior shivered as he moved his hand up and down, teasing hard flesh through its protective covering. The leather molded closely to Dannel's cock; Ander could feel the thick tube running the length of its underside and the flaring corona of the glans. The raffia oil slithered and slipped between leather and confined flesh, faithfully transmitting Ander's gentle manipulations almost as delicately as skin to skin.

"Forget the firestone," Ander said as he massaged the fighter's erection. "We can share pleasure like this. It's different, but still feels good. At least it did when Skorri did it to *me*."

Ander smiled as Dannel gulped. The youth was deep in passion's grip. "What you do in a tumble isn't as important as your feelings for your partner," Ander said. "That's the art's real secret. Giving your partner pleasure is more important than your own. *That's* where the magic lies."

Dannel nodded. His rapid breaths and rigid muscles showed the effort of holding excitement at bay. "You have a lot to teach me," he murmured. "And I'm eager to learn." He put a hand over Ander's, stilling the expert stimulation, then took a deep breath and moved Ander's hand away. "You've been a better friend than anyone I've ever known. It's time I showed my gratitude."

Leaning forward, Dannel put his hands on Ander's shoulders. Ander yielded. He was surprised and pleased by the new expression on the fighter's beguiling features. Desire was still there, as strong as ever, but the anxiety and suppressed defiance had faded. The youth truly *had* forgotten the firestone and turned his mind to demonstrating his love. It seemed as if a corner had been turned, and Ander sensed it brought an important change.

There was no time to ponder the new development. Dannel slid his arms around Ander's torso and eased him onto his back. He knelt at Ander's side a moment, gazing at him with unabashed sincerity, then lowered his head and brought their lips together.

The boy's kiss was tender but thorough. It left Ander's head swimming. The fighter's hands caressed his torso as their tongues explored, brushing the tan skin as lightly as a summer breeze. The dark nubs of Ander's nipples flared with pleasure at each touch, and his cock felt hard as iron.

At last Dannel began to explore further, trailing his lips over Ander's cheeks and closed eyes. His warm breath was fresh and sweet, a healthy animal complement to the raffia oil's sandalwood fragrance. The warrior paused to nuzzle Ander's ears, nibbling softly at the lobes. Precum drooled from Ander's cock and pooled beneath the glans as Dannel tickled his balls.

Rising from his crouch, Dannel turned his head and gave Ander a boyish smile. Playfulness shimmered in his eyes, mingled with lust.

"You're going to be popular at the Lyceum," Ander said, feeling dizzy.

"Never mind the Lyceum. All I care about is pleasing *you*." He shifted toward Ander's head, staying on his knees, then leaned down until the side of his face pressed against Ander's chest. His deep breaths played over Ander's skin like zephyrs. After a few motionless moments he moved his lips to Ander's right nipple and kissed it tenderly before pressing his tongue against it in a firm lick.

Ander was mesmerized by the youth's intensity. At the Lyceum he had grown accustomed to expert lovemaking and chivalrous partners, but the Torii Guardian was different. The initiates at the Lyceum were all experienced and sophisticated lovers, while Dannel was little more than a virgin. For him this was no mere tumble. It was a momentous occasion.

Dannel continued his determined exploration of Ander's athletic body. He licked and nuzzled, putting his hands on Ander's sides to hold him still. The fighter's combination of gentleness and masculine insistence was intoxicating. His tongue traced the cleft between mounded pectoral muscles, then followed the clean lines etched across Ander's lean abdomen.

As the warrior worked his way lower, he swung one leg around to straddle Ander's head. His oiled torso gleamed in the dim light and the scent of sandalwood was strong. Ander put his hands on the boy's sides, feeling hard muscle move beneath the skin. Suddenly Dannel's grip on his waist tightened. He waited, expectant, then felt the warm softness of Dannel's tongue lap at the underside of his cockhead.

Ander's back arched and his cock drooled, but Dannel's determination didn't waver. The fighter's tongue traced the length of Ander's cock from glans to root, tickling along the sides and bottom of the shaft as the engorged phallus lifted up from Ander's belly.

"Easy," Ander gasped.

Acknowledgment came as an additional squeeze and a muffled grunt. The fighter shifted still lower, leaving Ander's cock and moving his questing tongue to the youth's balls.

Ander moaned as Dannel's mouth engulfed one of his balls, then the other. His belly was slick with precum, and he could feel Dannel's spit seeping into the crack of his ass.

The fighter tugged gently at the scrotum, sending pangs of pleasure shooting through Ander's body. Dannel's hands moved to Ander's thighs, pulling up and spreading the legs as he lifted. The cleft between Ander's buttocks spread, revealing the rosette of his ass.

Ander felt light-headed, completely captivated. He knew Dannel wanted to fuck him, and would have welcomed it eagerly, but also sensed his companion's determination to pleasure him however he could.

Cool air brushed over Ander's scrotum as Dannel's strong hands spread his legs wider. The fighter pulled until Ander's lower body curled up from the floor and his knees almost reached his ears. Soon he was bent double, ass in the air, Dannel kneeling over his chest and holding him captive.

The warm swipe of Dannel's tongue over his ass made Ander moan. Sensation quickly escalated as Dannel licked and probed in a frenzy, his tongue penetrating deeply as it coaxed the ring of muscle to relax. Slippery spit drenched the hole, adding to the slithery thrusts of Dannel's tongue. Ander groaned, helpless, his toes curling and flexing as waves of sensation assailed him.

At last Dannel relented and lowered Ander's legs back to the ground. He swung to the side, still in a crouch, and pivoted to face Ander. He looked radiant. They kissed as Ander pressed a hand against the mound at Dannel's crotch, making the youth's erection shift and rub inside its slippery confines. Dannel moaned, closer to orgasm than Ander had guessed. When they broke apart the fighter looked sheepish.

"Ander . . . I'm sorry if I lack skill. I've only had dreams. Never practice."

Ander's soft chuckle was filled with warmth. Dannel's wide-eyed plea for pardon only emphasized his innocence. He was one of the most intensely sexy boys Ander had encountered, and he didn't even realize it. Ander reached up and tousled the youth's black curls.

"Don't fear. Nobody will ever regret a tumble with you. You're wonderful!"

A bashful grin lit Dannel's face, along with a blush. "The next part might be harder," he said. "I mean, taking you inside me. You're so big. And *hard*." He reached down and brushed his fingers the length of Ander's cock.

"You have nothing to fear," Ander repeated. "Pleasure springs from the mind even more than the body. Passion more than makes up for any lack of practice."

Dannel looked dubious, but still quivered with eagerness. "I'm glad you're my first," he said in a throaty whisper. "I'll do my best." He licked his lips nervously. "Um, what's the best way to do it?"

Another good sign, Ander thought. The boy wasn't afraid to ask questions. He would make a good initiate.

"It's easiest if you don't have to bend your neck," Ander said. "Straddle me like you did before, and go from there."

Dannel complied, swinging around so his knees straddled Ander's head, then bent forward and put a hand on each side of Ander's slender hips. He hesitated, breathing deeply.

"If you're not ready we can wait," Ander said. He put his hands on Dannel's sides, stroking the lean torso lightly. "We can satisfy each other without this."

Dannel shook his head without turning. "No more waiting. I don't want to disappoint you, is all."

"You haven't yet. Don't worry so much, Dannel. Just do what you please. I'm content with anything." Ander moved a hand to his companion's crotch and nudged the long phallus. It was still hard as oak.

Dannel answered with action instead of words. Bending lower, he brushed his lips over Ander's erection. First contact was fleeting, shockingly subtle for a novice. The boy's restraint was surprising.

Ander continued stroking the youth's sides and back, silently urging him on. His efforts were rewarded as Dannel's explorations grew less tentative. Ander felt soft lips trace the underside of his cock from root to tip, felt the boy's warm breath on his cockhead.

He closed his eyes and imagined Dannel's handsome features, intent with concentration.

The tip of Dannel's tongue touched the sensitive spot where glans joined shaft. It traced the underside of Ander's cockhead, following along the flared edge of the soft corona, tickling the arrow of flesh formed by the taut foreskin.

Ander's penis ached, rearing and bobbing under the delicate stimulation. Precum oozed from its tip onto Dannel's tongue, before being spread over the glans with careful licks.

"Feels good," Ander murmured.

The encouragement seemed to give Dannel the confidence he needed. He pulled back a little, then opened his mouth and slid his lips around the head of Ander's cock.

Ander held himself motionless, letting the inexperienced youth adjust to the new sensation. He was a quick learner. After a few seconds the fighter slowly slipped his lips an inch down the shaft, then another. His breath rasped through his nose. Another inch, and the cockhead reached his throat. He stopped, seemingly at a loss how to go further.

"That's good," Ander said. "*Really* good. It feels wonderful." The words were not empty praise; the warm sleeve of Dannel's mouth molded itself to Ander's cock. Soft wetness engulfed the sensitive flesh. Spit seeped from Dannel's mouth and ran down the shaft, tickling Ander's scrotum. "Maybe that's enough for now," he suggested. "You've done well."

Instead of backing off, Dannel slid his hands beneath Ander's legs, then up until his palms cupped the solid mounds of Ander's buttocks. He took a deep breath through his nose and slowly slipped his lips further down the shaft.

Ander tensed, amazed and delighted by the youth's control. Thane and the other initiates could accommodate the long phallus with ease, but they were masters of lovemaking while Dannel was a novice. Still, the fighter was equal to the challenge. Within a few seconds he reached the shaft's base and reversed direction. The gleaming column of flesh emerged from his lips as slowly as it had vanished. The cockhead emerged and Ander's penis slipped free, snapping back against his belly with a wet slap.

"You're a marvel," Ander said. "I'd wager not one in a thousand beginners is so skilled."

Dannel nuzzled Ander's cock, rubbing it with his smooth cheek while his strong arms pulled their bodies together tightly. "It's like we were made for each other," he said softly. Wonder filled his voice. "Having you inside me, *filling* me."

"People *are* made for love," Ander agreed. He stroked the boy's torso, felt his wide chest expand with deep breaths. "Everybody is, including you."

A strong squeeze signaled the fighter's agreement, and his desire for more than talk. His mouth engulfed Ander's cock again. This time there was no hesitation. He took the curving shaft into his throat in a single smooth glide, not stopping until his nose nestled in the soft skin of Ander's scrotum. His lips tightened as they slid back up, milking the cock with careful tenderness.

Ander surrendered to the youth's lusty attention. Dannel sucked him deeply, stroking the shaft and cockhead with his tongue, twisting his head, growling softly when the throbbing penis filled his throat. His hands kneaded Ander's buttocks, then slid down to stroke his strong thighs. His sucking quickened as his skill and confidence grew.

Ander closed his eyes as waves of pleasure washed his body. Dannel's physical perfection made him a natural lover, a healthy young animal at the peak of his strength. His single-minded concentration on their lovemaking was the greatest stimulant of all; the boy's passion burned fiercely.

The scent of sweat mingled with sandalwood as they strained against each other. Ander's hips lifted from the ground, meeting his partner's welcoming lips, and his hands clenched the youth's lean waist. His cock seemed to grow even longer as Dannel lavished passionate attention on it. A pleasurable itch started to grow, a spark of ecstasy that quickly swelled and pulsed. He ached, his cock's hardness nearing the border between exquisite pleasure and pain.

One of Ander's hands moved back to Dannel's crotch. Even through the soft leather, he could feel the boy's erection pulsing with powerful contractions. The oily confinement saved them from the firestone's spell, but did nothing to dampen the slick glide of cock against Dannel's own solid body.

Suddenly Ander felt something more. As his fingers traced the length of Dannel's phallus he felt the unmistakable echo of a psychic bond. Sensation from the warm slide of his cock down Dannel's throat mingled with the slithery feel of a rigid cock rubbing against oily leather. At first they were hard to distinguish. He put his palm against Dannel's cockhead, pressing it through the leather covering, and felt a corresponding squeeze on his own glans. There could be no doubt. Their anima had begun to reach out and mingle.

"Do you feel it?" Ander asked as he rubbed his palm in small circles over Dannel's cock. "Try to imagine what I'm feeling. Then see if you can feel it yourself. We've forged a bond, Dannel. Even without a trance. All you have to do is find it!"

Dannel's motions slowed, though Ander could sense the effort required. He felt a hint of inquiry through their link, of intellect emerging from a haze of lust. Carefully, trying to avoid surprises that would confuse the youth, Ander projected more of his anima through the fledgling bond. The fighter sensed his presence in a heartbeat and was drawn toward the bond like a flower to the sun.

Their minds touched. Confusion flooded the bond as Dannel suddenly became aware of Ander's sensations. The confusion was followed in quick succession by stunned wonder, then delirious arousal. Ander gasped as his companion resumed sucking. The youth now shared the benefit of his efforts, enjoying longed-for pleasures he had always been denied.

Ander fell back, arms extended overhead and legs spread wide, as Dannel possessed his body. It was like being in a room lined with mirrors as the sensation of soft lips gliding over his cock echoed between them. He soared. His lithe body trembled in Dannel's strong grasp, his balls pulled tight against the base of his rampant penis.

Pleasure spiraled, fanned by the flames of Dannel's rutting. The tickling itch in Ander's cock swelled and pulsed. Dannel felt it too. He stopped sucking, cradling Ander's cockhead on his tongue and trying to let the crest subside, but it was too late. The pleasurable itch exploded with searing ecstasy. Ander's cock spasmed and flooded Dannel's mouth with hot cum. He bucked as a wrenching orgasm tore through him and through their bond.

Dannel moaned deliriously. His hips moved in short jabs, as if fucking the air above Ander's face, as Ander's ecstasy triggered his own release. His lips sank to the base of Ander's cock as cum spurted into his mouth and throat. The sense of coming in a clenching throat sizzled between them, mingling sweetly with the sensation of ejaculating inside slippery soft leathers. The torrent left them exhausted.

At last their spasms subsided. Dannel collapsed on top of Ander. He turned his head and relinquished the still-swollen cock, cum smearing his lips as the shaft emerged. He rested, panting, his cheek against the slick flesh.

Ander waited for a time, sharing in the euphoric afterglow of Dannel's first real lovemaking, as their link gradually faded. The young warrior glowed with unalloyed happiness. Ander was humbled by the intensity of the boy's gratitude. At last he rolled to his side while holding Dannel in a snug embrace, then swung around to lie face to face.

Dannel gazed at him through half-shut eyes. A faint smile played on his lips as he touched Ander's cheek. "I was right about you," he said softly. "Somehow, the moment I first saw you, I knew fate had brought us together."

Ander leaned close and gave the boy a tender kiss. The ease they now shared with each other was uncanny. He could feel that Dannel's devotion was more than mere infatuation. The youth's life had changed forever, and Ander was now an integral part of it.

"Who knows what destiny holds?" Ander said. "If Thane succeeds, overthrows the zamindar, we'll have a new world to make. I'm glad you'll be at our side."

Contentment filled them. For the moment the firestone was forgotten, the powers loosened in the valley seemed no more than a dream. They snuggled together under the blankets and Ander soon found sleep, still wrapped in the fighter's arms.

12

THANE RAN back to the sweat lodge, brimming with ideas and news. Erik and Skorri kept pace; they were accustomed to the mage's boundless energy in the face of mysteries. And lately, mysteries were in plentiful supply.

The Torii Gates had been transformed by whatever happened when Dannel and Ander touched the kei. The entrance at the cliff face had become impenetrable. A swirling curtain of brilliantly colored motes, tiny points of intense light, filled the towering opening. Looking at the entrance was like peering deep into the night sky, a sky where the stars had gone mad and turned to fireworks. Approaching it was like walking against a tide, being tugged one way, then another, until the ground itself seemed to undulate.

When Thane had arrived at the Gates, Skorri had impetuously attempted running through the barrier. It was a mistake he would not repeat. He had bounced from the shimmering curtain like a leaf driven before a gale. Numbing cold had knocked him nearly senseless. They were able to revive him, but several anxious minutes passed before the blond's sense of touch returned.

Thane hadn't had any greater success with the barrier, but had seized on a new idea. Skorri's experience suggested a way to release Dannel from the firestone's spell.

They arrived at the sweat lodge and found the door ajar. Thane entered and paused while his eyes adjusted to dim light. All was quiet, the only sound the rapid breaths of Erik and Skorri at his back. He crossed the outer chamber and looked into the inner room. The fire had died to embers and the cavernous room was in almost complete darkness.

"Ander? Dannel? Are you awake?"

A soft rustle came from the middle of the chamber. He squinted and saw Ander stir among the blankets. A mumbled hello, followed by a huge yawn, helped him find his way to the sleepy youth. Thane crouched at his side and kissed the side of his head. The clean scent of Ander's hair was more appealing than any perfume.

"Where's Dannel?" Thane asked, feeling among the blankets.

Ander yawned again, leaning against Thane's strong body. "He was here when I fell asleep. Maybe he had to go piss, I don't know."

"You sleep like a stone," Thane said, mussing his hair affectionately. He turned to the doorway, where Erik and Skorri were waiting. "Would you fetch him back? I have some news he'll want to hear." Erik gestured with fingers closing into an upturned palm, his sign for affirmation, and the two boys left.

"What news?" Ander asked. He tugged Thane closer. His body was still warm from slumber and slick with oil. Thane settled into the blankets next to him and put an arm around his partner, basking in his warmth.

"Something's blocking the Torii Gates. It's like a curtain of anima, or a piece of the kei showing through to the everyday world. But different than I've ever seen."

"Different how?" Ander still sounded drowsy. He nestled against Thane's side like a tiger getting comfortable next to its mate.

"Skorri ran into it, right when I got there, and it knocked him off his feet. It was like he got frostbite. He couldn't feel his legs or hands, couldn't even stand. It was five minutes before he could feel Erik holding him."

Ander sat up straight, now fully awake. "Is he all right?"

Thane gave him a hug. "No harm done. Might have even scared a little sense into him. He rushed into danger without stopping to weigh the risk."

"He was probably wanting to show you what they'd found and forgot himself. You know how Skorri is."

The mage laughed and nodded. "He's an unpredictable creature, that's for certain. A virtue in bed, but not always when magic's afoot. Still, it *did* turn out helpful."

"See? Doing the unexpected comes in useful sometimes. Um, *how* did it help?"

"The way Skorri couldn't feel his hands, it made me think about Dannel and the firestone. We tried raffia oil to help him control pleasure. I thought if we dampened his sensations, he might be able to control the firestone's power when it was triggered. It didn't work."

"Well, it helped *some*. It delayed the spell, let him be touched more than he ever has before."

"But he needed the help of a trance, and even then the oil didn't save him for long. That's the key, Ander! We have to prevent the firestone's power from reaching him. It should be like there's no firestone at all. Like cutting it off."

Ander turned and looked at him sternly. "Dannel said that's been tried, remember? Torii Guardians have cut off their own ears to seek release from the curse. It always kills them."

"I said *like* cutting it off," Thane said, giving Ander's ear a tweak. "That's where Skorri's mistake gave me an idea. What if

Dannel's ear was frostbitten and he couldn't feel it at all? The firestone releases uncontrollable pleasure. But pleasure means nothing to numb flesh."

Ander looked skeptical. "Are you sure it won't hurt him? Maybe the spell would react to numbness the same way it does to being cut off."

Thane rocked back, sobered by his partner's thoughtful observation. It was easy to forget that Ander's inexperience didn't alter his intelligence; the young musician had a keen mind.

"There might be some risk," Thane agreed at last. "We'll have to tell Dannel, let him decide for himself. But remember, it won't be the firestone that's numb, it'll be Dannel's ear. The firestone and its spell shouldn't be affected. They'll still be linked to Dannel's body, sense his anima."

"That's another thing," Ander said. He was leaning forward now, fully engaged with the problem and thinking hard. The blanket had slid down to his waist, unnoticed. "Can you make a potion that deadens sensation that much? If the firestone is releasing power, you can't let *any* of it get through to Dannel."

"A difficult challenge," Thane admitted. "Our potions are designed to increase sensation, not deaden it. But I have some ideas that might work. Especially if we only have to numb a small area like his ear. And I saw some plants in the hierophants' garden that should be useful."

Ander shook his head, a bemused smile on his lips. "I wonder what Lord Tolmin would think if he knew what you'd end up doing with all the botany he taught you. The poor old man would probably have panicked and taken up music instead."

Thane returned the grin. "Gregory? Never! He'd approve of any use for plants other than poisoning. And besides, he's tone deaf." Turning sideways, he wrapped Ander in his arms and toppled him into the blankets. His partner yelped with pleased surprise, returning the grapple. They wrestled for dominance, muscles straining in a spirited contest. Soon Thane had Ander's arms pinned against his sides in a firm embrace. Ander licked the tip of Thane's nose and let his body relax, yielding to the victor.

Thane was about to claim his reward when Skorri appeared at the door. "We can't find him," he announced.

Thane and Ander rolled apart. "You looked everywhere?" Thane asked. "How about that copse of alder up the slope?"

"We looked there. No sign he'd even been there. Erik says he sees a trail heading across the meadow, though. To the west."

Thane sat up and ran a hand through his short hair. His brow furrowed. "This doesn't sound right. He was supposed to stay with Ander. And Dannel's not one to neglect a task."

"You're right," Ander agreed. He tossed the blankets aside and reached for his clothes. "We'd better search for him."

Thane was already rising to his feet. "Erik and I will go. You and Skorri should stay here in case he comes back."

"We don't both need to stay," Ander said.

The stubborn look in his eyes told Thane what was coming. Ander didn't lack for courage, and resisted when he thought Thane was trying to keep him out of harm's way. He wanted no special treatment on account of being the mage's beloved.

Thane raised a hand in a placating gesture. "I'm not trying to safeguard you. I've learned better than to try! But there are powers loose in the valley, manifestations we don't understand at all. Being alone might be dangerous. I fear that could be why Dannel vanished."

Ander's lips pressed together as if he still wanted to argue. Then he took a deep breath and the tension left his face. "You're probably right." He glanced at Skorri, who still stood in the doorway. The young blond had been examining Ander's sleekly muscled body with an appreciative eye. "But I'm not so sure it's safe around *here*. I've just cum, twice, and Skorri looks horny."

"Skorri is *always* horny," Thane said, walking to the door and patting the blond boy's rump. "Consider it a challenge."

Skorri's wolfish grin showed his approval for Thane's plan. Ander laughed, won over by the boy's frisky enthusiasm, and dropped his shirt back on the pile. "I'll manage, somehow. Be careful, Thane."

"Always." The mage thumped Skorri on the back, then turned and left. He felt some uneasiness as he left the sweat lodge, but attributed it to the ominous orb and spokes that dominated the sky. He had spoken truthfully; there *were* forces at work in the valley, and so far they hadn't been friendly.

Erik was standing a few yards to the west, scanning the meadow with a tracker's eye. Heather and phlox dotted the landscape, adding blue and purple highlights among the rocks and hardy grasses. Thane saw no signs of someone having passed that way, but then his survival had never depended on tracking game. Erik's rapport with the earth and the animals inhabiting it was unmatched by the other mages; the young hunter could work spells with animals that eluded even Thane.

Erik turned as he approached. "You think he went this way?" Thane asked.

Erik pointed west. "See the lighter green patches? The grass has been bent." He pointed with his toe to a small rock near their feet. "And this was moved, recently, from here."

Thane looked closely and saw a shallow depression near the stone where brown soil was still dark with moisture. "Can you tell how long?" he asked.

Erik turned his face to the sun, eyes closed, to judge the heat. He opened his eyes and looked at Thane with confidence that was striking in a boy of eighteen. "Half an hour, no more."

"We'd better hurry. Something's not right."

Erik set out across the meadow, pausing now and then to examine the ground and vegetation, even sniffing the air as if he could detect Dannel's scent. Thane followed and kept quiet. Tracking required concentration, and Erik was more easily distracted by talk than most. The hunter moved slowly but with great deliberation. When they reached the far side of the meadow, where grass met trees, there was an easily discerned trail where pine needles had been disturbed by booted feet. Erik had found his way to it with unerring accuracy.

"Good," Thane said, touching Erik's arm. "Let's hurry, now."

Erik nodded and they set off at a jog through the aromatic pines. There was little underbrush and the needles covering the ground muffled their passage. Thane let the hunter keep the lead, as the trail became muddled and hard to follow from time to time. They padded through the forest, heading up a slope, responding easily to the challenge. The air grew warm and sweat soon soaked Thane's shirt.

The slope became steep and rocky, almost like running up steps. Suddenly a pattern caught Thane's eye. Though it was cluttered with loose rocks and trees had taken root, they seemed to be ascending a series of narrow terraces. His gaze swept higher and the pattern held. The whole slope had once been a vast staircase.

Something stirred in the back of Thane's mind, making his hackles rise. It was bad enough that Dannel had wandered off. But disappearing to overgrown ruins, a place he had never even mentioned, was even more alarming.

The trees thinned as they neared the crest of the ridge. The construction of the terraces was now obvious. Large yellow stones were fitted together with meticulous precision, functioning as broad steps even though the rock had been rounded by untold years of weather.

As they neared the rim a menacing growl echoed around them. Erik froze, immobile as a stag waiting to see if it had evaded a pursuer's notice.

"What is it?" Thane whispered. "And *where* is it?"

"Mountain lion," was the soft reply. Erik turned his head slowly, one way and then the other, sniffing and listening at the same time. He looked puzzled. "Didn't sound right, though. I can't tell where it came from."

Thane's eyes narrowed. They had seen lion tracks in the desert as well as in the valley, though the beasts had avoided them. But changes had come over the valley and there was no way to guess what the effects might be. "I think it came from the other side of the ridge," Thane whispered. "Let's look."

A dozen yards brought them to the top of the slope. They were higher than the pass through which they had entered the valley, though still not as high as the encircling peaks. Instead of the ridge Thane had expected, he found a flat expanse curving away in both directions. Finely fitted blocks covered its surface, broken only by clumps of grass that had taken root in hairline cracks. The plaza was some twenty feet wide, and dropped off in a clean line on both sides.

The growl echoed again, this time escalating quickly into a full-throated roar. The angry sound rolled up from the far side of the plaza with chilling ferocity. Thane stifled an instinctive urge to flee and walked across the curving roadway. As he approached the rim, a strange vista appeared before him.

The flat area on which he stood formed the broad lip of a huge bowl. Steps descending the bowl's steep inner curve were wide enough to serve as seats. Channels were cut at angles to the seats, zigzagging in a complex pattern that connected a platform at the center of the depression with dozens of points on the bowl's rim. Water flowed from spouts at the top of each channel and cascaded down to vanish beneath the central platform. The design was similar to the exercise area near the hierophants' temple in Skarn but on a vastly larger scale. Sunlight glittered on the water, making it look like streams of jewels poured from the rim and flowing to the center. The place pulsed with unseen energies.

Erik moved to the mage's side and pointed. "There, in the center. See it?"

Thane shielded his eyes and looked at the circular platform far below. At first the complex structure at the bowl's bottom was hard to fathom. Ten pillars carved from opalescent stone formed a circle around a pyramid some fifty feet across at the base and fifteen across at its flattened top. The tops of the pillars rose about ten feet higher than the platform at the pyramid's apex. Then

Thane saw what Erik had noticed.

A lion lurked in the shadow cast by the pyramid, its tawny head swinging back and forth as it sniffed the air. It growled again, a rumble from deep within its chest, then sank to a crouch preparing to spring.

The predator's muscles bunched, but its prey was quicker. Dannel sprang from behind a pillar and raced straight for the lion. The startled cat hesitated while Dannel leaped and landed on its back. The beast roared and immediately started rolling, but Dannel had already wrapped an arm around its neck and his legs around its body. A cloud of dust engulfed them, penetrated only by snarls and outraged feline howls.

Thane found himself running down into the bowl, bellowing an incoherent challenge. Erik raced at his side, silent and determined. The hunter had left his bow and quiver at the lodge but still carried his hunting knife. It was a toy against a lion's slashing claws, but better than nothing.

Roars echoed around them, amplified by the curving bands of rock circling the amphitheater. The noise showed the struggle wasn't over, but Thane had no time to ponder what more it might mean. His dash down the slope had gained momentum. He ran in long strides, his booted feet racing over treacherous stone with bone-jarring impact. A misstep would send him tumbling down the steep ledges, but he didn't slow. Sweat stung his eyes by the time they reached the bottom of the depression and plunged into the cloud of yellow dust. Echoes vanished and the sound of struggle was suddenly close.

The dust thinned enough to reveal Dannel still astride the lion, clinging desperately as the cat twisted and screamed. Blood smeared his torso and red stained the dust as they rolled. Releasing his grip on the enraged beast would have meant quick death.

"Watch its claws!" Erik shouted, pulling his knife from its sheath.

Thane signaled his agreement, circling to the left as Erik went right. There was nothing in sight to use as a weapon.

Erik dashed within twenty feet of the combatants and threw his hunting knife at the lion's stomach. But the blade was made for skinning game, not throwing, and wobbled in flight. It struck its target broadside and fell harmlessly to the ground.

The lion roared, an ear splitting bellow of rage at the intrusion, and rolled away with Dannel on its back. Thane rushed forward to reclaim the knife, moving inside the ring of pillars.

A sound like a bell rang in his ears, seeming to come from all around him. The tone was pure and strong. His whole body reverberated in response. He felt something build within him like an onrushing wave.

"Stay back!" he shouted to Erik. "There's a nexus here. Maybe I can use it!" He held his hands chest high with his right cupped in the left, palm up. Ignoring the nearby snarls and howls, he closed his eyes and focused on the sensation of power springing from the air around him. The land itself seemed to come alive and flex granite muscles deep below the surface. Something tickled the palm of his right hand, as delicate as a butterfly's landing. In the space of three heartbeats the sensation grew, becoming a faint itch and then a numbing tingle like hundreds of tiny pins pricking his flesh.

Energy coruscated up through Thane's feet and into his hands. He opened his eyes. A translucent ball the size of a plum hovered above his right palm, resembling a glass globe containing a tiny orange sun.

Curling his fingers around the manifestation, he spun and sprinted toward the lion. "Let go!" he shouted. "*Now*!"

Dannel released his hold and rolled aside, tucked into a ball. The lion flipped and twisted, swiping at its nemesis with two-inch claws, drawing a new line of red across the youth's back. At the same moment Thane threw the globe.

The ball of self-contained energy Thane had wrested from the kei hit the lion squarely on the shoulder. It exploded with an intense white flash and a sound like water hitting red-hot metal. He blinked and rubbed spots from his eyes. Where the lion had been, only ash and a few charred remnants of bone remained.

Dannel lay on the ground a few yards away. He faced the sky, unmoving, but his chest rose and fell with shuddering breaths. He looked utterly exhausted. Thane went to his side and knelt in the bloodstained sand.

The young warrior was battered and bloody. Thane pulled off his shirt and used it to wipe blood away from the gashes on Dannel's bare torso. The boy groaned and looked to the side, his face a mask of misery.

"Nasty cuts," Thane said, daubing gently. "But not too deep. They'll heal well if we wash them out quickly."

Dannel nodded, tight lipped, avoiding Thane's eyes.

"What happened?" the mage asked. It was obvious the boy was upset by more than the combat.

Dannel groaned and raised an arm to cover his eyes. He swallowed as if choking back bile. "I failed you." His voice was a hoarse whisper.

Erik arrived at their side, carrying water in his cupped hands. "Drink," he offered. Dannel sighed, then moved his arm and raised himself on his elbows to accept the offering. Water cut rivulets through the yellow dust caking his face, but he managed to drink most of it. When he was done he raised his gaze to meet Thane's.

"Where's Ander?"

"Ander's fine," Thane answered. "We found him at the sweat lodge, fast asleep."

Relief flooded Dannel's face. "No trap, then. Just my blundering."

"Let's wash your cuts," Thane said. "You can tell us what happened."

They helped Dannel to his feet and out of the ring of pillars at the structure's center. Water swirled around the platform where the pillars stood and disappeared into concealed drains. It was clear and icy cold, and quickly revived the battered fighter. Haltingly, he began his story.

"We were lying together, in the blankets. Ander was sleeping. I was trying to stay awake in case something happened. Then I heard something outside, or thought I did."

"Animal sound?" Erik asked.

"No. I'd never heard anything like it. Like chanting but with no words. A slow and deep sound. Like the sea would make if it could sing."

Thane leaned forward, intent. "I heard something too. Like tuned bells in a deep cavern."

Dannel shrugged, having no explanation to offer. "I decided to look outside, see if there was something coming. When I opened the door it got louder." He pointed at the red orb and spokes that still spun lazily in the sky like a giant wagon wheel. "I glanced up at that *thing* in the sky and suddenly everything got . . . different."

"Different how?" Thane urged. "This could be important."

"It was like I was dreaming. But not exactly. I could still feel sun on my skin, weight on my feet. The sound pulled at me. I had to follow, even though this hill has always been forbidden ground for Torii Guardians. I couldn't help it, my legs moved by themselves. It was like riding a horse that's made up its mind where to go and won't heed the bit. And I . . . I was distracted by the voices."

"What voices?"

Dannel licked his lips, frowning with concentration. "The sound I told you about, like chanting? I was starting to hear words in it.

I couldn't understand them, but I still felt the meaning." He gulped, looking confused, but plunged ahead. "Somehow they were telling me to come here. To meet somebody."

Thane rocked back on his heels. Unless Dannel was addled by exhaustion, what he said offered unexpected opportunity. "What happened when you got here? Did you see anyone?"

"I don't remember. My head was full of voices and music, I couldn't think of anything else. It seemed like I stood among the pillars a long time. Until the lion came over and swatted me to see if I was alive. Then the voices vanished and I didn't have time to think about anything except lion claws."

"You fought well," Erik said. "I've never faced a lion without weapons. I've heard of men defeating one barehanded, but the lion usually wins."

"I didn't defeat it. Thane did, remember?" He turned to the mage and bowed his head. "Thank you for coming to my aid. I don't deserve it. I've led you into danger instead of protecting you. I . . . I hope you'll still let me be your apprentice."

Thane clasped the youth's forearm and held it until the clasp was returned. Dannel's heartfelt relief at the kindness was like the sun emerging after a downpour. "I have no reason to regret my decision," the mage said. "Besides, you hold more promise than most initiates."

Dannel's eyes turned questioning.

Thane gave his arm a squeeze, then released it. "If something or someone in the kei wants to meet you, there must be a reason. If we can learn what it is, the riddle of this place might be solved."

They finished washing and tending to wounds, then started on the hike back. While Dannel seemed hopeful about the day's events, and buoyed by his friends' confidence, Thane remained silent. Drawing the attention of forces in the kei might offer promise, but it offered peril in equal measure.

13

ANDER PULLED down on a springy branch, bringing clusters of spiky blue flowers at its tip into Thane's reach. The mage started twisting the clusters off with practiced snaps and dropping them into a basket. They had already harvested the materials they needed for the numbing oil Thane wanted to make, and were collecting a few additional specimens from the hierophants' garden while they had the opportunity.

"I still don't understand," Ander said, afire with curiosity. "You pulled power right out of the kei without using the art? How is that possible?"

Thane kept working as he replied. "It wasn't anything *I* did. There was so much power all around it almost manifested by itself. I bent the kei a little, the way you do to make a telos light. But instead of getting a trickle, there was a flood. It was like expecting a firefly and getting a forest fire."

Ander was so distracted he let go of the branch with one hand, nearly whacking Thane in the face with it. He restored his grip and pulled it back down, not even noticing his partner's reproachful glance. "Then it's like the fastness back at the Lyceum? Where earth, fire, water and air all come together at one place and make a focus? Could you tell if it—"

Thane stopped harvesting and raised a hand. "Did you hear something?"

Ander had been too full of questions to notice anything, but he dutifully cocked his head and listened. Wind whispered through leaves and insects buzzed among the blooms. He could hear Dannel and Skorri a short distance away, engaged in muted conversation. Nothing seemed out of the ordinary. Then he heard it. A low hum pulsed like the beating wings of a giant wasp. His hackles rose.

"What *is* it?" Ander whispered, slowly reducing his pull on the branch and letting it swing back into the air. He looked around apprehensively. "Um, lions don't make sounds like that, do they?"

Thane turned slowly, squinting against the late afternoon sun, then shook his head. "I don't see anything. It sounds like it's coming from all around us. You look that way." He pointed toward the garden's main gates. "I'll get Dannel and Skorri started looking, then catch up with you. Yell if you find anything. And be careful."

Ander nodded, then started down the trail toward the setting sun. Golden light bathed the garden and dust motes swam in the afternoon haze. The air was heavy with the sweet scent of roses and persimmons.

Fronds waved in the gentle breeze, finely cut leaves like giant fans casting bizarre shadows across the trail. The garden suddenly seemed alien and ominous as the buzzing grew louder. Looking over his shoulder, Ander saw that Thane had finished with Skorri and Dannel and was coming down the trail to join him.

A queasy feeling filled him as he neared the tall obelisks and pyramidal capstone at the garden's entrance. There was still no sign of what could be causing the sound. The high wall enclosing the garden blocked the view of anything beyond. He cautiously stepped through the gate.

Ander's stomach lurched as something caught him in mid-step. The sixteen-foot obelisks that flanked him seemed to become partially transparent, as if they were riddled with thousands of tiny holes and light poured through from a source within the rock itself. Faint blue lines writhed and flashed between the obelisks. They held Ander like a ghostly spider's web.

Ander heard Thane yell, a panicked shout that alarmed him even more than his sudden immobility, and heard the pounding of booted feet sprinting toward him. The obelisks pulsed with shafts of red light. There was a jerk, like a giant's hand encircling his body and snatching him from the air the way a boy catches a butterfly. Then darkness.

Ringing in his ears was followed by the discomfort of cold marble beneath his back. Ander opened his eyes.

A baleful red eye stared at him, an eye set in the head of a bird with a long hooked beak. The bird's head rested on a man's shoulders. The creature was eight feet or more in height, a giant. Black feathers covered it except where leathery skin hung between its arms and body like a bat's wings. A sword hung from its belted waist, its only clothing aside from a gold necklace holding a medallion set with a blue sapphire.

"*Vermin*!" The creature's voice was a raspy shriek, but somehow Ander understood its meaning perfectly. "Who dares trespass in the Sacred Grove? I'll pluck your eyes out!"

Ander recoiled from the beast's fury. At first he thought they were in a fiery cavern of some kind, but as his eyes adjusted to the ruddy light he realized they were in the underground temple's cylindrical chamber. A single flame flickered in midair twenty feet overhead and was reflected in the numberless glass tiles covering the walls. Dark slits marked the distant entrance and exit.

The creature leaned over Ander and snapped its beak within an inch of his nose. The stench of carrion was overwhelming. "No, I'll rip out your liver first. You'll live long enough to watch me eat it!"

Ander rolled to the side, his heart pounding. He scrambled to his feet, trembling with sick dread. The entrance door was fifty feet away, and the creature looked fast. He started backing toward the entrance, slowly.

The birdman tilted its head back and shrieked. The sound echoed around the echo chamber and sounded like a whole flock of vultures descending on helpless prey. It raised an arm and slashed its talons through the air. Dried blood stained the razor-like fingers.

The urge to run made him quiver, but he stood fast. *What would Thane do? He wouldn't panic, that's for certain.* Though he felt like a mouse waiting for the slash of an owl's beak, he stood up straight and met the enraged creature's gaze.

"We . . . we meant no harm," he stammered. "We thought this place was abandoned. We didn't—"

"Liar! You woke the Sentinel! It warned you to leave, yet you did not!"

"The sentinel? I don't—"

The creature hissed like a lizard, spittle spraying from nostril slits in its beak. It raised an arm overhead and made a complex gesture with its talons. The upper part of the cylindrical chamber filled with an image of the hub-and-spoke apparition that brooded over the valley.

"You were told!" it screamed. "Even vermin can understand the Sentinel's warning!" It drew the sword from its scabbard and advanced toward Ander.

His mind clamored with the urge to run. But even if he escaped into the subterranean labyrinth, his friends would be vulnerable.

Instead of running or preparing to fight, Ander bowed his head and held his arms out, palms up. "I beg forgiveness. We didn't know we were intruding on someone's home. We only wanted to learn."

The birdman towered over Ander with sword uplifted, but the blow did not fall.

Ander looked up, hoping he had won a reprieve. What he saw left him speechless.

The avian nightmare had vanished. In its place stood a man who appeared perhaps five years older than Ander. He wore cream-colored leathers, and a tunic that looked like thousands of green fish scales sewn together with black silk. The elegant hauberk glistened like butterfly wings. Thick golden hair fell to his waist. Though his features were youthful, his purple eyes held preternatural wisdom and his stern expression made him seem older. A rosy aura surrounded him, glittering with silver sparks, as though his body was formed out of the kei itself. He shed power the way men throw away spent breath.

Ander slowly lowered his arms, then licked his dry lips. "Who are you?" he asked, his voice shaky. "*What* are you?"

The man returned his sword to its scabbard and stepped back. His eyes never left Ander's. "An inquisitive one. Not a common thief, I think." He frowned. "What should I do with you?" His deep voice had a lilting quality, rising and falling almost like music. The words were unlike any tongue Ander had heard during his years working at Lady Tayanita's brothel, yet he understood their meaning.

"Your pardon, sire. But what happened to the, um, the one who was here before? The one with feathers?"

The man's frown faded and he examined Ander more closely. "Curious. Before, men have always run. But *you* ask questions. And you had enough courage to master your fear. A virtue." He dipped his head in a slight acknowledgment, though his expression remained stern. "I am Pallaton. What are you called?"

"Ander, sire. Thank you for coming. I was in danger, and you seem to have banished it. I'm indebted to you."

Pallaton shook his head, his severe dignity unwavering. "You are in danger only when I decide it. Only I have been with you. What you saw before was illusion, a test. I am as you see me now."

A test? Ander's mind bubbled with questions, but Pallaton's haughty manner restrained him. It was clear he was no ordinary man or even an ordinary mage. No hint of blood magic tingled the air, but the erotic tingle Ander associated with Thane's art was also absent.

Pallaton circled Ander, examining him like a bug stuck in amber. Suddenly he stopped and fixed Ander with an accusing stare. "Several scrolls are missing from my library. Sacred texts not meant for your kind. Who took them?" The last question was low and soft, filled with menace.

Ander gulped. *If punishment is required, let Thane be spared.* "I . . . I did," he answered. "I'll gladly return them. I didn't know what they were, only wanted to study them."

Pallaton was watching him through narrowed eyes. Time

stretched painfully and Ander began to sweat. He began to doubt his ability to conceal anything from this creature.

At last Pallaton took a step backward. "You're a clumsy liar."

Ander went white, expecting the worst.

Pallaton looked at him sternly. "Skill in lying is not a virtue, Ander. And you were trying to protect your friends. Loyalty *is* a virtue."

Ander felt faint. "Do you know everything?" he asked in a weak voice. "Are you just toying with me?"

"I am deciding what to do with you. Death is the usual fate for those foolish enough to intrude. But I will take a look at you before deciding. Seasons change, spring returns after a long winter. Perhaps you carry the seeds of a new beginning."

"I don't understand," Ander said, at a loss to guess what Pallaton was seeking. Despite the threats, he sensed a yearning. *He could have killed me easily, if that's what he wanted. He's searching for something else. But what?* The precariousness of his situation was painfully clear, but he sensed a current of opportunity as well.

Remembering his lover's fearless determination when discovery beckoned, Ander trusted his instincts and plunged ahead. "Maybe . . . if you'd talk with my friend Thane, he could tell you what you need to know. He knows far more than I do about—"

"You will serve my purposes. You and your friends can tell me nothing. I will see for myself what fate you deserve. This time no beasts can interrupt my inspection, and my judgment will be final."

Ander felt faint, but resolved to make the best of the situation. He bowed his head submissively.

"If I can be of service, I offer myself. I would make amends for our offense if you permit it."

Pallaton appeared pleased by the offer. He stepped close and put a hand under Ander's chin, tilting his head so their eyes met. His symmetrical features were princely, an effect strengthened by his functional yet elegant clothing.

Ander's pulse quickened, wondering if the gleam in Pallaton's exotic eyes sprang from the same desires as the smoldering gazes he had received from countless enamored visitors at Lady Tayanita's brothel.

"One more test," Pallaton said, leaning even closer. "There is virtue here, more than I have found before among your kind. That alone doesn't separate you from the beasts. I need to know if you see beyond the veil."

As Pallaton's eyes burned into him, Ander realized the next test had nothing to do with the erotic. Whatever Pallaton was, he wasn't truly human. He felt the presence of a massive intellect, probing yet gentle, touching his mind without the benefit of bonds such as those he had formed with Thane and other initiates. What touched his spirit now moved on a deeper level and with infinitely greater power. His knees felt weak but he found it impossible to move. Pallaton's hand released his chin and brushed his cheek, then moved to the back of his head.

"I seek balance," Pallaton continued. "Creatures of the mountain and the plain have a virtue of their own, but they see only the surface of things. They cannot even imagine that something lies beneath the surface. Some men can imagine higher truths, but they lack the balance to live in harmony. Perhaps enough time has passed for man to change. I intend to find out."

"How old are you?" Ander managed to ask. Pallaton's touch was having a strange effect on him, as if he were drugged. He felt helpless yet at the same time relaxed. Somewhere deep inside his mind protested and tried to raise an alarm, but his body paid no heed. His fate was in Pallaton's hands and no amount of worrying would change it.

"Save your questions," Pallaton said. "I have a task for you. Tell me what you sense, if anything."

Ander's vision clouded. In moments he seemed to stand in the middle of a howling blizzard. Swirling whiteness surrounded him like wind-driven snow. He could no longer feel the floor under his feet or Pallaton's hand at the back of his head. Disorientation threatened to spin into panic. Then the blizzard's voice changed, becoming unified and pure. A line of music composed of eight notes floated through his mind with crystal clarity.

"Music," Ander gasped. "I hear music!"

"Good." Pallaton's voice whispered through the white void as if it bubbled up from deep under water. "Those who can see beyond the veil perceive what lies there in different ways. What is important is that you perceive it at all. Now, *do* something with it."

Trepidation filled him, but there was no turning back. The melody repeated, like a challenge. Ander took the theme and sang it in his mind. The notes sounded a third time in his ears. This time the sound had a different quality, warmer and more full-bodied. The effect filled him with wonder and delight. He added another five notes to the theme, then inverted it so that notes went up where they had previously gone down, and down where they had gone up.

"So, your mind can speak as well as hear." A sense of grudging approval tinged the words. "But we are only beginning. Show me more."

An instant later the music Ander had constructed was repeated, but this time a countersubject answered the theme and completely changed the music's direction. The two voices danced around each other with delicate precision.

Ander felt himself grinning, irresistibly drawn to the music. His skill with intricate counterpoint had taken years to develop and had earned a well-deserved reputation throughout Pella. He doubled the speed of the original theme and reintroduced it with an overlap to create a fugue.

If Ander had thought in the first few moments that Pallaton's final test would be easy, he soon learned otherwise. They took turns adding to the musical construction. Augmentations, inversions, modulations and additional subjects grew from the original melody like an ornate temple growing from its keystone. Ander forgot everything else as the music filled his mind. Complexity beyond anything he had imagined threatened to overwhelm him, and the beauty of the growing creation tugged for his attention like a siren.

Ander thought he could keep up until Pallaton's turn came again and he added a fourth subject to a fugue that had already reached the limits of what Ander thought was possible. The fourth theme fit together with the rest like a key in a lock, bringing harmonies and rhythms together in a way that made Ander want to weep with joy. He surrendered to the experience, leaving Pallaton to work out the inconceivable intricacies. He could only marvel as revelations of infinite beauty spread before him.

The improvisation came to a towering conclusion that seemed to fill the universe. As the sound faded Ander grasped at the memory. But it was like waking from a dream, impossible to hold. His vision cleared and he found himself supported in Pallaton's arms. He ached with loss.

Pallaton waited until Ander's dazed expression faded, then effortlessly eased him to his feet. Then he stepped back and smiled faintly.

Ander gulped, suddenly remembering that he hadn't been able to keep up. He had failed. His stomach knotted and hot disappointment filled him.

"There is hope for your kind after all," Pallaton said at last. "I had begun to doubt. But now I see an infant has been born at last. Wonders await you, if you survive."

Ander felt tears in his eyes, and a welter of emotions too tangled to sort out. *Have I failed? Is he going to let us live?* Pallaton's cryptic verdict left him confused and frustrated, and despite it all he still felt a desperate yearning for the beauty he had seen. Most of all he wished Thane was with him.

Pallaton saw his confusion and, for the first time, a hint of sympathy softened his regal expression. "Many have come before you," he said. "Only a few had strong enough spirits to awaken the Sentinel and summon me. And none before have entered the library. That is why I put you to a test. I was not disappointed."

"Does . . . does that mean you'll pardon us?" Ander could imagine Thane's frustration at the mysteries they would have to leave unsolved, but there was nothing he could do to prevent it. Escaping with their lives would be boon enough.

"I have seen enough of your spirit to believe you meant no harm in coming here. Even to hope your kind might someday join the great venture on the other side of the veil."

Now that their continued survival seemed assured, Ander's fear faded and curiosity roared back to life. "You keep speaking of my kind," he ventured. "If you'll pardon my asking, what do you mean by that?"

Pallaton regarded Ander thoughtfully, then seemed to reach a decision. "Knowledge can be a dangerous thing. But an inquiring mind joined with a gentle spirit should be nurtured. If you have the balance to live wisely, knowledge could help you find the right path. So I will tell you this much." He extended his right hand and touched his thumb to the middle finger.

Ander felt a moment of vertigo and blinked with surprise. They no longer stood in the cylindrical echo chamber. The towering walls of the gallery inside the Torii Gates soared above them on both sides. The glyphs sparkled with light and shifted shape as if they had come alive. Pallaton indicated them with sweeping gesture.

"These tell the story," he said. "What you have been told of the past is wrong, Ander. The world is far older than you know. There were uncounted eons when it was a speck of dust surrounded by vastness you cannot imagine. Life finally emerged from chaos. Plants and beasts filled it for more ages, but none of them could see beyond the surface of the world."

Ander grinned, hearing the absolute certainty in Pallaton's words. "I always *thought* the priests' stories sounded like moonshine. The stories are all different depending on what cult you listen to, even though there's no way more than one could be true.

So I doubted *all* of them."

Pallaton smiled. "I judged you right. But the story is just begun. After the beasts came man. Men began to suspect there was a veil and that something might lie beyond it. But they lacked the balance to understand what was under the surface. Greed and fear twisted their spirits and clouded their minds."

"*That* hasn't changed," Ander said. "Well, mostly. Thane's not like that at all."

"As I said, things change. It is the nature of the world. Mankind grew powerful, became obsessed with machines. They gained more power than their corrupted nature could control."

"Machines? Like clocks? How could that be dangerous?"

Pallaton shook his head. "You still do not understand. How could you, when you know so little? When I say the world is old, I mean truly ancient. The age of machines is more than a thousand thousand years past, Ander. All traces of it have vanished. They were destroyed."

"A thousand thousand?" Ander tried to think how many generations would pass over such a time, and quickly decided the question was futile. "If the machines were so powerful, who destroyed them?"

"Such a simple question, but there is no simple answer. History was lost in the war that ended man's dominion. But this much we know. Man sprang from the beasts of the field, as a child springs from its parents but sometimes is stronger or wiser. In the same way the hsien arose from man. Perhaps it was fate, the way man arose by chance. Some think men *created* the first hsien. Perhaps as a weapon, or because some of them realized their own race was destroying the world. They had the means to do it. Men being what they are, once they had the power they would not have been able to resist using it."

Ander felt numb. Pallaton's story was nothing like the teachings of the mystery cults. But the assurance in his voice, and the grim inevitability of what he described, carried the ring of truth.

"You said there was war," Ander said. His voice shook. "What happened?"

Pallaton saw his distress and put a hand on his shoulder. "It was for the best, Ander. You would not be here now if we had not prevailed. Mankind, with its wars and machines, would have killed everything."

Ander realized he was shivering, tried to calm himself. "So the hsien fought man, and won? Then why are there still men?"

"Does a child kill its parents, even if the parents are mad? At first we fought to defend ourselves; mankind tried its best to destroy us. When they realized defeat was inevitable, the survivors begged for mercy. We moved them to a vast island in the south and took away their machines. They were glad to live quietly, close to the land. We sealed the place off so they could not leave, then rooted out the machines and poisons that had polluted the world. We built our own cities using powers you call the kei."

Ander felt as if the lynchpin of everything he believed about the world was working loose. He was sure Pallaton spoke truthfully but still couldn't make sense of the story.

"But there are men everywhere, and you're the first hsien I've ever seen." His voice was anguished. "How can what you say be true?"

Pallaton stepped back. He looked amused.

"So young. I wonder how it feels to see the world through such fresh eyes." His grin widened, and suddenly he looked much less threatening. His scaled armor glinted with twisting reflections of glowing glyphs. "You still have no conception of time, Ander. As I said, man's dominion ended more than a thousand thousand years ago. The history of the hsien is longer than man's. The tales I could tell you! Stories of bravery, laughter, beauty that would make you weep. But the hsien are not immune to change. We have traveled beyond the veil, Ander. The Portal I guard, in the chamber at the end of the Hall of Ages, leads to realms deep in the kei. We dismantled our cities and released mankind from its confinement. I remained here to guard this sacred place, waiting in a place outside of time except when the Sentinel summons me, but all the rest have been gone for millennia. Someday your kind might follow. At last I have seen a beginning. I wish you well."

"Could you help us?" Ander asked. "I'm sure we'd learn faster if you'd show us the way. And there are dangers, enemies who—"

Pallaton raised a hand to stop the entreaty. "First you must grow stronger. Touching the forces I wield would destroy you, like an infant playing with fire. You are not ready."

"Thane is much stronger than me, the most skillful mage of all. I'm only an initiate, a beginner."

"Enough!" The ring of authority had reentered Pallaton's voice and would brook no argument. His aura flashed with silvery streaks like tiny bolts of lightning. "I have seen into your mind, felt your beloved's spirit through the bond you share with him. He has glimpsed what lies beneath the world's surface, nothing more. The forces are too great for him as well. You may stay the night in the Sacred Grove, but must leave with sunrise."

"But—"

"I have spoken!" The steel in his voice showed the hsien were still a warrior race. Argument would be futile and unwise. Ander bowed his head in acceptance of the decree.

A boom like a thunderclap echoed sharply through the vast gallery. Pallaton vanished in a flash of white light and Ander felt himself pushed backwards. He stumbled, almost falling, and found himself between the pillars at the entrance to the hierophants' garden.

Within three heartbeats, Thane was at his side and grabbed him in a fierce hug. Ander protested weakly, gasping for breath. The mage broke the embrace and held him at arm's length. His eyes were panicked; through their bond Ander felt acute terror and grief that had only begun to fade. Skorri and Dannel stood nearby, looking vastly relieved.

"Ander . . ." Thane whispered, his voice hoarse. He held tight, as if fearing Ander would disappear again. "I thought we'd lost you. Are you all right?"

"I think so." Ander rubbed his eyes, fighting the fatigue that suddenly filled him. "Let's get back to the lodge. There's much you need to know, and little time to tell it."

14

"THAT'S ALL I can remember," Ander said. "I think it's everything." His eyelids drooped and his head tilted to the side as he fought a losing battle with drowsiness.

Thane's mind still raced at Ander's tale. There was no doubting its truth, or at least that Ander believed it without reservation.

Deep blue sky was fading to black and stars were starting to appear in the patch of sky visible through the smoke hole in the lodge's roof. They were all sitting around the fire pit, the air full of spicy smoke as Erik and Skorri grilled fish for dinner. Thane barely noticed the aroma. He leaned forward, elbows on his knees. His mind still swirled with visions of a world filled with mages born of man, but changed. Firelight played across his distracted features. "We thought we knew so much," he said, humbled. "But we know nothing. The underground temple should have been enough to make us suspect. Men have never had the skill to build such a place, or even to imagine it."

"The hierophants spoke of elder gods," Dannel offered. "There are legends handed down from times before writing. Tales of monsters and fury, punishing mankind for transgressions. They don't sound like this Pallaton that Ander met, though."

"Maybe the legends grew from a seed of truth, but the truth got lost after so many retellings. Ander *did* say there was a bitter war between the two races." Thane shook his head, then sat up straight. Ander leaned against him and yawned. He was already half asleep. The mage put an arm around his shoulders and supported him carefully. Ander's success at meeting Pallaton's tests filled him with pride. A blissful smile brightened the musician's face as the surge of affection flowed through their bond.

Thane picked up a wooden bowl containing seedpods and other ingredients he had ground with a smooth rock. Thick brown paste that smelled of leaf mould formed a layer half an inch thick in its bottom. He examined the contents, then tilted the wooden bowl so Dannel could see inside. "The philter is nearly done," he said. "A little more blending and refining, then we can give it a try."

Dannel's eyebrows lifted. "After what happened to Ander? What if Pallaton objects? It didn't sound like he wants us meddling with the powers his race left behind."

Thane nodded, his seriousness showing he shared the fighter's concerns. "There might be risk. But this could be our only chance. Ander didn't say we'd been *forbidden* to touch the kei. I'm willing to try, Dannel, but it's your decision. The art depends on love freely given."

"I don't fear risk. My whole life has been spent learning how to fight." He chewed his lip, his brow knitted. "This is different, though. It's not just *my* risk. Pallaton might punish us all. I'd be a poor apprentice if I brought the wrath of an elder god down on your heads."

Ander half opened his eyes. "Pallaton is a warrior too," he said. "He said courage is a virtue, so maybe he won't get mad. Besides, we're your friends. You need help, so we offer it. Risk doesn't change that."

Dannel looked at Thane and Ander with unguarded longing. He was breathing from his mouth, struggling with the decision.

Silence stretched as Thane gave him time to make up his own mind.

"You offer more than I deserve," Dannel said at last, his voice thick. "I've never had such comrades. I . . . I don't know what to do. I don't want to see you come to harm, but also don't wish to spurn your gift."

Thane gave Ander a gentle squeeze and touched their heads together, an unconscious token of their bond. A sense of peace filled him. He looked at Dannel and smiled contentedly. "Part of friendship is learning to trust. We'll always stand by you, as you'd always come to our aid. This is what makes us strong."

A grin grew on Dannel's lips, spreading until he overflowed with happiness. Thane had never seen such fierce joy in the youth's eyes.

"Trust is hard after what my family and the hierophants have done to me. But you have it. If you think making an attempt with your new potion is wise, then I want to try." He paused, then cleared his throat and continued in a subdued voice. "Thane . . . what will I need to do? Is it complicated?"

Thane heard the anxious note in Dannel's question. The fighter was hunched forward, his hands clenched together. Even in the fading light Thane could see uncertainty in the youth's eyes. *I let myself get distracted again*, he thought, chastising himself. In his excitement over Ander's discoveries, he hadn't thought about Dannel's failed attempts at lovemaking. The fighter's assured bearing made it easy to forget his inexperience with intimacy. Making love was second nature to the mage, but to Dannel it was a forbidden land filled with mystery and trepidation.

Thane eased away from his sleepy partner and moved beside Dannel. They stared into the fire for a time, watching orange sparks swirl in the rising currents, until Thane saw the tension ebb from the fighter's interwoven fingers. He turned his head and smiled apologetically, his gray eyes showing an understanding that belied his youthful appearance. "I don't suppose Ander has told you about my many faults," he said. "One of the worst is that when I get too busy I sometimes neglect my friends."

"That's *one* of them," Skorri offered, looking up from the grilling fish. "Want me to tell him about the others?"

Thane laughed and used the tip of his boot to direct a small cloud of dirt in the blond's direction. "Later, beast. I have to warn him about *you* first." The jest was only partly idle. Skorri was notorious for telling lurid stories that often had more to do with his randy imagination than reality.

Skorri snickered and turned back to Erik, who was tending to the cooking with the single-minded concentration of a truly hungry boy. Thane's stomach rumbled at the savory aroma of wood smoke and fish. He noticed that Dannel seemed oblivious to it, a sure sign of his preoccupation.

"What would you like to know?" Thane asked. "Don't be afraid to ask. The art won't work if you're nervous. And besides, think what it means if we succeed! Your first time, a night to remember always. We should make it a good memory."

Dannel shook his head slowly, looking at Thane in wonder. "I've heard men in Skarn talk of sex. They joked and bragged but never said anything about pleasing their partner. They just took what they wanted."

"If that's what you feared, put your mind at rest. Half the art is learning to please the one you're with. Pleasure grows strong enough to work magic only when both lovers share that goal."

Dannel gazed into Thane's eyes as if entranced. "You and Ander are perfect for each other," he said softly, as if to himself. "Will . . . will I get to take Ander's place tonight? Will you touch me the way you touch him?"

Thane grinned, his virile features radiant. Though he was serious about the art, his body and spirit still burned with a teenager's enthusiasm for sex. "Everyone is different," he explained. "What Ander likes best might not be what pleases you the most. We won't know until we try. No pain, I promise. Only pleasure. Pain is anathema to the art."

"I hope your potion works," Dannel said. A corner of his mouth lifted in a quirky smile. "You remind me of a stable boy I knew in Skarn. He's strong like you, though not so fair. What I liked best about him, though, is how he tamed horses. He didn't break them to his will like other riders. Instead he made friends with the horse, only mounted when it was sure of him and not afraid. It took longer, but the horses he trains are the best in Skarn."

Thane laughed and squeezed Dannel's leg. "That's the first time I've heard lovemaking compared to riding horses."

"That's not what I meant," Dannel said, blushing. "You just reminded me—"

"I know. Don't worry, I'm not offended. But what you say makes sense. Riding a horse and making love both need trust." He paused, meeting Dannel's anxious gaze with a steady eye. After a while he sighed and leaned forward again, elbows on knees. He looked dejected. "I know what the problem is," he said. "It's happened before. You look at me and think about magic, instead of just seeing *me*. It makes everything so much more complicated. I wish there was a way to avoid it."

Ander stirred, opening his eyes and yawning. "It's true," he said. "The first time I met Thane, I didn't know who he was. I thought he was just a sexy kitchen boy. We seduced each other so fast it still makes me flinch to think about it."

"A kitchen boy?" Dannel's surprised smile seemed to light the room.

"A horny kitchen boy who wanted to share a kiss," Ander amplified. "How could I say no? *You* wouldn't, would you?"

Though embarrassed, Dannel shook his head. "No," he said softly. "I wouldn't." Hesitantly, he reached over to Thane and touched his arm. "I can forget about magic. Would you give me the same offer you gave Ander?"

Thane looked up, desire for simple friendship clear in his eyes. He touched Dannel's cheek in a wordless invitation. Dannel leaned close and they kissed.

Thane let the young fighter set the pace. The chaste kiss gradually deepened as they unconsciously turned toward each other and moved into a full embrace. Dannel's wiry frame felt like a bundle of energy in his arms. Soon the boy's tongue grazed his lips, seeking admittance. Thane parted his lips. Dannel's tongue slid into his mouth with youthful urgency, lacking any timidity. Whatever the fighter lacked in experience was overcome by pent-up desire. He leaned against Thane and kissed him as thoroughly as the mage had ever been kissed.

A thud followed by muted giggles, coming from near the fire, interrupted their intimacy. Thane reluctantly broke the kiss and turned to look. Skorri and Erik lay on the ground in a tangle.

"They were inspired by your example," Ander said, mirth filling his voice. "But Skorri forgot how close the fire is. His rump got a little warmer than usual."

Thane sighed and shook his head. Erik looked chagrined, but the curly-haired blond wasn't fazed at all. His sunny disposition found cause for laughter in most situations, even when it came at his own expense.

"Perhaps it's for the best," Thane said, letting go of Dannel's athletic body. "It smells like the fish are done, and we have a long night ahead." He brushed his fingertips across Dannel's lips, felt the boy's warm breath against his hand. "You surprise me," he said. "I never doubted your spirit, but didn't expect your skill to match it."

Dannel blushed, flustered by the praise, but Ander laughed softly. "He's had a little practice with kisses. I was impressed too. He's well suited for the art. Or he *will* be, once that damned firestone is tamed."

The reminder of unfinished work spurred the mage. He stood up and inspected the fish fillets. "They're done," he announced. "Let's eat."

Dinner passed quickly as they debated the meaning of Pallaton's tests and compared his version of history to legends they had heard from near and far. Throughout it all, Thane felt the tug of Dannel's sidelong glances. He did his best to put the youth at ease but couldn't help responding to the youth's desire. Anticipation kept him hard through the meal.

"Can I help you finish the potion?" Ander asked as they cleared the table. He leaned close and cupped the hard mound at Thane's crotch, giving him a friendly leer. "It *looks* like you need some help. Were you watching Dannel at dinner? I've never seen anyone so eager."

"He has me aching," Thane admitted, his cock pulsing under Ander's light squeeze. He glanced over his shoulder. Dannel was helping Erik bank the fire, crouching with the stiff awkwardness of a boy with pinched flesh cramming his leathers. "Who can blame him for being eager?"

"He's been horny as a rutting stag for eleven years," Ander agreed. He gave Thane's crotch another rub while brushing his ear with a kiss. "He's lucky in one thing, though. Having you for his first real lover. Nothing could be better."

Thane grinned and groped Ander in return. "You'll help me, won't you? He fancies both of us. If he can feel our bond, it might help him understand us better."

"Generous as always, jirí." Ander beamed, strands of raven hair partially concealing his eyes. His fresh-faced countenance was more sensual than ever in the fire's fading light. "What about the potion? Need help?"

"It's almost done," Thane said. "Rest awhile. I haven't forgotten how tired you are."

Ander looked like he wanted to argue, but a yawn chose that moment to escape. He nodded and went to the sleeping ledges, where the others had already retired for a nap.

After creating a small telos light and positioning it above the trestle table, Thane settled down for the final steps in creating the numbing ointment. The task was more demanding than he had admitted, requiring repeated tests pricking the underside of his forearm with a knifepoint after dabbing the skin with ingredients mixed in slightly different proportions. He wasn't satisfied until he could draw blood without the slightest sensation. He judged dawn was still three hours away.

He carefully wrapped the thick ointment in a broad leaf, then left the table and went to the ledges where his friends were sleeping. Erik and Skorri were curled together front to back, as they always slept since banishment from their boyhood home. Dannel was on his side, his blanket knocked to the ground, an erection making a long mound beneath his soft leathers.

Arriving at Ander's ledge, Thane sat beside his lover. The boy slept with lips parted, his long lashes fluttering as he dreamed. Sleep had stolen the cheerful smile from his lips, but revealed an innocence that was usually concealed. Thane wished he could protect that innocence, shield Ander from the brutality and pain that filled the world, but knew it was impossible. He stroked his partner's luxuriant black hair, his breath catching as Ander's eyes opened and engulfed him in a warm gaze.

"It's time?"

"The potion is done. I hope it works. I don't know what else we can try if it fails."

"It will work." Ander knuckled his eyes, then sat up and stretched. His trust in Thane's abilities was flattering, though the mage wasn't sure it was justified. But there was no point in fostering doubts; confidence in the potion's effects might be as important as the actual physical effects. Thane had found that *belief* in magic was half the battle in making it work.

"We still have a few hours until dawn," he said. "I decided we should go to the place Dannel went when he was entranced. The kei is close to the surface of things there. If we can touch it, we might be able to understand the ancient magic Pallaton spoke of. And we might not get another chance."

Ander nodded, but looked doubtful. "I understand. But if your philter works this will be the first time Dannel has even had sex. How can someone so inexperienced hope to touch the kei? There'll be no trance to help him this time."

"Remember, he's like a conduit. His problem isn't with his capacity to experience pleasure. It's with his ability to *control* pleasure. Before, the firestone always prevented control. If we neutralize the firestone and forge a bond, who knows what might happen?"

Ander shrugged, then slid to his feet. "We might as well try," he conceded. "As you say, this could be our only chance." He flashed a grin. "And I doubt Dannel will care. He'd fuck in the treetops if that's what you wanted."

"That's a really hard way to do it," Skorri said, stirring nearby. "Ask Erik. We almost fell out of the tree."

"Why were you . . . no, never mind." Thane shook his head. "I don't think I want to know." He went over to Dannel and nudged his shoulder. The fighter woke instantly and sprang up with fists raised. Thane jumped back at the unexpected reaction.

"Sorry," Dannel said, lowering his fists. "Habit. Sometimes you have to fight as soon as you waken."

Thane gave him a wry smile. "Useful for warriors, I'm sure. And likely to keep your lovers from getting careless." Fatigue left him as he started to contemplate the adventure ahead. "Tonight is a new beginning for you, Dannel. And for us as well. Get ready to ride!"

Two hours remained before dawn. Preparations were complete and there was no time for second thoughts. A sense of mystery and enormity hung in the air. Like other focal points where earth, air and water came together, here the connection between the everyday world and the kei was almost palpable to one who knew what to seek.

They stood on the platform at the center of the crater-like depression. The bowl retained heat so that even in the final hours before dawn it felt like a comfortable summer evening. Silvery fog wafted from the channels of rippling water, reaching halfway up the truncated pyramid. It was as if they occupied a small island in the clouds. Above them the Sentinel continued its stately rotation and cast reddish light over the ancient landscape. For the first time Thane felt the truly alien character of the temple's builders. They had not been exotic ancients; they had been something other than men. Something greater, beyond a doubt.

They had left their clothes at the base of the pyramid and ascended with only the numbing ointment, a jar of slick oil and blankets to spread as a cushion over the smooth stones.

Dannel looked up at the stars, his finely honed body gleaming like bronze in the ruddy light. He seemed subdued by the surroundings, but unafraid. *He has the courage to defy the firestone's curse*, Thane thought. *Where he does it is a smaller thing than accepting the challenge in the first place*. He smiled, feeling satisfaction. Dannel would be a strong addition to their brotherhood.

A few moments passed in silence, broken only by the soft splash of water racing down stone channels around them. Thane unwrapped the folded leaf and went to Dannel's side. Tearing an edge off the leaf, he rolled it into a cylinder and daubed one end in the ointment. Dannel watched, lavender eyes full of apprehension.

"I've already tested it on myself," Thane said. "It doesn't hurt. Flesh that it touches feels nothing, until it's washed off. If we guessed right, it will keep the firestone's spell from triggering. But there could be dangers."

Dannel nodded, solemn. "What dangers?"

Thane looked him in the eye. "The firestone's spell might still be triggered, and we'd fail. It's also possible the spell could mistake numbness for the firestone's removal. If that happens, it could harm you. Maybe even kill you."

Dannel swallowed, and his nostrils flared.

"It's your decision," Thane said. "It's a gamble. You're a freeman, Dannel. We won't question your choice."

Apprehension faded from Dannel's face, replaced by quiet pride. "You treat me as an equal, even though I'm pledged to you. For the first time in my life I *feel* free. I choose to go wherever you're willing to lead, Thane. Use the potion." He stood straight and stiff, mastering fear with a warrior's iron will.

Thane handed the folded leaf to Ander, then put one hand on Dannel's shoulder. With the other he painted the firestone and earlobe around it with a coating of ointment. Dannel trembled beneath his touch.

Thane held his breath, heartbeat drumming in his ears, trying to lend encouragement through his steady gaze. The ointment acted fast. Ten seconds passed, then twenty. Dannel's rapid breathing slowed and the rigid set of his shoulders eased. They broke into wide grins at the same moment.

Thane squeezed Dannel's shoulder, feeling lightheaded with relief. "The worst is over. The firestone hasn't harmed you. Now let's see if our ruse deceives the spell." He put a hand behind the boy's head and kissed him gently, keeping the rest of their bodies apart for the moment.

Thane slid his hands from Dannel's shoulders to his chest as the kiss lingered. The fighter shivered beneath the light touch and his breath quickened. Thane reacted strongly to the boy's excitement, his cock growing thick and hard in a few heartbeats. His hands slid lower, almost to Dannel's waist, as their kiss deepened. Their tongues met and jousted. The fighter started to tremble. Carefully, barely grazing the skin, Thane slid his hands to Dannel's hips.

Dannel gasped, breaking the kiss, closing his eyes and shaking like an exhausted runner on the verge of collapse. His long erection reared like a spear from his crotch.

Thane tightened his grip on the boy's hips. "It's working!" he said in an urgent whisper. "You've beaten the spell!" He took the final step, boldly pressing a hand against the belly of the boy's rampant cock.

Dannel opened his eyes, amazement and disbelief quickly shifting to jubilation. Laughing out loud, he wrapped his arms around Thane and squeezed him fiercely.

"*You* defeated the firestone, not I! You did it!"

The others crowded around them, pressing against Dannel and stroking his sleek body. The young fighter couldn't stop grinning.

Ander moved behind Dannel and wrapped his arms around the youth's chest. His upthrust cock aligned itself between the solid mounds of the fighter's buttocks as he nuzzled the boy's ear. "You've only begun to discover Thane's skills. It was lovemaking that led him to magic. And now pleasure can open the gates for you as well. Open your mind to it, Dannel!"

Skorri and Erik stepped back and sat at the edge of the platform, the blond nestled between his lover's legs and embraced by his strong arms. Thane stood alone before the fighter. The mage's sultry smile showed no hint of mysteries. He radiated sex, an earthy enthusiasm for fucking that could never be smothered by abstractions. He moved closer until their bodies pressed together. Their cocks throbbed, nudging each other and drooling precum, slicking their taut skin. Dannel closed his eyes and moaned softly. Thane was as breathless as his new initiate.

"Try to relax," Thane said. "This is new to you, and you've waited far too long. We'll go slow."

Dannel nodded, watching Thane through half-shut eyes. He trembled with desire. Ander stayed behind him, arms wrapped around his broad chest.

Thane sank to his knees, trailing his hands down the fighter's lean sides. Hard muscle etched ridges across the youth's abdomen as he tensed.

The boy's thick phallus reared upright in front of Thane. It was already slick with precum and reflected a wet sheen in the Sentinel's reddish light. It twitched in time with Dannel's heart, as rigid a cock as Thane had ever seen. He placed one hand on Dannel's hip and with the other traced the long muscles of the boy's inner thigh. Balls churned in the lightly haired scrotum. Another glistening bead of precum seeped out and drooped slowly from the glans. Thane leaned forward and caught it on his tongue, licking the sensitive spot where glans and shaft joined.

Dannel moaned, leaning back as his knees bent.

"You can do it," Ander said, squeezing the boy firmly. "You've defeated the firestone. Now it's time for your reward."

"I'm ready," the boy said, gasping. "Just give me time."

Thane nuzzled the rampant cock, rubbing his cheek against the shaft's underside. His fingers moved higher, tracing with feathery delicacy the line that divided Dannel's scrotum. Then he gripped the base of the shaft and angled it downward. He brushed his lips against the wet glans, kissing it lightly, until his lips glistened with precum. Dannel went rigid. Slowly, giving the inexperienced youth ample time to prepare, Thane parted his lips and let the glans enter his warm mouth.

The cock twitched between his encircling lips, oozing precum into his tongue. Thane moved both hands to the boy's hips, holding him steady, and let more of the straining penis slide into his mouth.

Dannel's back arched and he rose onto his toes. His hands grasped Thane's head, fingers enmeshed in the thick brown hair. "Slower," he gasped. "It's better than I ever dreamed!"

Ander chuckled softly, loosening his grip on Dannel's torso and raising a hand to fondle his right nipple. "That's because your dreams never contained Thane. He's the best lover in the world."

Thane paused, letting Dannel adjust to the new sensations, then resumed his slow glide down the rigid cock. The soft tip reached the back of his throat and slid past, filling him completely. Soon Thane's nose nestled in curly black pubic hairs. Dannel shivered as the mage tightened his lips around the shaft and reversed direction. The rigid penis emerged slowly, seemingly too big for the place it had occupied. Thane repeated the cycle, sucking with provocative deliberation.

"You're very lucky," Ander murmured in the boy's ear. "He's

the best lover, and the most beautiful."

Thane let Dannel's cock slide free and looked up at the dazed fighter, smiling seductively. "You'll have to decide that for yourself, and now you can. But tonight we complete your initiation. Now that you can share your body, you need to learn how pleasure forges bonds. Magic requires sharing body *and* spirit."

The glazed look faded from Dannel's eyes and he took a shuddering breath. "I want to learn," he said. "What should I do?"

Rising to his feet, Thane gazed into the youth's lavender eyes. "The strongest bonds are forged when flesh is fully joined. Since you lack experience, it would be best to let me take the more active part." He slid a hand down Dannel's muscled torso, barely grazing the smooth skin. "Are you ready for that? It won't hurt, I promise."

The fighter's glance darted to Thane's thick phallus, revealing apprehension, but he answered without hesitation. "I've learned to trust you. And even if there *is* pain, I don't care." He smiled nervously. "I trust Ander, too. He says no one could ask for a better lover than you, so I believe it."

Grinning, Thane moved his hand to the fighter's erection and gave it a gentle squeeze. "Ander is biased," he said. "In a way this is new for me too. I'm not sure I've ever been someone's first partner. I doubt it." He looked at Ander, eyes full of affection. "You're ready to help, jirí? I think Dannel would welcome it as much as I."

"More than ready," Ander replied. He released Dannel and stepped back. "Lie on your back," he instructed the fighter. "And don't worry. Sex with Thane is a priceless treasure. You'll see."

Dannel gave him a grateful look, then gracefully reclined on the layered blankets they had spread over the ancient stone. Any unease he felt at their exotic surroundings or the next phase of his initiation was more than offset by lust. His erection stretched across his hard belly from crotch to past his navel, still glistening with spit.

Thane knelt at his side, bending low to give Dannel a kiss, then swung around to straddle his body. He held most of his weight on elbows and knees as their chests touched lightly and their cocks jousted. The kiss lingered, growing more intense as each responded to the heat of the other's flesh. Thane waited until he felt Dannel begin to calm before doing more. Then he broke the kiss and let a little more of his weight press against the youth's solid body.

"Try to relax," Thane said. "Ander will take care of the lubricant. Concentrate on what you're feeling. If you can, imagine what

I'm feeling too. And let me know if there's anything you need or want."

Dannel's smile was ecstatic. "Feeling you against me is almost enough. If touching is this good, fucking is more than I can imagine. But I'm ready to try!"

Thane moved his knees between Dannel's legs, then drew them forward and pushed against his thighs. The boy's long legs spread wide. He wiggled excitedly as Thane's rigid penis rubbed against his cock. "First Ander will make us slick," Thane said, gently rocking against the lithe youth pinned beneath him. "Then he'll make you ready for me."

Dannel nodded once, his trusting gaze never wavering.

Thane slid his hands beneath the youth's shoulders and held him firmly while Ander took the jar of lubricant and moved behind them. A moment later the mage felt warm fingers, coated with slick oil, brush against his balls. Ander's wrist pressed against his scrotum as he funneled lubricant into the cleft of Dannel's ass. Mild fragrance like freshly cut hay filled the air.

Ander's finger tickled the rosette of the fighter's ass. Surprise flickered across the boy's handsome features and his lips parted in a soft gasp.

Thane grinned, happy to share in the youth's discovery of his body's capacity for pleasure. Dannel squirmed beneath him as Ander's slick finger slipped inside the ring of muscle.

Suddenly Dannel's eyelids fluttered and his eyes rolled back. His body seemed to vibrate in Thane's arms. At the same moment the mage felt a warm rush of pleasure mixed with overwhelming anticipation.

Within a heartbeat Dannel's eyes opened wide. "What happened?"

It took Thane a moment to answer. He could scarcely believe it, but the sensations he was experiencing were impossible to deny. He could feel the gentle probing of Ander's finger as it slid deeper into Dannel's ass. A bond had already started to link him with his new partner.

"We're forging a bond," Thane said. "Faster than I've ever seen, by far. Your flesh is a conduit for anima even *without* the firestone. You're going to make an exceptional mage!"

"I feel it too," Ander said, sounding breathless. He continued his slow caresses, working lubricant deep inside Dannel.

Thane used his knees to push Dannel's legs further apart, giving Ander easier access to the tender flesh. The young fighter gripped him tightly, looking bewildered by the torrent of sensations.

"You're doing fine," Thane murmured. The boy's cock pulsed against him, making their skin slick. "Give it time. There's no rush."

"I'll try to make it last," Dannel replied. He licked his lips, his eyes half shut. "It's all so new."

Another surge of quivering pleasure shot through Thane as Ander slid a second finger inside Dannel's ass and stroked the tight channel. The bond was growing stronger by the second. He felt Ander's gentle touch as if his own body was being penetrated. Slow twisting motion gradually loosened the muscle as it clamped on the slippery fingers. Using the newly formed bond, Thane provided calm reassurance to the nervous initiate.

Soon the clenching stopped and Ander used his fingers to funnel more lubricant into the opening. When the channel was thoroughly coated he poured more oil onto his palm and reached between the embracing youths. Slimy fingers wrapped around Thane's hard cock and gave it a slippery stroke, coating it from root to tip.

Dannel gasped and went rigid as shuddering waves of pleasure echoed back and forth through the link. It was plain sensations were flowing freely through the bond in both directions.

Thane slid down a few inches, letting his cock slip free of its confinement between their bodies. Ander gripped it lightly and pulled it down until the glans rested against the rosette of Dannel's ass. The well-lubricated opening encircled the tip in a warm circle of oily flesh.

Thane paused, his heart thudding. Dannel clung to him fiercely. He felt the boy's tension, and through the bond felt the presence of a cock touching his own ass. "Trust me," he said in a whisper. "I'll wait until you're ready."

The night was quiet, with a light breeze that caressed Thane's back like a silk sheet. He felt Ander's fingers circling and lightly stroking his slick cock, patiently holding it in position until the fighter was ready to accept it. Gradually, the youth's muscles relaxed. Dannel gazed into Thane's eyes and gave a small nod.

Slowly, carefully feeling for sensation through their bond, Thane increased the pressure of his cock against Dannel's ass. Skin moved across oiled skin without friction. The glans slipped inside the ring of muscle and Thane stopped. Dannel's eyes widened and a delighted smile lit his face.

"Feels good," he murmured.

Thane returned the grin. "I know. I feel it too, remember?" He rocked his hips, moving his cockhead back and forth an inch deeper in his partner's ass. Dannel gasped, arching his back and pressing his erection against Thane's abdomen.

Sizzling rapture throbbed through the bond, far out of proportion to the pleasure Thane was causing. Years of longing were being washed away in the youth's first real lovemaking. The mage's heart raced in sympathetic union; restraint was difficult.

Even without the bond, Dannel's ecstatic expression showed he was ready for more. Thane tightened his embrace and slid his cock another inch into the muscular youth. The glans nudged the sensitive spot a little inside the opening, eliciting a heartfelt moan from Dannel. A bloom of pleasure echoed in Thane. He had forgotten what the first time felt like, but was now experiencing it again by way of the fighter's virgin body. Barely able to control himself, he slowly slid his cock the rest of its length into the clenching ass. Dannel's muscles squeezed at him, as if trying to seize the slippery shaft of flesh, making their mutual pleasure soar.

"It's all in," Ander said softly, moving his hand to rest on one of Thane's solid buttocks. "Smooth as you please." He paused, then continued in a hoarse voice. "I still share what you feel, just from touching you. I'm so hard it hurts!"

Thane understood the sentiment. His cock throbbed as he slowly withdrew from Dannel's ass, then slid back in with a single smooth glide. The sensation of being penetrated with a long cock mingled with the tantalizing effect of Dannel's ass milking his rigid penis. They began to move against each other with a single mind. Thane started to lose himself in the young fighter's frenzy. Sex had always been terrific, but fucking the young fighter was like being in a whirlwind. Anima seemed to spring from the earth itself and flood his body with tickling filaments.

Dannel's head lashed back and forth. He wrapped his arms around Thane's back and curled his body in time with the mage's thrusts, his legs splayed wide. Silvery specks of light began to trace his body from head to toe, following lines of muscle. Thane felt as if he was on a runaway steed, gaining momentum. Whatever forces Dannel was tapping were gathering too fast. Breaking the pace took every shred of his will.

He shifted position, releasing his grip on Dannel's torso and rising to his knees while keeping his cock ensheathed in the boy's ass. He put a hand behind each of the fighter's knees and lifted the legs so Dannel's heels rested on his shoulders. The increased separation of their bodies seemed to help. Dannel blinked and looked at him as if dumbfounded.

"Is it always like this?"

"Only at the end, when you cum." Thane continued to fuck with slow strokes, pulling his cock out until only the glans remained inside, then sliding back in until his pubic hairs brushed his partner's balls. Traceries of light continued to race over Dannel's body. The boy's quivering erection confirmed what Thane already knew: the youth loved his first experience with fucking. "Maybe I shouldn't be surprised," Thane said. "Your capacity for pleasure is incredible. It might even be part of what you were trained for, and why the firestone was so important for controlling you. But now you're free of the firestone and the pleasure remains."

Dannel smiled blissfully. "It does! And I feel your pleasure too. It pleases me." He paused, concentration flitting over his face, then continued. "And I think I feel Ander, too. He feels wonderful!"

Ander answered with a shaky laugh. "Almost too wonderful. You're very sexy, Dannel." He had been maintaining contact with the lovers through a hand on Thane's rump, and was as aroused as they.

The fighter lifted his head enough to give Ander a sultry look. "Could I give pleasure to both of you at once? I'm not skilled, but I'd like to share with you as well."

"We could try," Thane said. Now that he had regained control of his body, confidence was growing again. The fighter's potential was unprecedented and he was eager to explore it. "Join us, Ander. Let's show Dannel what he's been missing."

One invitation was enough. Ander moved around to kneel above Dannel's head, then leaned forward, putting his hands on the youth's chest. "I have a favor to return," he said. He brushed his lips against Dannel's. "Rest easy. Thane and I can take care of things for now."

"Whatever you say," Dannel said. He stretched luxuriantly, arms overhead, as Thane's phallus slid into his slick ass. His lean body glistened with fine traceries in the reddish light.

Leaning further forward, Ander kissed Dannel's neck, then his chest. He moved to a nipple, lapping at it with delicate licks, as his hands moved down the youth's sides.

Thane watched, fascinated, as Ander skillfully tantalized the new initiate. A new layer of complexity was added to their lovemaking as the link between Dannel and Ander strengthened. Soon the mage felt Ander's licks as if there were no intermediary. He slowed his thrusts even further, trying to quell the mushrooming flurry of sensations.

Ander moved lower. He concentrated on the well-defined ridges of Dannel's abdomen, at first avoiding the quivering cock stretching across the youth's belly. Thane shuddered, sharing the fighter's terrible anticipation.

At last Ander stopped teasing. Placing his hands on Dannel's waist, he bent down and licked the underside of the boy's glans.

Dannel jerked like a hornet had stung him. But the sensation he experienced was no sting; an intense stab of pleasure raced through all three of them like lightning. They teetered on the verge of orgasm.

After a moment the sensation passed. Thane slowly let out the breath he had been holding. "That was *strong*. But having you share the bond helps, Ander. There were more places for the anima to go."

"Should I try again?" Ander asked.

"Just go slow. Ready, Dannel?"

The fighter murmured consent, though he seemed distracted by Ander's rigid penis above his face. Thane sympathized. Ander's cock was as perfect as the rest of him.

Ander traced the length of Dannel's cock with his tongue, starting at the base and working his way to the tip. The fighter's ass clenched on Thane's shaft as the mage resumed his deep thrusts.

Their bond was strengthening by the moment. Dannel seemed able to draw strength directly from the kei, and to use the bond to sense how his partners controlled their pleasure. His lifetime of physical discipline, and his capacity to forge bonds with unprecedented speed, soon enabled him to react to Ander's caresses with more restraint.

Ander took the boy's cockhead in his mouth again and let it rest on his tongue. This time the fighter responded by reaching between them and angling Ander's cock down so the glans touched his lips. Tilting his head back, he took the slippery cockhead into his mouth.

Dannel's legs tensed and his hands gripped Ander's hips tightly, but the surge of pleasure sweeping through their bond passed.

They began to make love in earnest, their athletic bodies moving with effortless coordination. Thane's head swam. The depth of their union was deeper than he had ever experienced. His consciousness seemed to flow between their bodies. He closed his eyes and felt himself lying on his back with a long cock gliding in and out of his ass. In the next heartbeat he felt himself crouched on hands and knees with Dannel's erection filling his throat while his own penis was lashed by the boy's avid tongue. His companions' minds swirled through the mix, sharing his awe and delight at the merger of their bodies and spirits. Their thoughts united, coordinating their joined bodies to coax every possible pleasure from their joined flesh. Their erections throbbed, almost painfully hard.

Thane opened his eyes and gasped. The pillars surrounding the platform glowed with warm yellow light, making the flowing water descending from the rim sparkle like molten gold. Their bodies were enveloped in a red halo that had expanded to fill the whole platform. Erik and Skorri, engulfed by the anima, had yielded to its power and were sucking each other avidly. Sweat sparkled on their bodies like rubies.

Thane started thrusting with faster strokes. He took Dannel's ankles and lifted them from his shoulders, spreading the youth's legs wide. His hips moved without conscious control. The surrounding pillars blazed like torches as their pleasure soared beyond the point of turning back.

With a single thought, the three youths surrendered to the blazing ecstasy coursing through their bodies. Their cocks convulsed in unison, spewing thick jets of cum. Thane felt his cock jerking and sliding deep inside Dannel, slithering through hot semen while still spurting with strong jolts. His mouth filled with the familiar taste of Ander's cum and the musky tang of Dannel's seed.

They were caught in a web of pleasure as anima channeled from Dannel's body coursed through them. Light streamed from the fighter in shimmering waves. The air seemed to vibrate with deep tones as the curtain between the kei and the everyday world wavered. Erik and Skorri moaned, wrapped in a tight head-to-toe embrace, as each emptied his seed in the other's throat.

At last their straining bodies relented, releasing them from climaxes extended nearly beyond endurance. Thane withdrew his cock from Dannel's ass and collapsed on top of his partners in an exhausted heap.

Ander rolled onto his back and moved around to make room for the mage. They kissed deeply, sharing traces of Dannel's cum that smeared Ander's lips, before aligning themselves with the fighter and bringing him into their embrace.

The youth looked dazed. "Is it always like this?" he asked, his chest still rising and falling with rapid breaths.

Thane laughed and tousled the boy's curls. "With you, maybe. That was no ordinary tumble. Perhaps it was the firestone, or your training. It might have been your long deprivation. Whatever the cause, I've *never* seen so much anima from a new initiate! Defeating the firestone hasn't changed your ability to channel energy from the kei."

Ander put a hand on the fighter's sweaty chest. "And you're

good at sex, Dannel. Already better than most companions, and you've only started to learn about love."

"You have nothing to worry about," Thane agreed. He reached down and cupped the fighter's genitals, still warm and moist from Ander's sucking. "Now that you're free of the firestone you're going to be very busy!"

"Thane." Erik's voice was low and soft, the voice he used during a hunt. "Take a look."

Thane turned and saw the hunter pointing up. He looked toward the sky.

The Sentinel had changed. Its spokes had stopped spinning and the orb at its center had darkened.

"What does it mean?" Ander asked, unconsciously sidling close for reassurance. Thane put an arm around his shoulders. "Maybe it was affected by the anima we created. Or maybe it's signaling something else. I think we'd better find out."

The air cooled rapidly as they descended the pyramid and donned their clothes. Mist arose from the waters flowing around them and thickened. Thane was seized by a sudden conviction. Danger was near.

15

ROCKS BOUNCED down the slope as they hurriedly descended from the ancient mound's summit. The Sentinel hovered above them like an unblinking eye. Ander could tell Thane was worried by its change, and felt a shiver of premonition. He glanced at Dannel. The fighter still looked amazed by his first real love-making. The bond they had forged lingered, unusually strong for a new lover, and conveyed the youth's profound happiness.

They reached the clearing where their horses were tethered. Before mounting, Thane signaled for the others to gather around. "Keep your eyes open," he said. "There's something strange in the air. Something *other* than that Sentinel."

"Can you tell what it is?" Ander asked.

"No. Maybe Pallaton is watching to make sure we leave with the dawn. Maybe it's something else. It's like there's something moving in the kei, and it feels dangerous. So be careful."

His unease growing, Ander mounted his horse and turned it into the forest. Losing sight of the Sentinel and its unnatural light seemed to help. They rode silently, senses straining, in unspoken agreement to collect their belongings from the warriors' lodge and leave the valley without further delay. Even Thane had said it would be unwise to test Pallaton's patience.

They soon emerged from among the pines. The valley floor lay below, the lodge to their left and the Torii Gates to their right. Erik reigned in his horse and pointed. "There," he said. "At the pass. See it?"

Ander stopped and stared. At first he saw nothing; the hunter's eyesight was keen as a hawk's. Then he saw what Erik had noticed. A short distance below the pass, the Sentinel's light glinted off metal. A moment later he saw the indistinct shapes of robed figures moving down the slope.

Dannel exhaled through clenched teeth, a strange hissing sound. "They must have left Skarn as soon as the Sentinel appeared and driven their horses until they foundered." He looked sick. "The pass is the only way out, as far as I know. They'll post a guard there while searching the rest of the valley."

"Is there a place we could hide?" Ander asked.

Dannel shook his head, scowling. "They'll know we're here and won't stop searching until they find us. They'll have dogs, get our scent from the lodge. There's no escape. We lingered too long."

"Then we fight," Erik said. "If they don't leave many men at the pass and we take them by surprise, we might get through."

Dannel shook his head. "They'll leave more than enough guards. And they'll all be Torii Guardians. Even if you had your bow, you couldn't get them all before they overwhelmed us. I could hold off a few, but not for long."

"You're forgetting something," Thane said. "We know a place where they can't follow. Not unless they've learned to open doors with magical keys."

Ander stood up in his stirrups, grasping at the shred of hope. "Pallaton's lair beneath the temple!" A moment later he frowned and settled back into his saddle. "But the entrance is on the wrong side of the Torii Gates. We can't reach it."

"We can try," Thane replied. His determined expression was almost enough to calm Ander's fears.

"Whatever you decide, you'd best decide it fast," Dannel said. "They'll be sending out scouts. Before long we'll have to fight just to reach the Torii Gates."

"You're right," Thane agreed. "Let's go!"

Moments later they were galloping across the clearing at breakneck speed. Ander bent low over his horse, hugging it with his legs as his bones shook to his mount's jarring stride. They plunged into the forest again, this time following a narrow trail. Tips of branches grazed his head and pine needles clung to his hair.

Soon the forest cleared. A cliff rose majestically before them, its stone appearing to glow beneath the Sentinel's eerie light. They pounded down the sand-swept road at the cliff's base. Ander squinted as gritty sand flew, stinging his face. The air smelled of horse and dust. Rounding the shoulder of a bluff, they entered the courtyard at the foot of the Torii Gates.

Ander was taken aback when he saw the barrier blocking the Gates. The descriptions he had heard didn't do justice to the thrumming curtain of energy filling the huge doorway. Low vibrations shook the earth, making their mounts raise their heads and look around with wild eyes. Ander calmed his horse, then swung out of his saddle. Anima whipped him like searing desert winds. Looking up at the towering rip in the world's skin made him feel like an ant before a bonfire.

Thane dismounted and handed his reins to Erik, then joined Ander a few yards from the threshold. A line in the sand, slowly weaving like an undulating snake, showed the barrier's perimeter.

"I had no idea," Ander said, feeling queasy. "It's *huge*. How can we hope to overcome it?"

Thane reached toward the barrier. Ander's hand tingled with

the pricking of a thousand tiny needles as the mage's sensations flowed through their bond. He clenched his fist and grimaced, biting his tongue as the mage probed the fingers of the barrier.

At last Thane stepped back, looking thoughtful. "You're right," he said. "We can't force our way through. And I can't tell how to undo the spell."

A knot formed in Ander's stomach. "Then we can't take refuge here. Erik's right. We'll have to take our chances trying to fight our way through the pass."

Thane's expression turned stubborn. "Maybe. But you saw how many men were at the pass. Most are probably Torii Guardians. Dannel's right about our chances against them. It would be folly."

"What choice do we have?" Ander said. He felt trapped, savagely suppressed a surge of panic. "We have to do *something*."

Dannel had been standing to the side, watching silently, but now joined them. "Ander's right," he said. "If our time has come, we should give them a fight and hope for luck."

Thane's gaze rested on Dannel, a far-away look on his face. For a moment Ander thought his lover was overcome by the looming defeat and was losing his reason. Then a gleam lit the mage's eyes and he stood taller.

"If we're going to try something desperate, let's try something that might work," Thane said. "We can't force our way through the barrier guarding the Gates and we can't undo the spell, but anima is still anima. We could try draining it away."

The suggestion seemed laughable, but the mage's expression was deadly serious. Ander took a deep breath, feeling like he was diving from a cliff into unknown waters, then nodded. "I can't imagine what you're thinking, but I'm not going to start doubting you now. How can I help?"

Thane put a hand on his shoulder and squeezed hard. "Thank you, jirí. I don't know if this will work, but it's our best chance." He turned to Dannel. "You're the key," he said. "We've seen how you channel anima. You've never been able to control it before, but things have changed. You've subdued the firestone, and you've started to form bonds with Ander and me. I think maybe *you* could defeat the barrier, with our help."

Dannel gaped. "But . . . I don't know anything about working magic! And there's no time to learn. The hierophants and Torii Guardians will get here before the sun's up."

"Our bond is strong enough for me to help. All you'll need to do is let the power flow through you, drain it away from the Gate. I'll worry about trying to control it." His expression was grim. "It's a gamble, though. If the power overwhelms you, or I lose control, we won't survive."

Dannel held his gaze. "I never expected to live forever. If this is our best chance, let's take it now, while there's still time."

Thane smiled fleetingly. "The spirit of a true warrior. I'm glad you joined our cause." He turned and extended a hand to Ander.

"Your bond with Dannel is as strong as mine. Help me link with him. Between the three of us, we might succeed." He tugged his shirt off and dropped it on the ground. "Bonds are strongest when flesh touches flesh. Take off your shirts and we'll begin." He turned to Erik and Skorri, who stood beside the huddle of nervous horses. "You two stay back. If something goes wrong, try to get back to the Lyceum. Tell Sorel and Nicolai what happened. I'm counting on you."

The boys nodded, looking somber.

"Water should help dissipate the anima," Thane said, pointing at the shallow streams flowing from openings at each side of the Gate. "We'll stand there, try to draw the anima into the water."

Ander led the way, stepping into the clear water and walking to the center of the channel on the left side of the Gates. The water was only ankle deep but it still sent a chill through his boots and conjured images of icy underground caverns. He turned and waited for guidance from the mage.

Thane took position next to Dannel, facing the anima barrier an arm's length away, then gestured for Ander to stand on the fighter's other side. They each put an arm around his waist.

Ander felt Thane's arm touching his own, felt the reassuring warmth of their bond renewing itself. A few seconds later he grew aware of Dannel's more muted presence in the link. Though the youth was new to the art, he slid smoothly into the sharing of feelings. Thane was right; it was as if the fighter had been made for this purpose. Only the hierophants' compulsive secrecy had prevented them from tapping the boy's power.

They allowed the bond to grow and deepen, opening their awareness to the strange forces surging across the Gate's portal. Thane's intelligence, Dannel's strength and Ander's empathy flowed together to create a new balance. It was a wonder, unlike anything Ander had ever experienced, but Thane left him no time to savor it.

"We're ready," the mage said. "Try touching the barrier, Dannel. Go slowly. Ander and I will direct the energy into the water."

Moments later a telos light appeared in the water at their feet. Ander had never seen one beneath water and was momentarily distracted by its beauty. Light shimmered and refracted in the water's ripples, like a circular rainbow behind wavy glass. Thane fed more anima into it, strengthening the pathway, until the water flowing past their feet looked like a path made of jewels.

"Now," Thane whispered.

Dannel raised his right hand and slowly moved it forward. Air seemed to thicken around it, like a clear liquid, as his fingers touched the magical barrier.

A wave of vertigo hit Ander. His legs felt weak. Dannel staggered but maintained contact with the sparkling curtain.

"You're doing fine," Thane said, tightening his grip on the fighter's waist. "Think about the water. Imagine the power flowing through you and into the stream. I'll show you."

Though the advice was meant for Dannel, Ander followed it too. He calmed his thoughts and concentrated on his bond with Thane. Soon he sensed Dannel's confused struggle with the welter of impressions and forces. He reached out with his mind, felt a jolt of surprise followed by relief when Dannel sensed him.

Ander brought their inner sparks together, introducing the fighter to the elusive trick of merging consciousness in a bond while simultaneously acting independently. The youth adapted with startling swiftness despite the strong current of anima buffeting his body.

"Good," Thane murmured. They began to breathe deeply, in unison, as the mage showed the others how to guide anima without being engulfed by it. Ander lost himself in the challenge, even forgetting the urgency of their task. It was like the boyhood game of making a ball on a stretched sheet go where you wanted by tugging and tilting the sheet, only this time they were bending the fabric of the world itself and directing forces he could scarcely comprehend. Only Thane's calm assurance kept them from disaster.

"You've got it," Thane said. A warm glow of approval surged through the bond. "Open yourself to more power. We have to do it *now*. Time is running out."

Dannel took another breath, held it in, and pushed his hand fully inside the curtain of energy guarding the Gates.

The anima cascading through the fighter's body became a torrent. Ander held tight and concentrated on maintaining the precarious balance of forces in the kei. It was like walking a tightrope through a gale.

Tremors shook the ground. Ander heard the horses whinny, heard Erik and Skorri trying to soothe them, but had no time to look. His mind, along with Dannel and Thane's, had forged an unstable chute through which power roared like a river suddenly squeezed into a narrow chasm.

Dannel raised his other hand and thrust it into the barrier. The rumble got stronger and rose in pitch, like a giant's roar. The water at their feet grew warm, sand swirled around them in spiraling eddies. The curtain changed from sparkling blue to brilliant gold. Dannel stood motionless, barely breathing, his body rigid as a statue. The firestone at his ear sparkled brilliant white. His unguarded expression revealed fear as well as the iron discipline that held fear in check.

Mist wafted from the stream as it flowed past their feet. Sweat ran into Ander's eyes; he felt himself tiring but didn't dare distract the others from their task. The barrier hissed like a geyser.

Pressure built in Ander's head. It felt intolerable, even though he recognized it as a mere echo of Dannel's sensations. He wanted to scream. Instead he ground his teeth together and threw his last shreds of strength into constraining the forces ripping through the fighter's body.

There was a loud *crack*, like a mighty tree snapping in half. Cool air washed over them as the barrier dissolved in rippling circles centered on Dannel's hands. The fighter lurched forward as resistance vanished, but Thane and Ander caught him as he staggered. Sweat drenched their torsos and Dannel shook from fatigue.

"You did it!" Skorri shouted. He and Erik ran to the portal, relief filling their faces.

"We'd better not linger," Thane said. "The spell's power might be replenished from whatever source it draws on. We don't have the strength to drain it again."

"You're right," Dannel agreed. "And any nearby scouts will have heard the noise it made. We'll have company soon."

"Send the horses off," Thane said. "They can't go underground with us, and we don't want them to draw attention to the Torii Gates." Erik obliged, swatting the horses on the rump. The startled animals bolted for the forest.

Ander watched the departing steeds until they vanished among the trees, then turned and followed the others into the high gallery. They moved quickly, pausing only briefly when darkness forced them to create a telos light. The glyphs beckoned for attention but Ander kept his eyes downcast, searching for the concealed passage to the subterranean chambers. Winds had shifted the sand and swept away all traces of their previous visits.

The gallery seemed to go on endlessly. Ander grew disoriented, unsure how quickly they had traveled during their earlier explorations, knowing that pursuit was making his mind race. He was brushing sand from a likely looking area when Erik appeared next to him and made a covert gesture. Glancing up, Ander saw the others were already gathered near the wall. The hunter gestured for Ander to follow.

Once they were all together Erik drew them into a close circle. "We're not alone," he whispered. "I heard something between us and the entrance. Very quiet. Maybe men, maybe not. Keeping just beyond the light."

Ander resisted the temptation to turn and look. "For how long?" he asked.

Erik shrugged. "I heard a sound like footfalls about a minute ago. If it's men, they're just watching so far. That might change once they know we've heard them."

"Scouts," Thane guessed. "We can't let them see where we're going or we'll be followed. We'll have to fight."

"Can you make the light vanish, then come back brighter?" Dannel asked. "It would help if we can surprise them."

"You have a plan?" Ander asked.

"Give me ten seconds of darkness. I'll try to get close without being heard. Then make the brightest light you can. You'd better do it now. If they're scouts, they'll be getting suspicious."

"And if it's not scouts?" Ander asked.

Dannel grinned fiercely. "Then I'm the one who'll be surprised. Come to my aid if you can, but don't follow until there's light again. It would be dangerous."

"I understand," Thane said. "Good luck. Ready?"

Dannel nodded once. An instant later the telos light vanished and total darkness engulfed them. Ander held his breath, his fear of underground places surging. He counted to ten, feeling as if demons stood directly behind him. If Dannel was moving, he was too stealthy to be heard.

Suddenly a telos light blazed overhead, five times brighter than the light Thane had been maintaining earlier. The thud of colliding bodies echoed between the tall stone walls, followed by a sharp *snap*. Ander spun around to catch a glimpse of Dannel flinging a man's limp body aside, his head twisted at a grotesque angle. The fighter immediately moved toward the entrance, blocking retreat by a second man who had been lurking in darkness.

Instead of attacking, the leather-clad man crossed his arms and sneered. "You're a coward as well as a traitor, Dannel. Were you afraid to face a challenge?"

Dannel remained in a crouch, his expression stormy. "You didn't come here for a fair fight, Zevon. And you won't delay me with trickery."

The older man assumed a fighting posture but didn't advance. His sneer turned into a glare of pure hatred. "Too bad they want you alive," he said. "You betrayed us. I won't get to kill you myself, but I'll see you screaming in the dungeons. They're planning tortures they haven't used in a hundred years."

"Threats are for slaves like you," Dannel replied. He moved forward, balancing on the balls of his feet and watching his opponent warily. "I'm free now, Zevon. Free of the hierophants and released from the firestone. Your loyalty to your masters was misplaced."

Zevon growled and raised his fists. "Liar! You were always a fool. What you say is impossible. Time to stop dreaming and pay for your treachery."

"Enough talk, Zevon!"

Dannel leapt forward. The fighters engaged, lashing out with vicious kicks and spinning like acrobats as they dodged blows. Zevon was older and slower, but Dannel was fatigued from breaching the barrier at the Torii Gates. His torso glistened with sweat while his more heavily muscled opponent moved with assured strength. Both landed bruising blows. The pace changed, momentarily slowing. Dannel's face was impassive, his attention totally focused on combat.

Erik moved toward Zevon, coming from behind, getting within twenty feet. "Stay back," Dannel said, his eyes never straying from Zevon. "He knows you're there. He'll use you as a weapon. Leave him to me." Erik looked uncertain.

"Do as he says," Thane said.

The hunter started to step back. Before he moved more than a yard Zevon whirled and sprang at him. Erik raised his arms in belated self-defense. At the same moment Dannel yelled and charged.

Blows fell in a blur. Erik fell and rolled to the side, bleeding from a split lip, as the Torii Guardians continued to pummel each other. Dannel was at a disadvantage from his lighter weight but attacked with such ferocity Ander was taken aback.

Suddenly Dannel landed a rabbit punch in the middle of Zevon's chest as the man inhaled. An agonized expression flashed across his face. He momentarily dropped his defenses. Without hesitation, Dannel joined his hands into a doubled fist and delivered a crushing blow to his opponent's neck.

Zevon fell onto his back. His breath rasped horribly as he

clawed at his crushed windpipe. The rasp turned into a gurgle and his struggles stopped. Dannel got to his feet and stepped back, his chest heaving. When he looked up, Ander was surprised by the sorrow in his eyes.

"I've known him since I was sold to the temple," Dannel said. "In a way, we were friends. He had almost finished his indenture. I'm sorry we had to fight."

Ander went to the fighter and put a hand on his arm. "It wasn't your choice. You did what was needed. He was a warrior, he'd understand."

"I know." Dannel put a hand on top of Ander's. Their eyes met, and Ander could see the youth's acceptance of what fate had demanded. "We're not out of here yet," the fighter said. "We'd best continue our search."

"Found it!" Thane called, his voice tight with urgency. Fifteen minutes had been required to locate the concealed entry, though to Ander the time felt like hours. The rest of the Torii Guardians would not be far behind the scouts.

They clustered around the mage, hurriedly brushing sand from the intricate mosaic, revealing the hairline crack that marked their goal. Escape beckoned and Ander began to breathe easier.

"Keep still," Thane said. "I need to concentrate." He closed his eyes and took a deep breath, dimming the telos light to a mere flicker as he gathered his strength. After a few seconds he extended his right hand and moved it as if caressing an invisible ball directly in front of him. He paused, then repeated the gesture. A puzzled expression flit across his face, settling into a frown. His eyes opened and fixed on Ander.

"Something has changed. I'm not finding the spell we used before. Help me look?"

Ander moved behind the mage, putting his arms around his torso and pulling their bodies together. Their bond deepened and strengthened.

"Try now," Ander said.

Thane closed his eyes again while Ander shared anima through the bond and opened his mind to the mage's perceptions. The feel of swirling currents was strong as ever. But there was no hint of the pivot point they had used to operate the concealed entrance. They searched together, with increasing desperation, but soon there could be no doubt. The psychic key for gaining entry had vanished.

Ander opened his eyes and stepped back, cold sweat on his

brow. "It's no good. The spell's *gone*. Pallaton must have sealed the passage." His throat was dry. "Where do we go now?"

"Wait," Erik said, holding up a hand for silence. "Do you see it?" He pointed in the direction of the Gates. "Douse the light, Thane."

Thane snapped his fingers and darkness engulfed them.

At first Ander saw nothing. Darkness wrapped him like a smothering blanket. Then a dim glow materialized in the distance like fire beyond the horizon. Moments later the murmur of voices reached them as faint echoes.

"Sounds like a dozen or more," Ander whispered. "They're not trying to hide."

"What now?" Skorri asked, his voice timorous.

"Three choices," Dannel said. "Go back and meet them. Wait here. Or go deeper and hope we find something that could help us."

"We keep going," Thane said. "At least we'll gain some time. Use it, think of a plan!" He conjured another telos light, a tiny red orb that barely provided enough light to see by, and beckoned for the others to follow.

They retreated as quickly as they could without making noise. Soon the corridor began sloping down. Faint vibrations in the floor grew stronger and a thrum of power filled the air. Ander noticed that the glyphs covering the high walls glowed faintly. It was as if the power dwelling at the temple's heart brought the stone itself to life.

Ander felt wisps of the disorientation that had snared them the first time they visited this place. A rectangle of pulsing red light appeared ahead of them, marking the entrance to the circular chamber where the portal into the kei stood.

"Wait," Ander said. "We should think a minute before going further."

Thane stopped and turned. The mage was fighting to control his expression, but there was no way to conceal the despair. Ander's heart ached. He was more saddened by his lover's defeated look than by his own likely fate.

"Remember what happened last time we went in there?" Ander said. "You and Dannel were both possessed. What if it happens again?"

"What choice do we have?" Thane asked. "Do you have a plan?"

"No," Ander admitted. He gazed into his lover's eyes, almost unable to continue. Thane had suffered so much, fought so hard. Now that their remaining time together might be numbered in minutes, he couldn't bear the thought of losing even a second of what they had left. He clenched his hands into fists, struggling to keep from trembling. "I . . . I don't think there's anywhere left to run. We might as well make our stand here, jirí. Where we'll at least be able to put up a fight."

Thane nodded, looking as desperately unhappy as Ander had ever seen him. Then he held his head high and took a deep breath as the others gathered around him. "You're right. We should be together now. Fight well, friends. And remember, the kei is full of mysteries. A part of Lucian survived there after his death. If we lose this fight, I hope we find each other again. Somewhere else, someplace better." His gaze returned to Ander and his voice softened. "I'll never stop searching for you. Not ever."

Ander took Thane in his arms and held him tightly. There was no time left for words, none were needed.

Angry shouts echoed behind them, followed by the clatter of booted feet on stone.

"They've found Zevon and Aremis," Dannel said.

They formed a line and waited. Tumultuous voices quickly grew louder and the flickering light of torches cast distended shadows on the soaring walls. Ander felt strangely calm as destiny rushed toward him. He wouldn't have traded his time with Thane for even a hundred years of a quiet life.

Suddenly men boiled down the gallery like bats swarming from a cave. Most wore the black leathers of Torii Guardians, but men wearing red and yellow robes moved among them. Ander raised his fists, feeling as futile as a hare defying wolves, but Thane stood at his side and he was determined to meet his fate with honor.

The clamor was deafening, the air thick with the sour stench of men who had traveled hard for days.

The onrushing tide of men abruptly slowed and came to a stop fifty feet away, like a wave cresting on a beach. There were at least two score, a third priests and the rest fighters. They spaced themselves across the wide corridor, muttering and glaring with murderous intensity. A man stepped away from the mob and strode toward them. Torchlight glinted on his steel skullcap.

Thane lowered his hands, stunned. "Varian! What's *he* doing here?"

Ander was speechless. Somehow the approaching priest of Yataghan was more terrifying than the phalanx of warriors. Death in combat was one thing; but the followers of Yataghan inflicted slow death by torture as their chief sacrament. Varian approached to within ten feet and stopped in front of Thane. The mage glared at his nemesis, not deigning to speak.

Varian examined Thane from head to foot, from all appearances more curious than hostile. At last he looked Thane in the eye. "You're a mystery to me," he said. "What they say must be true, the zamindar has lost his reason. Why else should he be so concerned over a pretty boy? But I don't care. The reward is mine. That's all that matters."

"You've earned no reward," Thane said. "We spared your life and this is how you repay us. You're lower than a dung beetle."

Varian's lip curled with a cold smile. "You're trying to provoke me. Is that why the zamindar wants you? To avenge some stupid insult before he dies?" He laughed, a guttural sound filled with malice, then took a step back. "You can't escape," he said, gesturing at the men behind him with a sweep of his arm. "I've brokered an agreement with the mystics from Skarn. They'll do my bidding in return for a share of the prize. But I need you alive to collect the reward. Preferably undamaged, since the journey is long and time is short. The zamindar's enemies could topple him or his body could fail him any day. Either way the reward would vanish. I can't permit that."

Thane hesitated. "Topple him? He rules with an iron fist."

Varian smirked at the mage's confusion. "That was when he was an ordinary tyrant. Now he's a madman, a dying one at that. He tore his kingdom apart in an insane search for *you*. His cronies abandoned him once they saw his mind weaken, and the peasants have seized their chance. Half the manor houses in Izmir have been set to the torch." He laughed again, seeming to take sadistic delight in the chaos sweeping the kingdom.

Ander gaped, shocked by the turn of events in Izmir. If the zamindar's health was finally failing, he would be desperate for the secret of immortality his sorcerers had promised. But Thane had defeated the chief sorcerer and snatched away the zamindar's prize. It was no wonder the tyrant was willing to risk everything to recapture Thane.

Thane looked at Varian defiantly. "You're wasting your time. Fight, or leave us. You have no other choices."

Varian's eyes narrowed. "Brave words, boy. But you're worth a king's ransom and I need you intact. So I'll give *you* a choice. Come with me peaceably and on my word as a priest of Yataghan I swear I'll let your friends go free. Or fight and lose. And after you lose you'll watch me skin your companions alive, one by one. It will delay our journey but you'll likely need mending before you can travel anyway."

Thane paled. Ander felt the mage's sick dread. There was no doubt Varian would make good on his pledge.

Thane wiped his forehead with a shaking hand. "I . . . I need a moment. Give me a minute with my friends."

Varian gave a curt nod. "Be quick about it." He turned and walked back to the men standing guard.

Thane retreated a short distance down the corridor, then drew the others into a grim huddle. "What do you think?" he asked. "Whether we fight or not, I'll be taken prisoner. The only way to avoid it is for one of you to kill me now, while you still can. And then Varian will take his revenge on you." He glanced at Dannel, his dark thoughts obvious. Only the fighter had the skills to kill a man quickly and without risk of failure. "If I surrender, I think he'll keep his oath to let you go free. He gave it in front of others, and followers of Yataghan are fanatical about keeping their word. It sounds like the zamindar is near death. With luck he might die before we get back to Izmir."

"There might be another way," Dannel said softly. "While you were talking with the priest, I was hearing the call of the power in the next chamber. I can feel it, Thane. I think I could release that power from the kei. Like we did with the barrier outside. You and Ander showed me how to do it."

"It's not that simple," Ander said. "How could you control it? It took three of us to drain the force from the Gate, and even then we barely managed. Varian won't give us the time we need."

"I know," Dannel's voice was hushed. "All I can do is breach the dam between the kei and the world. I sensed anima's nature when we were draining the barrier. It's a force, like an arrow in flight. It goes straight unless something shoves it aside. Everything in front of the portal will be swept away. But if you're *behind* the portal you should be safe."

No one spoke. Dannel plainly understood the consequences of his plan.

Thane broke the silence. "Dannel, I remember your pledge, but I can't—"

"You gave me freedom and I want to use it! I'm still a fighter and now I have something worth defending." He gazed at Thane with unguarded longing. "You and Ander should never be parted. I want to do this, for both of you. *Forget* my pledge, Thane. Accept this as my gift."

Ander put a hand on Dannel's arm, the ache in his chest making words impossible. A few moments later Thane did the same. The fighter gave them a solemn nod. "On my signal, run for the inner chamber and get on the platform behind the portal. Don't look at it when you enter the chamber or it might ensnare you. And don't look back."

"Give me your answer!" Varian shouted. "I grow tired of waiting!"

Dannel took a last look around the circle of friends, giving them an unsteady smile. "Think of me sometime, around the campfire on dark nights. But now it's time to act. When the count reaches three, run like the wind. One . . . two . . . *three*!"

Ander turned and sprinted for the inner chamber, cursing the tears that blurred his vision. The roar of outraged men resounded as Varian and his warriors gave chase.

As they entered the inner chamber, the portal's rumble almost drowned the sounds of pursuit. Ruby light bathed the walls and streamers of red light writhed from the portal like beckoning arms. Ander forced himself to look away, careening around the huge artifact just behind Skorri. Out of the corner of his eye he caught a glimpse of Dannel leaping onto the platform in front of the portal.

Strong hands grabbed Ander and pulled him up. He found himself on a wide pedestal in the portal's shadow. Thane put an arm around his shoulders and tugged him to his knees. Skorri and Erik huddled a few feet away.

"Hold on!" Thane shouted, pulling Ander against his body.

A deafening crash like thunder boomed around them. Spears of searing white light bathed the chamber. Even behind the portal, reflections etched lines in Ander's eyes. Screams filled the air before being cut short. The stench of burned hair and flesh clawed at his throat.

The chaos ended as suddenly as it had begun. Ander looked up and blinked. Colored streaks of light still danced before his eyes, but the chamber had grown still. Even the portal had fallen silent. He felt Thane's embrace and returned it fiercely.

"He did it," Ander whispered. "He succeeded."

Thane's body shook. Grief flowed through their bond in a river of anguish.

"Don't blame yourself," Ander said gently. He touched Thane's cheek, felt hot tears. "He had found what he sought. He was his own man at last."

Thane took a ragged breath. "So many have died. So many friends lost. When will—"

Footfalls echoed around the chamber, slow and deliberate. Thane looked over Ander's shoulder, eyes wide with shock.

Ander turned. Pallaton appeared from the other side of the huge stone block and walked toward them. He glowed with a silvery nimbus and carried a limp figure in his arms. When he saw Ander he nodded gravely.

"Perhaps I judged too hastily. You and your companions have more strength than I thought. When this one unsealed the portal, I decided you were worth saving. But you must leave now. You have much to learn before you can safely touch hsien powers."

Ander got to his feet. "Dannel . . . is he dead?"

"I shielded him," Pallaton said. "A simple thing if you have understanding." He extended his arms, holding the fighter effortlessly. "Take him. He will awaken soon. Where would you and your companions go? The Sentinel is destroying the intruders in the valley and closing the pass. But I will send you where you wish."

Thane stood and helped Ander support Dannel. The fighter was feverishly hot, but still breathed.

"Home," Thane said. "The zamindar's death is near. There will be troubles, struggles for power. Our friends will need our help."

"Come." Pallaton beckoned, and they followed him to the front of the portal. Its tumultuous surface had calmed and turned jade green, like the surface of a gently rippling pond. He turned to Ander. "I know your mind best. Show me where you call home."

Ander thought of Thane's estate, its weather-softened castle nestled along a river and surrounded by gardens. A moment later the portal chirruped. The rippling jade was overlaid with a view of the courtyard between the castle's great tower and the stables. Dawn blazed in rose and gold glory beyond the old fortress wall.

Skorri whooped and slapped Erik on the back.

"Go ahead," Pallaton said. "That is where you belong, not here."

Thane nodded and Skorri walked through the portal with Erik. A golden shimmer limned their bodies as they crossed the threshold, then Ander saw them standing in the courtyard laughing and hugging.

Ander and Thane stepped up to the portal, supporting Dannel between them. Ander turned his head and met Pallaton's steady gaze.

"Will we see you again?" he asked.

"I cannot foresee the future. Anything is possible."

Ander grinned at Thane, his heart soaring. Together they carried Dannel through the portal. The sweet smell of spring welcomed them home.